I0744180

Broadway

Broadway

a Charlotte Smart Mystery

STAN CHARNOFSKY

HAWKSHAW PRESS | LOS ANGELES

Hawkshaw Press is an imprint of Devil's Party Press, LLC.
hawkshawpress.com

ISBN: 978-1-957224-07-7

Cover and book design by Dianne Pearce and David Yurkovich

This third Charlotte novel is for my two
grandchildren, Molly, studying in New York to
become a Broadway star, and Jack, a Ventura high
school basketball, baseball, and chess star.

SC

Also by Stan Charnofsky

Accident: A Charlotte Smart Mystery
Charlotte
Famous
Morpheus
Old
Ruthless

This is the first man I have killed with my hands, whom I can see close at hand, whose death is my doing. But every gasp lays my heart bare. This dying man has time with him, he has an invisible dagger with which he stabs me: Time and my thoughts.

All Quiet On The Western Front

Broadway

PART 1
Something's Rotten in The Big Apple

1

"Jesus!"

"No, just Charlotte, though there may be some similarities."

"How does she know those things?" Detective Cavanaugh asks.

"Part of the package. Call it intuition, savvy, whatever. She listens to flowers, sees concertos, smells beauty, is able to climb into a tale and ferret out the deceit. I've only been around her less than a week, and already I've seen the calm, steady talent. I'll bet she'll bring this whole crazy scene into focus in a matter of days."

Broadway Farivar has become, as have others before him, a devotee.

Charlotte Smart is his heroine.

She tried to eat a banana without removing the peel; she had never seen a banana before. Twelve was a young age to be uprooted, leave everything familiar, and, with her doting, pear-shaped, four-foot eleven-inch mother, traipse off from a small village in Ukraine in stealth and fear (the Soviets did not permit people to leave), hiking along hostile plains, wading across dark creeks, sailing over an endless ocean, retching and miserable, to the monster, New York City.

Sarah's mother had a relative in Hoboken, New Jersey, and his family met the new arrivals, beaming at them as if, beyond a doubt, they were the luckiest two people on the planet to view Miss Liberty, strip naked on Ellis Island, have their ears and throats invaded, get dumped in a misty rain on the cruddy pier at the foot of the City of Baltimore's creaking gangplank.

The New World, it was called. To Sarah, it was more like an old nightmare.

In the blink of an eye, fifty years flit by. That's the way it is, always in retrospect; where in the hell did my life go?

Sarah was at first terrifying, but, in the end, accommodating, married to good-looking Jacob Farivar, her plodding yet industrious Persian-Jewish husband, she birthed two children, the boy, perhaps oddly by American values, named Broadway, the girl Brooklyn.

He was older by two years, was not born until Sarah's thirty-eighth year, and because the family lived a good part of their American lives in a modest apartment on the most famous street in the country, his mother, despite Jacob's resistance, insisted they dub him Broadway. They moved to Brooklyn after Broadway was born, and that is how and why Brooklyn Farivar got her name.

Jacob died of pancreatic cancer when the children were ten and twelve. Both winsome and clever, Broadway, perhaps influenced by the constant referral to his name, became an aspiring actor, Brooklyn a runway model.

"You will be famous," Sarah told them.

She had learned to be a seamstress and, with her husband's death, earned a satisfactory living, at first repairing gowns and dresses and later designing unique clothing that caught the attention of the garment trade. By the time the children were grown, she was an acknowledged designer, her income substantial even by American standards.

Brooklyn and Broadway attended New York University, he setting the pace and she following, majoring in the performing arts. Nice to have an older brother greasing the skids, the name of Farivar recognized and appreciated by the faculty.

A success story so far, but early in the twenty-first century, the Farivar family hit a bump in the road—not a total crash and burn, but nonetheless a tragedy—that punctured Sarah's heart and detoured her children's careful plans.

Enter Charlotte Smart.

2

Broadway, at the age of twenty-seven, had performed in eleven stage productions, including one just off Times Square, a small part in a play that was nominated for a Tony. In college, he played Harold Hill in *The Music Man*, a challenge and, in the end, a triumph.

Now, tall, tan, and talented, lithe as a sprinter, he is represented by Mark Angel, a respected New York agent, hoping his persona will fit some ambitious producer's exact needs.

Brooklyn, at twenty-five, is modeling for a middle-sized agency, often in swimwear, since she looks, as the industry likes to say, delicious when mostly naked. She is only five feet five inches, a bit too short for the major companies, but a stunner, with blonde hair she keeps braided down the back and her grandmother's pale blue eyes.

On a Sunday, brother and sister are in Central Park, on a bench beside the ice-skating rink. It is a cold day in November, clear and breezy, the deciduous trees clutching their last remaining leaves as if disinclined to become…mostly naked.

"He's a prick," Brooklyn says. "I don't know why I got involved with him in the first place."

"So, kiss him off."

"Not so easy. He has connections. It's an entrée to better work."

"Yeah, but if he treats you like shit…"

"He does. I feel as if I'm faking it with him. Big man, Donald Stout, every model's dream date, but, when you get to know him, two-faced, caustic, and a first-class manipulator." She shivers, not so much from the cold as from the ugly reality of her situation.

"Look, Sis, you don't have to stick it out. Life isn't meant to be painful—well, I mean, you have to expect pain, but not from someone you're supposed to like."

"Thanks for the wisdom, Bro, but frankly, I'm damned scared of him. He once told me nobody ever leaves him. Always his choice. He's had a hundred babes, is generous as a come-on, then becomes the date from hell."

"What would he do? You think he'd be violent?"

"Without a doubt. Last time I was with him, his exact words were, 'Don't get it into your head to walk out the door. It could be your final exit.' Then he picked up a kitchen knife and jammed it into a pillow no more than five inches from my head."

"Who in the hell does he think he is, Al Capone? He can't get away with threatening you. The police ought to be in on this. Anyway, a boss is stupid for sleeping with his hired hands."

Something riles up a swarm of swallows in an evergreen cedar tree a few yards away, and there is suddenly a cacophony of chirping that drowns out their voices. They rise and saunter over to a bench on the opposite side of the rink, busy with skaters circling, spinning, speeding, slipping.

"You walked away from your supposed girlfriend, that Monica babe, just last year, and I know it was hard for you. I don't have that kind of courage. Donald is quixotic, and I'm not sure what he'd do."

"Monica wasn't threatening; she was a most appealing, to-die-for beauty, but with an addictive personality. Our little mother, who abhors your bizarre boyfriend-boss, admonished you and me to stay away from drugs—and it stuck. But Monica was a snorter. I hated it. She wouldn't change, so I split."

"That's what I have to do if I could only figure out a way."

Two little girls, each wearing a red, tasseled, floppy hat, skid by the new bench, and their skates send up a splash of splintered ice. They giggle and glide off, leaving Broadway and Brooklyn giggling back at them.

"I tell you, falling in love is a mixed bag, aromatic as a costly perfume, disturbing as pounding rain. I learned something with Monica: that when I bare my heart, I ought to expect nothing in return; truth is personal; the other person sees things differently; crying is okay."

"The philosopher. Sure, but if it's a coercive thing…if one

partner dominates the other, how does one cope? I know I don't love the asshole. I think I became addicted to him, and he, I'm sorry to say, has all the power."

"You're not helpless. There has to be a way to pull out."

Broadway stops, his handsome face a mask of concern, and gazes about the peaceful scene—couples and singles, children and families, relishing a day in the park, two squirrels squabbling at the base of a fir tree, the brisk air a tonic. In this idyllic setting, it is easy to feel power, as if one needs nothing more in the world or from the world.

Back to reality as a grizzled old man, clad in layers of dark cloth, face wrinkled as a prune, approaches them, hand cautiously extended. Broadway thrusts a dollar bill into his instantly closing fingers and sees the man's grin, toothless as a pug boxer.

"Maybe I need to step in. I'll go have a talk with Donald Stout."

"No!" Her response is instant, firm.

"I want you safe and healthy, and that means you dump the guy."

"I'll handle it myself. Not sure exactly how, but not with you interfering."

"Here's my pitch again: life is fleeting. You and I have ambition, but time is not on our side, not on anyone's. Mother Sarah is already old. No one part of life is preparation for another; we have to live fully every moment, experience each day; roll in the grass; skate on our own pond."

"Wow, Bro, you're having a good day! Love the images."

She pauses, leans over, and kisses him on the cheek.

"Why can't I find a man like you?"

Three days later, in the middle of a rehearsal for his gig as the gentleman caller in a one-week production of *The Glass Menagerie*, Broadway's cell twitters and his mother's voice screeches in his ear.

"He's done it! The bastard crapped on your sister. She's in Mount Sinai Beth Israel Medical Center at Fifth Avenue and Sixteenth Street. I'm on my way. Get there as fast as you can."

—

Mount Sinai Beth Israel is famous for its Albert Einstein College of Medicine. It has received awards as one of the premiere hospitals in America. That is all to the good, but a small consolation to

Broadway, heading there in the dark about his sister's condition. She is his soul mate, the lyrics to his music, salve to his wounds, the only person he can tell on himself to without fear of judgment. Tears come, and he tries to remember his own admonition that crying is okay as his taxi wheels up to the parking area in time to see Sarah striding into the Emergency entrance.

As he approaches, his mother is leaning over a green Formica counter, demanding information. Taller than her mother, Sarah is still a small woman, but, as a designer, conscious of her figure, and, though her face has sagged and rounded, hips broadened, she tries to stay slim as if she might have to model her own creations. As her son knows, she is a no-nonsense person.

"They won't let me see her; tell me she's in surgery." She says this with both anger and panic, showing little patience for clerks or aides.

"What happened? Do you know?"

"Only that a girlfriend found her at their studio and called an ambulance. I decided to see her first before calling the police."

"You think that Stout fellow attacked her?"

"I wouldn't be surprised."

A bell sounds, not loud but repetitive, and a door that bears the sign *Hospital Personnel Only* swings outward. A young man with dark stubble, the Hollywood look, all in white, moves toward them.

"You Brooklyn's family?"

"We are," Sarah replies, a barb in her voice.

"I'm Doctor Landry. She's still in surgery. It's her spine. Seems she fell down some stairs."

"Her spine?" Broadway says.

"Might have severed something. It doesn't look good."

3

"I live in Pennsylvania," Charlotte says on her cellphone, proud of her connection to present-day technology. "It's quite a trek for me to get into the city. …Well, yes, I could, but I'm not a real detective, you know. …At the Sheraton, in Times Square? Really. Hmm, that would be an adventure."

She pauses, looks at a calendar on the wall in her tidy little apartment in Bigelow Retirement Village, memories of her last crime investigation suddenly vivid, and immediately says, "All right. I'll do it. Meet me at Penn Station tomorrow at noon."

When she places her phone on the cradle, she waits only a few seconds, lifts it again, and punches in her brother's number in California.

"Say there, Greg," she says to his voice mail, "I know you won't like it, but I've taken on a new case. Well, I think it will be a case. A young man called from New York and wants me to look into a terrible accident that happened to his sister. He and his mother are willing to put me up in the Sheraton, at Fifty-Third and Seventh Avenue, for as long as it takes. That's at about three hundred a night. Can you believe it? Oh, he said they read about me in the newspaper, said the sister's nasty boyfriend likely hurt her on purpose. So, we'll see. I'll miss not having you around for this caper. Send your good energy to me. Love to Meredith. Bye, little brother."

She already knows Greg's arguments: "You only did your first case because the poisoned person was a longtime friend. The second one gripped you because it was about little children. Other than a free week or two in New York, what in hell would tempt you to jump in on this one? Sixty-nine is not the ideal age to be trying to track down a criminal. When do you plan on really, truly retiring?"

In one sense, she is glad he hadn't answered the phone; leaving a message spared her the burden of countering his quite accurate points. She sits in her cozy, familiar apartment and decides to toast her new adventure with a glass of California merlot, brought by her brother on his last visit. In her alertness, she recalls that in the delightful movie *Sideways*, merlot is a no-no. She likes this wine and, about once every two weeks, she indulges, and, yes, this is a proper occasion. What, indeed, stirred her to say yes to Broadway Farivar? Her last murder–mystery lifted her spirits; the bizarre carnival of events, the disparate clues, denials, affirmations, the final clinching moment! Damn it, there is a definite thrill in the chase.

—

The New Jersey Transit ride from Hamilton Township Station in New Jersey to Penn Station in New York is an hour's trip. Charlotte has made the journey a hundred times, does not relish it, dislikes the cruddy scenery in depressed Jersey towns along the railroad tracks, and finds her spirits lift only when the New York skyline comes into view. For years it was the Twin Towers that caught her eye; now, after nine-eleven, the Empire State Building is the main attraction.

It's good exercise, she tells herself as she climbs the forty stairs to the vast Penn Station lobby. The only way the young man would know her is by the butterfly pin she told him she would be wearing on her left shoulder.

She stands for a moment, wide-eyed as usual in the bustle of this garish edifice, wondering how our culture manages, constantly on the go, scampering from one planetary locale to another, some folks traversing a hundred miles each day of their lives.

A gorgeous fellow ambles up to her with his hand extended: "Strange name, I know, but I'm Broadway. My mother and I are delighted you are willing to help us."

"A pleasure to meet you, Broadway. However, you need to add the word 'try.' I shall *try* to help you. In cases like this, there are no guarantees."

They move off to the spill-out on Eighth Avenue, in front of the famous Madison Square Garden, an attached neighbor of Penn

Station. A small-town girl, the pedestrian jungle of scurrying humanity is bewildering for Charlotte as Broadway garners a cab from the cue of half a dozen lined up at the curb.

"My sister, Brooklyn, is one of the most beautiful people in the world. She's been a model but got herself into a relationship with the guy who runs the agency, a first-class abuser. It was almost like the way pimps operate. Once hooked in, you can't get out. We just talked about this a few days ago and I wanted to confront the guy—his name is Donald Stout—but she didn't want me to. And now this."

Charlotte, in her usual way, has been an avid listener, tuning into every word, despite the cacophonous ambient noise of the Manhattan traffic.

"Explain what you mean by 'and now this.'"

"My mother got a call that Brooklyn was in the emergency room of Mount Sinai Beth Israel. When we got there, we were told by a doctor that she had fallen down a flight of stairs."

He pauses, looks away and around; Charlotte sees at once that he is about to burst with grief. He picks up, "…That her spine was damaged. There was an extensive operation, and now she is in recovery—but the medical people don't think she'll walk again."

His breath catches, like a child in tears who can't get the words out, and he lowers his head, hand over his mouth and chin.

Clearly, Charlotte realizes a powerful bond between this young man and his sister, and since she is a model, this injury is devastating. Well, it would be for anyone, and when one's occupation involves physical dexterity and flawless beauty, a monstrous tragedy.

After a moment, Broadway resumes: "We contacted the police since Brooklyn managed to tell us that she didn't fall but was pushed. A deliberate act of hostility, and we can think of only one person who would do something like that. But this Stout fellow denies having anything to do with it. Yes, they had argued over something, but then she left, is his position. Her word against his, and the cops said they couldn't hold him on that."

"Yes, of course. The police are tied to the ADA's agenda; no clues, no charges." Charlotte smiles at her own awareness—after only two cases, mind you—of the justice system's language.

"Brook told us that just before she was shoved down the stairs, she had gotten up the courage to kiss the guy off, that he was livid, and said she would be sorry."

"One question," Charlotte begins. "I am curious if your sister claims she actually saw the…uh, guy push her."

He hesitates, frowns, and rubs his forehead. "Well, not exactly. You would have to ask her, but I gather that when she reached the top of the stairs, she suddenly felt hands on her back and a hard shove—and down she went."

"Ah. So, discovering the mystery pusher is to be my task."

Broadway looks at this little, nearly seventy-year-old lady, about the same age as his mother, though pretty in a way his mother no longer is, and nods slowly.

"We'll be glad to pay you whatever you wish."

"Oh no. Putting me up at an elegant hotel is ample pay. I'm not a professional, so I don't charge for services."

The driver pulls into the drop-off area under the Sheraton Hotel, a wide expanse for loading and unloading, comes to a stop at a white-painted curb, and, in a thick, Middle Eastern accent, announces, "We get here."

"Your name is at the desk," Broadway says. "And here." He hands Charlotte a rolled stack of bills. "For food—a couple of hundred for the next several days. Eating in New York can be expensive. You might want to rest for a few hours. Mom and I will pick you up right here at three. Then, if you like, we can take you to see Brooklyn."

Charlotte laughs. Serious business, this, but boy, it sure is fun.

4

Her first impression of Sarah Farivar is mixed: attracted by an obvious style in clothing, yet put off by her officious manner.

They pick her up in a shiny, blue Lexus, which Broadway is driving, his mother in the passenger spot in front, and Charlotte motioned to sit in the back. As is her way, she acquiesces but stores away what she sees as the mother's self-serving attitude.

"I want you to know, Ms. Smart, that since my son read about you in the newspaper, he requested that we engage you for this activity. You will find me a very direct person, so I will tell you that I have my doubts. If the police were willing to do their work, you would not be here."

"Oh, dear me, I understand. I am not, however, a substitute for law enforcement people. If any progress is to be made in solving this mystery, the police will have to be included."

"Yes, well, good luck with that."

"My mother is frustrated with the cops," Broadway says. "They refuse to pursue what they say could be the 'perp' unless there is substantial evidence. And since there were no witnesses—at least as far as we know—there is simply no evidence at all."

A profound silence fills the car for a time, Broadway maneuvering his vehicle through late afternoon, stop-and-go traffic, two-thirds of it yellow cabs.

"I wonder," Charlotte says, "if either of you knows the people at the agency where Brooklyn worked."

"I do not," Sarah says bluntly. "My daughter is a private person. I did meet the loser one time, this Stout fellow. Didn't like him from the start. Arrogant. No warmth."

Hmm, a lot like you, Charlotte thinks, but says, "And you, Broadway? Do you know her colleagues?"

"Her best girlfriend is Kyla Pino, the person who called the medics. She's also a model, about as beautiful as Brooklyn, taller, with darker hair and eyes. A woman who's easy to like. And there is also Brent, a male model, who cares a lot for Brook. He's gay."

"Ah, I wonder if they would be on hand later, if the agency has any activity in the early evening. I'd love to meet those folks."

"Might be," Broadway replies. "They sometimes have pep-talk rehearsals in the evening. Unfortunately, Donald Stout conducts them."

"Oh, I want to meet him as well. It would be grand to have access to them all at the same time."

A giant big rig, its massive side-panel advertising Gerber Baby Food, blocks their way, seemingly parked on Thirtieth Street, but actually stuck in traffic as well.

"Oh, you went the wrong way, son. This is the busiest street in New York."

She says this with a scold in her voice, and Broadway shrugs but says nothing, apparently used to his mother's criticism. As the crow flies, the hospital is less than two miles further, but with the congestion, it will be a laborious task to get to the adjacent parking area.

"If you don't mind, another question," Charlotte says. "Do you know if this Donald Stout fellow has any, what the police call, priors? A criminal record of some kind?"

"If he has, I don't know about it," Broadway replies.

Quiet for an instant, Sarah says, with a snarl, "I guess I'm a meddling parent, but when Brook told me about him, I hired a private detective to research his background."

Broadway tosses her a quick glance—obviously unaware of this information.

She continues: "Police were called two separate times for domestic violence issues. No arrests since the women decided not to press charges."

"Just like with Brook," Broadway says. "I'm sure they didn't want to lose a career opportunity. You take a little abuse if it means getting ahead. Some women simply sleep with the guy; others take a beating.”

"Quite a lovely fellow,” Charlotte says. “I can't wait to meet him.”

Another silence is broken by Sarah as she notes, “Evil is everywhere. I'm an immigrant, and I came here with nothing. There is ample opportunity for success in America, and people get there either morally or immorally. I climbed my ladder the honest way, and believe me, it was hard. This Stout fellow got to be head of an agency with treachery and by using women.”

Would not like to be Sarah Farivar's enemy, Charlotte thinks. *For now, she is tolerant of me, though not welcoming. If I misstep, she could turn nasty. Wonder what Broadway meant when he said, no witnesses, "as far as we know."*

Broadway says, as if thinking aloud, “It's not black and white, Mother. Good people sometimes do bad things and vice versa.”

"Well, I agree with both of you,” Charlotte says. “Is there anyone else in Brooklyn's life who might have issues with her? I mean, the implication is that Stout did the dirty deed, but one must not eliminate others prematurely.”

Mother and son seem stuck for an instant, and finally Broadway says, “She really didn't have enemies. A couple of failed love affairs a few years back, one with a guy named Batchelor, Aaron Batchelor, but I don't think she's seen him for over a year. He's a stockbroker. Loves money the way Wall Street people do. That's what broke them up; aside from being a chauvinistic pig, he was addicted to the green stuff.”

He stops, concentrating on his driving. For a minute, there is a clearance, and he speeds up his Lexus to thirty before again slowing for a yellow light. Mother Sarah frowns. No doubt, she would have gone through the yellow. *Not immoral,* Charlotte thinks, *but a skilled cutter of corners—a seeker of the crease.*

"Oh,” Broadway resumes, “there was a girl—a woman—who sort of competed with Brook for a couple of gigs. Not quite as talented, and certainly not as pretty, so I don't think Stout tried to get into her pants.”

"Watch your language, Son!”

Ignoring his mother's admonition, Broadway adds, “Her name is Corrine, with a funny last name of Gelly, spelled with a G. I think she may have resented Brook's getting ahead, though she was never openly hostile.”

The Mount Sinai Beth Israel complex appears on the left, and Broadway steers his elegant vehicle into the underground garage.

Charlotte notices the sign that reads, *Parking For Mount Sinai Beth Israel, $8 An Hour, $25.00 All Day.*

Welcome to New York values, Charlotte thinks.

5

"She's in room 3117," Broadway says. "Another two days and we may be able to take her home. We already have a wheelchair. I have to warn you, she's pretty broken up about all this."

"Of course. Dreadful, simply dreadful."

When they enter the room, Brooklyn is staring in the opposite direction, toward the window that looks out on the Lower Manhattan panorama of towering edifices and windows. She hears them and turns her head, eyes pale blue and lifeless.

Despite cheeks red-tinged from tears, the beauty of her face captures Charlotte's attention. Brother and sister, handsome and lovely; the mother not so much. Wonder about the father. Must have been an Adonis.

"Hi, Sis. This is Charlotte Smart. She's agreed to look into what happened to you."

As if revving up all her courage, Brooklyn smiles wanly and says, "Thank you. I know what happened to me, but I don't know who made it happen."

"Hello dear. Yes, I understand you were assaulted from behind. I hope you don't mind if I say you are a stunning young woman."

"Stunning and a cripple—for life."

"We don't know that," Sarah says. "People sometimes fight through these things. You have the Farivar willpower."

"How do I will myself a new spine?"

"Not a new one, Babe," Broadway says. "A healed one."

"Fat chance." She turns away, again gazing at the window as if the late afternoon light can offer hope.

"I wonder," Charlotte begins, sitting at a swivel chair raised to the level of the bed, "if you feel up to answering a couple of questions."

Pause, and Brooklyn says, "Why not. Can't guarantee I'll know the answers you want."

"All right, though there are no rights or wrongs here. My questions have to do with your perceptions."

A tedious sigh. "Go ahead."

"Do you have any enemies at your agency? Anyone who has shown resentment toward you?"

Instantly she replies, "Corrine Gelly-belly. She's a nut. I don't resent her, but she resented me because I got more assignments than she did. Then the big boss, Donald Duck Stout, finally let her go. She hasn't worked with us for over a month."

"This Donald Duck Stout fellow, who is your boss, well, I gather he was also your boyfriend."

"*Was* is right. He is pure poison. Broadway knows I was stuck and scared to kiss him off. But I finally did, and he blew a gasket. Told me I'd be sorry."

"He could have been furious enough to want to hurt you?"

"Sure, but he's not obvious. Covers his ass. Any ugly stuff on his part has always been camouflaged, so he could never be pinned down."

"So, are you saying you don't think he would operate in the…way your, uh, incident occurred?"

"If he did it, he would have made sure first that no one else was around, and second he would have hidden until I reached the top step."

"Sorry, I know this is painful for you, but the push—it must have been severe and sudden? You didn't even have time or the balance to turn your head to see the person?"

She sighs heavily and says in a monotone, "It was more than a push. It was a hard blow to my back, almost as if with a heavy object. I was launched off the summit and flew several feet before even hitting the steps."

"Ah, well, I do believe the police are being obtuse if they don't investigate this as…sorry to be so blunt, but…attempted murder."

"That is what I told them!" Sarah says fiercely. "The idiots can't make up their minds. One dummy told me it still might have been an accident, that Brook could have stumbled."

"She is a skilled dancer," Broadway inserts, "with marvelous balance. An athlete. Works out every day. She doesn't stumble."

"You need to put that in past tense. *Worked* out each day," Brooklyn says. "Those days are history."

"I hate to hear that," Sarah says. "My children don't throw in the towel."

Brooklyn begins to sob, her mother's sanguinity too painful to accommodate.

A white-clad young man enters the room, his name tag identifying him as the same Doctor Bruce Landry. Though somber-looking, he manages a brief smile and says, "Ah, the family…and a new person. I'm Doctor Landry, and you?"

"A friend of the family, Charlotte's my name."

"Yes, well, I think this lovely young woman will be able to break out of this joint tomorrow. What do you say to that?"

"About time," Sarah mutters.

"Super!" Broadway says.

"Ready for my new life." Brooklyn almost gags. "Need someone to push me around wherever I want to go. Nice way to live, huh?"

"We will have someone in twice a week for physical therapy. The somewhat good news is that the spine was not severed. The damage was extensive, and we are hoping the surgery, and the passage of time, will give you a chance to heal."

"And then what? I take up knitting? I learn ceramics? Oh…" She turns away again and weeps.

Dr. Landry leans in toward her and says in a tone laced with affection, "Look, Brooklyn, there are no guarantees. But I am optimistic that you have a chance to build up your surrounding muscles and compensate for the injury."

Well, Charlotte thinks, *how interesting. The prognosis is one thing, but the attention this medical person is giving is fascinating.* No doubt, in the last few days, he has gotten to know Brooklyn rather well. No doubt he is drawn toward her—who wouldn't be? Now that would be an irony: after being entrenched with a scoundrel Brooklyn was trying to discard, she finds him replaced by a caring healer.

Sarah says, "First good thing I've heard from you all-knowing medicine men. I've been telling my daughter that for several days. She will not be a cripple."

There is an awkward silence for a moment, and Charlotte says softly,

"Let us hope not. Yet, if she is, I'm sure the love will abide."

32

6

They go for dinner on a street nicknamed Restaurant Row, just beyond Eighth Avenue on Forty-Sixth, Charlotte aware that the roll of dollars in her purse will not be needed. Becco's has European/Italian style food, elegant yet casual, a place where theatergoers can dine before strolling over to one of the twenty plays within walking distance.

Sarah sits there, glowering, like a menacing cumulonimbus cloud.

"Two things," she starts out. "My perfect daughter is now maimed and her perfection compromised. And the sick person who did this to her is walking around free as a bird."

"That is why Charlotte is here, Mother. We'll go to the studio and introduce her to the menagerie. She has a sharp eye. Maybe she'll pick up something."

"Thank you for the compliment, Broadway. None of this will be easy. The bad guys are always so sincere, and any leads have to be pursued with caution. When a suspect feels cramped, he or she becomes much more dangerous."

"But, my Brooklyn was the person they were after, not anyone else. It had to be a vendetta of some kind."

"Well, Ms. Farivar, that is likely so; however, when the deed is done, the only thing that matters is to avoid being unmasked. In my limited experience, 'perps' get desperate if they sense they are about to be caught."

Charlotte stops, intent on her food, a veal dish with angel hair pasta, and comments, "Yum. This is tasty stuff."

"A little prep for the people you are about to meet," Broadway says. "Kyla Pino is close to Brook and a real babe. I mean, if she weren't already dating someone, I'd ask her out. She's majestic-looking, a skilled model, and also an actress. Makes me think of Amber Valetta, who has a foot in both doors.

"Brent is a sweet man, African-American, gay, and with a special connection to Brook. He's a well-built guy, formidable, who takes shit from no one. A couple of times, he's scared off would-be harassers. Has sort of a quixotic manner at times, which makes him hard to read.

"Donald, as you know, is the big man. He is officious and oppressive. I don't know anyone who likes him, though a lot do respect him. He knows the business and runs his shop with an iron hand. He takes up with each new model, initiates her into his culture, but then, if he loses interest, dumps her. With Brook, she decided to dump him. Unacceptable!

"Of course, there are a dozen more aspiring young people in the fold. It's a cutthroat business, and anyone might think she—or he—can get a break by removing the person one step ahead. My guess is that once Brook said no to Donald Stout, she might be demoted to trivial gigs. And, it could be that the rest of the entourage didn't know she was on the outs."

"Ah, so you are saying the entire modeling crew could be suspects that, at any moment, a given person could perceive Brook, or another model, as an impediment to her progress in the industry."

"Well, yes, in the modeling game, ambition is a must. These folks come from all over the country, the rambling farms of Kansas and the teeming inner neighborhoods of Detroit or Cleveland or Baltimore. Inhospitable as it is for most, New York becomes their second home. Brook is quite popular, and she is not a very competitive person. As far as I know, fellow models of both genders really like her."

"It had to be a real sicko to do this to my Brook. My vote is for Donald—the creep, the exploiter, the obvious womanizer."

"Yes, Mother, he would be the frontrunner, but I like Charlotte's notion of not closing the door to other possibilities."

"I wonder which of the models might be next in line? I mean, right below Brooklyn in Stout's eyes and most likely to move up to her rank?"

"Hard to know. Could be Kyla. Donald knows she has a boyfriend and is off limits for him, but Brook told me he's crazy about her. Maybe we'll find out when the next job is announced. Brook was at the top of the list since Stout appreciated her look and her skill. He'll have to elevate someone."

They finish their meals—the restaurant, its walls gaily painted with Italian landscape scenes, is, by now, crowded with theatergoers, bustling, and noisy—and Charlotte says, "Thank you for this wonderful dinner. Even though I'm older in years, I haven't lost my appetite for good food."

"Brook said the meeting starts about seven. That's less than an hour from now," Broadway says. "It's not far, only four or five blocks. I suggest we walk since our car is okay in the lot, and because of the theater crowd, finding another parking spot would be a bear."

"You're going to make your mother walk five blocks?"

"Hey, Mom, you're more vigorous than I am."

"I don't mind walking," Charlotte says.

Sarah scowls at her.

The building is an old, red brick edifice, long devoid of any elegance, in need of a scrubbing, its façade a faded pink, its entrance lit by a bulb that sputters and appears about to die. The title above the door reads *Antwerp*, which Broadway says is in honor of the man who commissioned the construction some sixty years ago, a man from Belgium, who is no longer around.

"As you must realize, the Stout Studio is on the second floor," Broadway says. "I doubt the big man will welcome us, but I think he will be careful not to treat us with disrespect."

They ascend the staircase, Sarah groaning with the realization that this is where her lovely Brook's body was broken.

Music drifts down to them from an interior room. The hallway at the top of the stairs is poorly lit, and Charlotte takes note of the door just to the right, labeled "Closet." They pause for a moment before Broadway points to the left to steer them to the meeting room.

Charlotte says, "Excuse me for one minute." She tries the knob on the old door, and it turns. Peering in, she says, "Cleaning supplies, brooms, brushes, fluids, those sorts of things. Also, a couple of metal buckets and a hefty canister sitting on the floor, which, from the label, looks like a supply of floor wax." She leans in and lifts the wax container, a bit heavy for her but manageable for a man or a woman.

"Where the creep was hiding out?" Broadway states as a question.

"Could be."

They hear people sounds from down the hall and an undertone of violin music. One male voice rises above the rest.

"People, you got to realize, vendors want their merchandise to be presented in the best possible light. No trudging on the runway. No slouching. You move with purpose, with a glint in your eye. No smiling. It's all business. A frown is okay; it catches the viewers' attention, gives you personality."

"The hero," Sarah murmurs.

They enter the open door, and the speaker pauses for an instant as he sees them. But only for an instant, and he picks up again—his message too important to allow intruders to distract him.

Donald Stout is tall and lean, not frail, but without bulk. Sandy hair spills over his left eye. He wears a thin mustache that makes him look, Charlotte decides, like the old swashbuckling actor Errol Flynn—though, other than Sarah, she is sure no one else in the room is old enough to know who that was.

She sees Broadway nod at a young fellow seated in the row of chairs outside the participants' circle.

"That's Andy Burrus," he whispers to Charlotte, "Kyla's boyfriend. He's a goofy little guy, kind of hard to warm up to."

She picks up resentment in his tone and, in her mind, finishes his sentence with, "…if only Kyla wasn't hooked into him."

There are some fifteen folks in the large, rectangular room, with three walls colored pale green and the fourth a massive mirror. A few feet down from the ceiling, two round portals are meant to allow light in, though now they are black with night. The floor is split in half; the part where chairs are positioned is covered with a darker green carpet, and the other a polished, well-maintained wood parquet.

As they take seats in the outer circle, Charlotte makes note of all the beautiful people, almost every one with a fresh, photogenic look. It makes sense that the public wants its models to be, as Sarah described Brooklyn, the embodiment of perfection.

As if reading her mind and adjusting the idea to fit his harangue, Stout says, "I want my models to be…aggressive. Most of you are of ample height and thin, the men with enough muscles to turn women on but not look like bodybuilders, the women with little tits and swiveling asses. It's a bump-and-grind exercise, and I want to see a lot of bumps and a lot of grinds."

"Pig," Sarah mutters, a bit too loud.

Stout stops. "I beg your pardon? Do you have something to say to me?"

Sarah stands at her chair. "Yes. You are a pig. The pig who crushed my daughter's future!"

One can feel the tension as a hush falls over the room, every pair of beautiful eyes on Donald Stout.

"Madam," he says with a cold stare, his voice laced with venom, "you are in my studio, I presume, as a visitor, and your idiotic accusations will not be tolerated here. If you cannot remain civil, then I suggest you leave."

Appropriately outraged, yet under control, Charlotte thinks. *Can't show weakness to his crew, yet won't be bullied.*

"Sit down, Mom," Broadway says softly, tugging at her arm.

She complies with a snort, done for the moment but perhaps not for the evening.

Stout resumes: "I know of several possible contracted jobs on the horizon. I hope to use all of you, some, as you already know, more than others. Keep your energy up since you never know when you will be tapped. It's like the substitute ballplayer, who, when his chance comes, must charge off the bench and perform flawlessly."

Broadway whispers to Charlotte, "I'm surprised. That's Corrine Gelly at the end of the row. She's no longer with the troupe. Must be a visitor."

Definitely not as pretty as Brooklyn, Charlotte sees. *Wears a bit of a smirk on her face. Glad she's here. Gives us many, if not all, of the suspects in one room.*

"I want some samples," Stout says. "My instructions will lay out the format and the situation, and we will assume the fashions. Kyla, you first."

Ah, the hierarchy. Kyla is indeed next in line. Charlotte feels Broadway tense up when Kyla rises. She glances at Andy, who seems disinterested, playing the way young people obsessively do, with an electronic device in his hands.

Stout moves to a sound box and switches the music to Tchaikovsky, a segment of his "Romeo and Juliet Overture"—a soaring melody sure to pull listeners into a romantic humor.

"The audience is here. The music rises. Your couture is elegant, the latest fashion, the mood intense. Show us how you display your garments in the most appealing light."

Kyla moves to the far end of the room. She is, indeed, an attractive woman, perhaps, as Broadway noted, two or three inches taller than Brooklyn, darker in complexion, with penetrating hazel eyes.

She begins her trek, legs swiveling across so that her path is straight as if there were a line on the parquet. Her head is high, and she has pulled her ebony hair across her left shoulder, hands on hips, lips as if painted in a firm, unsmiling line. Her waist is thin as a child's, and her hips swell outward several inches as they wag back and forth in matchless harmony with the music.

It is over in a minute and a half, as Kyla prances up to Stout's position on the floor, almost into his face—still not smiling—turns and struts back to her starting point.

"Bravo!" Stout shouts. "An 'in your face' performance. Now, there is a woman who knows how to move."

His look is salacious, Charlotte notes. Wouldn't he love to make Kyla his next conquest! Two men in this room wish Kyla were not partnered with the techno-whiz, Andy, whatever his name.

"All right, so Kyla has set a standard. I want a man now. Brent, you are up; let's see how you do it."

Brent White is an African-American with tan skin, clipped, curly hair that stops in a straight line across his forehead, and a smile showing a row of perfect teeth that aptly match his name. Hardly a feminine hint about his frame or his movement, he is a sturdy fellow who prefers men for his amorous activities.

Now he retreats to the same point in the room as Kyla and, with surprising lightness, moves in an athletic way as the towering Tchaikovsky melodies fill the hall. His jeans are tight, and in them he moves as if on the prowl.

Stout giggles with glee.

"Well done, Brent! I like it. You just seduced a room full of women buyers. Note, everyone, that you don't have to be sexual to be sexy."

This time too softly for anyone other than Broadway and Charlotte to hear, Sarah mumbles, "An exploiter of sex, that's what he is. Design means nothing to this gigolo."

Another way that Sarah resents Donald Stout; clothing design is her life's work, and she sees his modeling enterprise as an attempt to corrupt its purity. Charlotte, as always, files this new information away for future use.

Two other models are asked to walk the walk, and with one, there is praise, while with the other, number four on Stout's list, there is a rather cruel critique: "You look like a mouse. We don't want mice on the runway. Get fierce. Become angry—at someone. Think of a person you hate. Think of some asshole who dumped you."

Broadway whispers to Charlotte, "He equates anger with getting dumped. How's that for a smoking gun?"

"Yes," Charlotte whispers back. "But it is a generalized statement, not an admission of anything. Anger often follows an insult."

The music off, Stout announces, "A five-minute water break, then ten minutes of our gymnastics."

The majestic-looking Kyla Pino is held back for a moment as Stout consults with her, a smile on his handsome countenance, a look of hunger that he does not try to disguise.

After a minute, she turns away, her colorful face red with, what? Embarrassment? Insult? She joins Andy at a table in the left rear of the room where paper cups and a water cooler are set out.

Stout disappears through a small door near the front, labeled with the printed brass sign: *PRIVATE*. Others stand about, sipping water, gabbing quietly.

"Come," Broadway says.

The three of them approach Kyla and Andy, and Broadway does the introductions.

"Charlotte is a friend of Mother's," he says as an afterthought.

"Broadway tells me you are Brooklyn's best buddy," Charlotte says, her smile warm and welcoming.

"I am," Kyla replies softly. Her voice is lower than most, a contralto, and, at the moment, she seems subdued, likely, Charlotte assumes, a result of her little dialogue with Donald Stout.

"I'd like to understand the pecking order here," Charlotte says. "I can see that Mr. Stout runs everything, but it seems as if he has a hierarchy of modeling artists, and, at least from this evening's order, you are now number one?"

Kyla looks troubled, this time clearly embarrassed, and responds with, "Brook was number one. When she fell, he lifted me into that spot. It…could change tomorrow."

She seems not to want to be critical of her boss, and her explanation tends to excuse him.

Broadway says, "Kyla, he's a…scoundrel, and—"

Sarah interrupts, "He's a criminal!"

"Well," Broadway resumes, "that may be, but what I'm saying is that he plays favorites, and we all know he considered Brook his girlfriend, at least until she dumped him."

"Well, he's not going to dump me," Kyla says, with more energy, "because he's never going to get that close."

"Yeah," Andy blurts out.

One word and Charlotte pins Andy down as immature—a kid, really—with teen habits and an unsophisticated manner.

Wonder how old he is; can't be more than nineteen or twenty.

Not wanting to appear the investigator, Charlotte chooses her next words in a tentative way: "Broadway and Sarah tell me that Brooklyn's fall was not an accident and that, according to her, she was pushed. What a terrible thing. I wonder if that…uh, scoundrel, could have been so offended by being dumped that he would have tried to hurt her."

Kyla says, "She and I both thought that at first. But now, I'm not so sure. He kisses off his women every few months, and, after all, she was his number one, so why would he want to lose her?"

"Why yes, that makes sense. But, if she was pushed, who else resented her?"

Kyla waggles her head to the right. "Gelly-belly over there. The one with the plain look. She doesn't like Brook or me. I think it's an envy thing."

"What's she doing here?" Broadway asks.

"Good question. I think she's hoping Donald will reconsider and take her back—especially now that there is one less girl."

The *PRIVATE* door opens, and Stout emerges, striding energetically, his face serious as a stalking tiger. "All right, people. Line up in front of the mirror. We have work to do."

As if his voice were an electrical current, the entire modeling entourage scurries to positions, certainly rehearsed, with each attractive person in a prearranged spot, frozen, waiting for orders.

Whipped into shape, Charlotte thinks, *like the military. This tyrant tolerates no dallying, no private initiative. High in discipline, low in compassion.*

"Got to go," Kyla says.

"Have fun," Andy calls out, his Blackberry in his raised, waving hand.

7

"Mom and I will walk you to your hotel," Broadway says. "It's only two blocks from our parking lot."

"Thank you. I think this evening was most profitable, even if we didn't speak with many of the folks."

"Really?" Sarah says, her manner still distant, compounded by the frustration of being rebuked in the studio, used to having her way and, in this instance, held back by her son and the awkward situation.

"Two things," Charlotte replies. "Everyone there saw me, so my next contact will not be as a stranger. That includes Mr. Donald Stout. And second, I see how things line up. In intrigues such as this, relationships and pecking orders mean everything."

"So, can you tell us how you see the pecking order?" Broadway asks.

They are, in fact, walking down Broadway. It is well past nine o'clock and the streets are still people-jammed, vendors hawking their products, tourists crowding around musicians on corners, hoping, with whatever talents they have, for a few bucks to be dropped into their baskets. Most theaters have not yet let out, and when they do, the surge will grow and the vehicle traffic will double. In downtown Manhattan there is no visible sky, and folks confirm being outdoors by the weather, rainy, hot, and humid in the summer, cold and intermittently snowy in winter.

"Oh, it is not a good idea to presume too much at this stage," Charlotte says. "I can tell you that Brooklyn's friend, Kyla, is an exquisite woman and that her boyfriend, Andy, is, rather surprisingly, a nerd."

"Yes!" Broadway shouts. "That's how I see it, too. So what do you think holds them together?"

"Maybe chemistry. They both are handsome. One would be a fool to try to understand romantic chemistry."

"He's twenty and she's twenty-three," Broadway says. "They've been dating for several months. She hardly ever talks about him, but they almost always hang out together."

"Hmm. My hunch is something else is operating there. Maybe it will be uncovered."

They reach the entrance to the Sheraton, whose elevators are in the interior, the actual lobby up a few floors. Charlotte thanks them again and goes inside.

As they head toward their car, Sarah says, "Some detective. She's going to figure out why a girl and a boy like each other. What about figuring out who tried to kill our Brooklyn?"

In her room, Charlotte checks her watch, checks her address book, then lifts the phone and punches in a number.

"Augustus!" she says with a convivial tone, "my favorite officer of the law. …No, I'm in New York City. …Don't blow a gasket, but I agreed to help a family with a criminal event. …Oh, I know your jurisdiction is limited to Pennsylvania, but you were so accommodating to me in those two cases we explored that I decided to consult with you. …Well, it isn't a murder, but it could be attempted murder, and I need someone from the city here to help me with some forensics. …That's it. I wonder if you know of a good guy—or gal—on the Manhattan staff with whom I might consult? …Say it again."

She picks up the Sheraton pen and begins to write on the Sheraton pad.

"A woman? That's fine."

Meticulously, she writes, *Detective Shanna Cavanaugh.*

She waits and says, "How old? …About thirty, but smart. Okay, that'll work for me. …Sure, I'll mention your name. That way she'll be more likely to want to help."

After listening for a moment, she responds, "Augustus Hartunian, you know I always tread lightly. …Okay, no risks. Take care of yourself. I'll call again and let you know how it's going."

She loves her little apartment in the retirement village, but this five-star hotel brings a special panache into Charlotte's otherwise routine life. She snuggles down in the oversized bed under an opulent comforter, realizing that she is grinning, and finally allows herself to laugh aloud.

Morning brings a light rain, which Charlotte loves, and she regularly carries a small, retractable umbrella in her shoulder bag. Remembering a busy but elegantly scrumptious eating establishment a couple of blocks off Times Square, she hikes to Au Bon Pain, the one on Fifty-Fifth Street. The going-to-work crowds scurry along the canyon-like streets, most tourists still asleep or having breakfast in their hotels.

During her time living in California, she realized how spread out a place can be, getting from one spot to another often perilous— well, after all, in a heavy metal vehicle traveling at seventy miles per hour, it takes only an instant of distraction to bring on a life-threatening tangle of twisted steel and maimed bodies. In New York, the opposite floods in on her. To be sure, there must be numerous collisions, but the narrow streets and enormous number of vehicles keep the speed down and injuries less serious. *This,* she muses, *is the remarkable, man-made American Grand Canyon.*

At Au Bon Pain one selects her own food, pays at the register, and searches for an empty table; she finds one around the corner in the L-shaped café. While sipping on an aromatic herbal tea and munching a banana-nut muffin, she ponders her next activities: Call Detective Shanna Cavanaugh and meet with her; arrange a time to converse with Donald Stout—being certain not to threaten him with accusations; consult with the custodian at the Antwerp Building; get in touch with Corrine Gelly; ask Broadway for transportation to visit Brooklyn again, either in the hospital or where she lives.

Cats is still playing on Broadway. So is *Phantom of the Opera.* Her trek back to the hotel takes her past several theaters, doors open for ticket purchases, the plays themselves several hours away.

Back in her room, she calls Detective Cavanaugh, gets a voice-mail message, and explains her purpose, noting that Detective Augustus Hartunian referred her. It takes less than ten minutes for her phone to buzz, and Shanna Cavanaugh says, in a pleasant voice, "Well, well, Augie Hartunian, an old friend. So how can I be of service to you?"

They agree to meet at the Starbucks across the way from the Sheraton, Charlotte aware with just a hint of irony that a police person can park wherever she wants.

Charlotte's perception of Kyla's boyfriend has energized Broadway. Aside from being struck by her beauty, the fact that she is his wonderful sister's best friend seduces him to want more.

"How about meeting me for lunch at Fridays in Times Square? Nothing unique about the food, but it's clean and pleasant enough."

To his great joy, she agrees. Something cooking. At least maybe a better understanding of what pulls on her. Besides, maybe she knows something about Brook's accident she hasn't disclosed. *Nothing conspiratorial,* he hastens to tell himself. *Contemplating Kyla being furtive in any way would be offensive.*

Though unknown to each of them, there are two meetings, an hour or so apart, not more than two blocks from each other, neither Charlotte nor Broadway assuming to be detectives, yet both on the trail of information hoping to hold up to the light Brooklyn's tragic fall.

On his way to his rendezvous with Kyla, Broadway's cell plays its melody. It is Mark Angel.

"Hey, handsome, guess what?"

Aware that his agent likes him—likes him in more than one way—Broadway, nonetheless, welcomes his calls, his professional career brighter since he took Angel on.

"Tell me."

"They are auditioning for a new musical based on the movie *Sleepless in Seattle.* I already submitted your profile, pics and all, and they want to take a look. The part I suggested to them was not the Tom Hanks lead role, but Meg Ryan's boyfriend's one. I know you've studied voice, and you'd be involved in two songs, one a quartet, with the lead and two women, and the other a solo when you find out you're being dumped. Think you can handle that?"

"Oh, man, can I! When's the call?"

"Auditions begin in a couple of days. Opening isn't for three months. They believe they have the Shubert Theater. Big time! And they're ready to start building sets as soon as they sign. There are sixteen new songs, and the writers have great credentials, both with hits here in New York as well as Hollywood."

With this news swelling in him like a tsunami, he enters Fridays and sees Kyla already seated in a corner booth. It is all he can do not to blurt out the news—but, after all, that isn't the purpose of this meeting.

"You look…uh, great," he says.

She is dressed in a stylish amber-colored blouse, tied tightly below her breasts to show a bare midriff, the chilly weather ignored. On her head is a Mau cap, dark blue, with a tiny brim; her ebony hair is pulled back and braided the way Brooklyn wears hers.

"Thanks." She stops and, in a reciprocal gesture, replies, "So do you."

The ambiance is less than Broadway had hoped for, somewhat noisy, with the lighting like an acrylic painting meant to glow.

What I'd love to do, he thinks, *is dispense with all the cliché stuff, grab hold of this dazzling woman in a bear hug, and cover her soft mouth with the most erotic kiss in the history of the world!*

Pure nonsense, he acknowledges, *since she has no reciprocal feelings and is already spoken for.*

To his utter surprise, she says, "You like me, don't you."

"Of course I like you."

"I mean in a serious way."

"Uh, unless I'm mistaken, you're hooked in with someone— Andy, the computer guy."

"Situations don't eliminate feelings. I was asking you about your feelings."

He squirms in his seat, avoiding her eyes, and is about to say something when a smiling server looms above them with, "What can I get you to drink?"

After a moment, he realizes Kyla is still waiting for his response and splays his hands out in supplication. "Look, you are an astonishing woman. Brook loves you. I won't say you're not appealing to me. You are. But it's a tricky situation. I wouldn't presume to intrude on a relationship already going on."

"Shaky," she says. "Andy is…well, he's someone I owe a lot to. Can't say I'm crazy about him, but it's payback time for favors tendered."

"What does that mean?"

"It's a long story. I won't bore you with it."

Something penetrates, and he is aware that there are ifs and buts in her life schema. Unfortunately, it offers him no clear direction. Is she saying she is open to a new connection? After all, he called the meeting, and since he arrived, it's her agenda they've been discussing.

As if synchronized, she laughs and says, "Hey, handsome, you initiated this little get-together and so far it's been about me. What's going on?"

They are interrupted again by the server, this time Broadway noticing that she is an attractive blonde—tall, trim, and shapely. One, he is sure, of the thousands of young women who collect in New York hoping to hitch their wagons to an entertainment star. She wears a name tag: *Helen.* Lots of Helens in the world, each one special in her own way. *Wonder what she thinks is her salable quality?* He smiles at another badge below her ID, this one reading, *I'm working as a waiter, but I really am a star.*

The order given, Broadway again realizes it is his turn to speak.

"Doesn't have to be now, but sometime I'd like to understand what you and Andy are all about. The other thing is what happened to Brook. You must have some theory or, even more, some insight on the whole thing."

"Look, the goon who runs the show at our agency is capable of almost anything. He's an exploiter. I was glad when Brook told me she was getting out—even if it might cost her the top spot. Would that idiot deliberately try to hurt her? Who knows?"

"But Kyla, in your opinion, is one of the other folks connected with the studio at all likely to do this?"

She is silent for a time, then, in a lowered voice, says, "I mentioned Corrine Gelly, the girl who was recently let go. She hasn't been around, so I don't know how she could have been there that day without someone seeing her. Then, she shows up last night, as if guessing the goon will want to reinstate her."

"So, if she was seen by someone the day Brook was attacked, it would be news. I mean, it would be an important clue."

"Yes, but so far, no one has said anything. And I'll tell you something else you don't know that could be operating here."

She gets conspiratorial as if ears are open all around them and finally whispers, "Our lovely tyrant boss actually goes both ways."

"What?"

"Stout. He keeps it in the closet, but some of us—not Brook, by the way—have known he's been sleeping with one of his male models."

"Damn! Must have a hell of a lot of energy. All those women he's seduced and having a guy on the side."

"He lives for pleasure. Yes, he knows his business, and he's a tough taskmaster, but he's also totally self-serving, a bon vivant."

"You say Brook didn't know?"

"Well, she wouldn't have started up with him if she was in on his sordid history. I think she may have suspected something, which gave her more reason to dump him. But, think about it; it also gave him more reason to want to get her out of the way."

"Afraid she might blow his hidden agenda?"

"Any of us might, but maybe Brook said something to him when she kissed him off."

What a complicated mess! Thoughts scramble in his head: *My sister finally gets up the courage to get rid of the asshole and might not realize she was giving him reason to take revenge on her. I wonder if she did admit she knew about his secret life.*

"Do you know which model Stout was banging? I mean, as far as I know, there are only two men in the troupe."

Pause, and Kyla says, "It may surprise you because he's very protective of Brook, but…it was Brent White."

8

"I subscribe to *The Science News*, and I read in the last issue that scientists crushed the brains of locusts and cockroaches, put them under a microscope, introduced E. coli and staph bacteria, and let the mix sit overnight. In the morning, the bacteria were all dead. So, who needs penicillin if we have insect brains?"

Sitting across from Charlotte in the Starbucks in Times Square is Shanna Cavanaugh; she smiles and asks, "And you are telling me this because…?"

"Oh, Detective, I simply like people to know I am not a narrow person. I read and study all sorts of things." She hesitates and adds, "Isn't life just filled with fascinating new discoveries?"

Cavanaugh is a dark-haired woman, surprisingly pretty for one of New York's finest—though hard-looking female cops could be a stereotype tattooed on law-enforcement people by a cynical public, a stereotype beginning to break down because of all the beautiful FBI and police types portrayed on television. She is tall and slim, dressed in a tan pants suit with no visible display advertising her official capacity. Her smile is full and honest. Charlotte likes her at once.

When they met, the officer shook Charlotte's hand vigorously, a gesture that Charlotte relished: no deference to her because of her age. They ordered, the detective a hazelnut cappuccino, Charlotte her usual herbal tea.

"So, you know Augie," Cavanaugh says, appreciative of the connection.

"He and I have…well, we worked on a couple of murder cases

49

together."

"Hold on, are you the amateur lady who helped solve the so-called accident crime? Where a child was killed?"

She turns shy and says softly, "I guess you could say that."

"Hartunian told me about you. I didn't remember the name. He said you were a natural."

"Not sure what that means. I have a sort of intuition about things. I guess Augie respected that."

"Well, I need to know what in hell brings you into the Big Apple? Is there some murder we legal sleuths know nothing about?"

"Oh, it's not a murder, but it is, possibly, an attempted murder, and the local police are ignoring it. They say there is no evidence and the whole thing could be an accident. The family asked me to look into it."

She lays out the episode with Brooklyn, includes the dating connection between her and Stout, and ends with the kiss-off and the fall.

"I've spoken with Brooklyn. No doubt in her mind she was forcibly struck from behind and sent airborne. Damaged her spine. Here's an absolute beauty, a promising model, who may never walk again."

Cavanaugh is silent for a moment. One never knows the triggers a story sets off. She seems to turn inward; in her own life, a little sister was abused by a stepfather and ended up brain-damaged. This sordid event prompted her to go to the police academy and enter the field of law enforcement.

She frowns and says, "I make no excuses for the cops. We all work under the justice system rules: no proof, no prosecution. But, let's assume someone did this to…uh, Brooklyn, what do you see as my role in it?"

"At the top of the stairs, just to the right, is a custodian's room filled with cleaning supplies. Brook felt something bulky and hard hit her in the back, and my guess is that it came from that closet. I looked in there and saw a can, maybe five-gallon size, of floor polish that could well have been used. The pusher likely stuck it back in the room before hurrying away."

"Yes, so I'm beginning to get the idea. You want me to examine that little room?"

"Well, my thought is that since Brook has very long hair that goes halfway down her back, whatever was used to bludgeon her may have picked up a hair or two. That, at least, would take away the accident theory."

"Good thinking. I can see why Augie was impressed." She pauses and then tacks on, "Interesting, isn't it, how we women have a lot more subtle insight than the men."

"I've never been married, so my experience with men is from a cozy distance, though I have experienced a 'get to the point' attitude. Men I have known want the problem solved yesterday, while most conundrums are complicated and take time to unravel."

"Is the area marked off as a crime scene? You know, yellow tape and all that?"

"No. The police decided it wasn't a crime."

"Unless the owner gives permission, we would need a warrant for me to go in officially to search for anything. You, as a visitor, could get in, but what you find would be unofficial and likely not admissible in court."

"Hmm. Can you get a warrant based on what I've told you?"

"Tell you what. Let me check out the cops who did the investigation. If I can nudge a little suspicion out of them, a judge might favor us with a warrant."

"Another thing, Shanna—is it okay if I call you Shanna…?"

"I love it."

"Okay, then Shanna, it might be that the culprit, if there is one, forgot to wear gloves, and we could find fingerprints on whatever was used as the weapon."

"Would have to be either dumb or careless, but who knows. Sounds like an amateur perp, so anything is possible."

This Starbucks is noisy and crowded, not surprising for the heart of Times Square, and intermittently, a siren blares out on the street as an ambulance or fire vehicle speeds by. Their communication is challenged, and Charlotte decides it is time to close.

"The family has put me up at the Sheraton, quite posh as you know, so when you have something to pass on, you can reach me there; room 1840, with a great view of the skyline." Her look is a blend of delight and guilt— not her usual kind of lodging. "And, guess what? I also have a cellphone." She dictates her number.

Her mix of feelings isn't lost on Detective Cavanaugh. "Hey, Charlotte, live it up."

—

On her cute little plastic phone, Charlotte punches in Broadway's number, and after two rings, he answers, "Yes, Charlotte?"

Caller ID, she realizes—amazing how there are no secrets anymore—and replies, "Are you in the midtown area? I would love to visit with Brooklyn again."

"Just off Fiftieth and Seventh Avenue. Where are you?"

"Two blocks from there. Do you have your car?"

"No, but I'll meet you in ten minutes at the kiosk where tourists wait in line for twofer tickets for the shows. We can get a cab."

"Is Brooklyn home yet?"

"Came home this morning. Mother had one of her aides pick her up and take her to her apartment. We hired a twenty-four-seven nurse to be with her, at least for now."

The taxi drops them off uptown, just beyond Carnegie Hall and the Russian Tea Room; they might have walked, but it would have been ten or more blocks.

"She has a one-bedroom place on the third floor," Broadway says as he touches the button that opens the elevator door. "The nurse will sleep on the couch, which turns into a bed. You might have noticed this building has a mom-and-pop eating establishment on the first floor. Closes at three in the afternoon but serves good breakfasts and fresh fruit so one doesn't have to find a market."

"My kind of place. The retirement village where I live allows us to take bananas, oranges, and apples out of the dining hall. I stock up once every few days."

The nurse, with the incongruous—considering the names of her ward and her brother—but oddly synchronistic name of America, a woman in her fifties, with a large nose and close-set eyes, her hair in a bun on top, answers their ring. She gives off a pleasant grin and invites them in.

Charlotte, with a private, quirky smile, is aware that she is in the presence of three people named after places on the planet.

"The lady has been napping. I think she's up by now."

"How does she seem?" Broadway asks.

"Low. Cries off and on. It's tough to lose body movement. She's still a lovely woman, but it don't seem to lift her spirits."

The apartment is well appointed; Charlotte is not surprised, certain that a child of Sarah Farivar would not live in squalor. It is neat and spotless, and Broadway, catching Charlotte's eyes perusing the place, says, "Once a week, a cleaning person comes in and puts everything in order. Not that Brook is a slob, but keeping a residence tidy is not her thing."

They move into the bedroom, where Brooklyn looks small in a king-sized bed. She sees them, and her expression doesn't change.

As they approach, she says in a bitter voice, "Came to visit the cripple?"

"To visit my amazing sister," Broadway says, as he leans over and kisses her forehead.

"You have better color than when I saw you yesterday," Charlotte says.

"A chunky little guy was here this morning, moving my legs and arms. Said I need exercise so my muscles don't atrophy. Really! What difference does it make if my muscles atrophy?"

"All the difference in the world, Sis. I bet you'll be dancing up a storm in a few months."

His pronouncement brings out a sob from Brooklyn, and she turns her head away.

"I've been thinking this whole thing over," Charlotte begins, "and while I can't do anything about your injury, I'm hoping we can corral the awful person who did this to you."

"And how will you do that?" Sarcastic. Cynical.

"A New York detective and I have met—a woman, by the way—and she is willing to help us. But there are a few more things I'd like to know."

Broadway snaps to attention with this information while Brooklyn remains silent, her face a stony map of mistrust.

Resignation makes sense, Charlotte thinks, *especially when one believes she is maimed for life.* She flashes on the Hemingway statement that we must "…become strong at the broken places."

"Are you willing to describe to me how you…uh, dumped Donald Stout? I mean, what exactly did you say to him? And how long afterwards did your fall occur?"

Deep sigh, and then, "I told the prick that his threats won't dissuade me and that we were no longer a couple. I told him I was not a masochist and refused to be treated like dirt—which, I know, he does with all the people in his life."

"Ah, and did he then warn you or make any overt threat?"

"He did his usual. Finger in my face, eyes raging, words guttural and abusive. When I walked out, he shouted at me, 'You'll regret this!' I went into the restroom—there's only one for men and women—and locked the door. I stayed in there for about five minutes. I guess I was crying."

"And then you headed for the stairway?"

"Not right away. It was afternoon and no one else was around, but I went into the large, mirrored room—Donald's private office has one door that opens into it—and sat on the carpet for a few minutes. I needed to think things through. Pretty sure I'd get fired."

"No one saw you there?"

"Well, Brent poked his head in the door—he's a male model— and smiled at me. Must have seen how miserable I looked. I didn't feel like talking so I gathered my things, but before I finally left, maybe three minutes later, I saw Brent knock on Donald's door. It opened, and after he went in, I heard that door click, like being locked from the other side. I didn't see anyone. But here's something a little odd: Brent wears cologne, a fragrance I know rather well, and I could smell it in the hall, near the stairway."

"Brent is your pal, right? I mean, he's shown good feelings toward you."

She seems to be wearying of the dialogue and mutters, "Yes, he likes me."

Broadway says, "Hard for me to believe Brent would do anything to hurt you."

A good sleuth collects information, doesn't give it away, so Charlotte says nothing about Kyla's observation that Brent and Donald Stout had a physical connection. As she knows, patience is the key, and if a person is aware of something, eventually it will come out.

"I'm sure he didn't," Brooklyn says in a whisper.

"One more thing," Charlotte continues. "This Corrine Gelly model, the one who was let go, we saw her last evening at the studio, and I would love to speak with her. Do you object to that? And, if not, do you have her contact information?"

Mild surprise on Brooklyn's face animates her for an instant. "She was at the pep rally last night? Donald's little tribute to himself?"

Charlotte smiles at this deprecation, not uncalled-for, yet a unique way to describe Stout's evening session.

Broadway says, "I was surprised to see her there, too. Kyla thinks she was hoping to be called back into the fold now that they're one model short."

"I don't care if you talk to her. She's a spiteful gal, has some marginal talent. Probably better suited for the porn industry than as a model; if you've ever seen pics of the porn lineups, not too many of them have beautiful faces. Would she do this to me? Maybe. But as far as I know, no one saw her that day."

"Yes," Charlotte says. "But then, you noted that other than you and Stout and, later, Brent, no one else seemed to be around."

"She lives across from the park, on the west side. Her phone number and address are in my cell, over on the table."

Charlotte can see Brooklyn's fatigue, rises from the chair next to the bed, smiles her sweet smile, and says, "Okay, enough of this. Get some rest, pretty lady. And, though I'm no expert on this, do cooperate with the physical therapist. You'll be amazed how one area of the body can learn to compensate for another."

Broadway pokes around on his sister's cellphone and jots down Corrine's number. As he and Charlotte turn to go, the door-chime sounds. America responds, and, in a moment, former boyfriend, Aaron Batchelor, strides into the bedroom.

9

"Where to?" Broadway asks. They are on Fifty-Ninth Street, standing in a bright November sun, the long row of apartments, including Brooklyn's, directly behind, and the entrance to Central Park across the way, which gives the sky clearance to intrude in on them. Though the air is chilled, the sun's warmth feels like a stimulant on their necks. For Charlotte, it provides needed energy, for, despite their unremitting array of neon, the cavernous, murky alleyways of Central Manhattan act as a depressant.

"I'm thinking I would like to speak with Stout. He saw me with you and Sarah, but I doubt he would find me threatening—at least not at this point in our endeavor."

"And me? You don't want me with you?"

"Oh, I think he would find that threatening. If I go alone, he likely will look at me as a meddling but inconsequential old woman."

Broadway laughs. "You are anything but that. In the little time I've known you, I'm already pretty stunned by your clear focus. You seem to know exactly what to do."

"Now, young man, that is rubbish. Different from Robert Burns's mouse, when it comes to the future, '…I guess and fear.'"

"An aficionado of poetry, I see. But, I haven't seen you guess and fear too much yet."

"Everyone does at some time or other. Of course, we all have unique stimuli that set off our trepidation." She pauses and asks, "What are yours?"

He thinks for a moment as he spies an empty taxi and waves it down.

"That I'll be alone. My mother will go someday soon, and Brook is struggling. And, so far, I have no love person in my life."

"There is one you'd like to have."

"Okay, smarty, so there is. But, as of now, she's ineligible."

In the cab, he says, "I had lunch with her earlier."

Charlotte says nothing but raises her eyebrows and looks directly at him.

"Something screwy about her relationship with that Andy guy. She told me it was complicated and that she owed him something."

"Ah, yes. I could see the twist there. They are not a compatible couple. But she didn't tell you what the hold was?"

"No. Said she didn't want to bore me."

"Patience. She'll tell you."

Different from Broadway, Charlotte is not familiar with New York cab drivers, and her body tightens and leans at each sudden turn. A picture of the cabbie smiles at them on the back of the front seat. He is Armando Flores, mustached, dark-skinned, black-haired, probably in his twenties, probably from the Caribbean, and with a gleaming white, toothy smile. To Charlotte, the taxis seem in competition, and it will only be a matter of time before they collide, hopefully without her in one of them.

"What do you think this Batchelor fellow wants?"

"Beats me. They haven't been together for a year or more. At first he was resentful that Brook wanted to break it off with him, but she told me he got over it and found a new woman rather quickly. He dotes on women but needs to control them."

"Could have read about her in the paper—or could have been carrying a subterranean grudge," Charlotte ponders aloud, "and wouldn't that be something."

They are deposited in front of the Antwerp Building—in one piece—and pause at the door.

"You know I'm here, in case you need me. You have my cell number."

"I'll be fine. Enjoy the sunshine—if any of it manages its way in here."

She climbs the stairs rather easily for her age, her legs sturdy and still strong, which she attributes to the Jazzercise classes at Bigelow Village.

It is afternoon, and, again, no one seems to be around.

Feeling her way about, she enters the large exercise room with the wall mirror, remembering that Stout took his break through a door marked *PRIVATE*. Typical of her assertive style, she raps sharply four times.

Faintly, she hears a voice inside call out, "Enter."

When she does, she sees Stout, his back to her, focused on a computer screen. He says dryly, "Leave it on the table."

"Sorry. I have nothing to leave."

He spins about sharply. "Who? Oh, I know you. The lady with the Farivar family. What do they want now?"

"I'm here on my own, not because they sent me."

"Okay, so what do you want?"

So abrasive, this narcissistic man, so unwelcoming. The reports did not exaggerate: not a pleasant fellow.

"I'm sort of a distant friend, and I am saddened by Brooklyn's injury. I would love to find out more about it. Don't mean to intrude on your busy afternoon, but perhaps you can help."

"Look, lady, Brook was my best model. If you're her friend, you know she and I were involved as well. What happened to her was a first-class tragedy. I'm sorry for it. And that's all I can say."

"Mr. Stout, you run a tight ship, and you seem to know your team of models rather well. Brooklyn has told the family that she was—and this is a horrendous accusation—shoved down those stairs. Is there anything at all that would make someone so outraged as to do such a thing?'

Looking distressed, he rises and walks toward Charlotte. She does not see his approach as threatening and holds her ground.

A few feet away, he stops and says, "This fucking business is a monster when it comes to competition. My outfit is modest in size, but it has been the jumping-off place for a few beauties, and they've now become world celebrities. All my girls—or men—know the payoff for rising to the top in this profession: millions of dollars, fame, acting gigs, you name it. Brooklyn had the best chance of all. Her looks are to die for, her style flawless. She was a brilliant learner. A break for her was just around the corner. Her fall was the ultimate tragedy. Who did it? I haven't a clue."

"You promoted Kyla to the number one spot."

"Next best. Kyla has many of the same qualities."

Charlotte hesitates and asks, "What happened with the woman

named Corrine Gelly? I'm told she was here last night but is no longer in your fold."

"That's right. Corrine is a fierce competitor. I like that about her. Unfortunately, she doesn't quite have the look or the…uh, body of my other models. She wants back in, but I don't plan to let her. Could she be pissed? Sure, but more at me than Brooklyn."

He looks at Charlotte curiously and asks, "What's your real investment in all this? You come in here acting like Sherlock Holmes. What's it to you?"

"I assure you, I am a total amateur when it comes to sleuthing around. It's just that I care about Brook and her family, and they are too wounded to even ask questions. Oh, I know, the mother can be blunt and annoying, but believe me, she and her two children are devastated."

"Yeah, I get that. So am I." He wheels about and heads toward his computer. "Got work to do. Show yourself out."

"One more question, please, Mr. Stout. You say that you and Brook were involved, and I take that to mean—in the very specific language of the day—that you were lovers. I don't mean to trivialize that fact, but the word is that she was…closing you out and that you were outraged. Any truth to that?"

A sound like an animal growl comes from him, and he says, "You ever been dumped, lady? It's no fun. Sure, I was upset. But would I cut off my nose to spite my face? Hell no. Like I said, she was my best model." He puffs up like a towering cloud and blurts out: "It would be stupid for me to want to hurt her. Now clear out of my office before my outrage spills over on you."

"I doubt, sir, that you would do harm to an elderly woman, so your threat is empty, though I'm not convinced your threat to Brooklyn was empty. Get what I mean?"

He actually spits on his carpet, fuming with rage.

"All right, I'm going. Thanks for your time. As they say in the movies, don't leave town. I may have more questions later."

She places her hand on the doorknob, turns, peruses the room—about a dozen close-up portraits of Stout's models line one wall, marked, she notices, by the absence of Brooklyn's—and, taking a calculated risk, says, "By the way, Donald Stout, your secret is out."

His stare is acrid as his brows wrinkle, a slow burn reddening his cheeks. "What the hell you talking about, lady?"

Again, her smile was wry and mysterious.

"Stout and out," she says to herself, and as she exits, she can't help but smile at her propensity to make rhymes.

10

Outside, in the sunlight reflecting off high windowpanes, she sees Broadway standing in the street next to a pair of autos, clearly engaged in an accident. A female figure is sitting on the asphalt and Broadway is holding her hand.

A siren, distant at first, grows in decibels, and, in a moment, an emergency vehicle arrives.

It takes several minutes to untangle the event, and no one, it turns out, was seriously injured. The woman's face is bruised from the front airbag that exploded. The person in the other car seems unscathed. Both autos are badly damaged, and each driver makes a public statement of appreciation for Broadway's quick work in getting them out and tending to them.

"You're a hero," Charlotte says.

"I'm always afraid when a major collision occurs that something could explode, so I coaxed and pulled each occupant away. Luckily, what you see is not too bad." He stops, spreads his lips in a beatific smile, and adds, "The woman whose hand I was holding—at her request, by the way—is an actor. I didn't know her, but when she told me what she had been in, I recalled the name."

"Anyone I'd know?"

"I doubt it. It's 'China Olivier.' She's a singer-dancer, too."

"Did you get her number?" Charlotte asks with a whimsical shrug.

"As a matter of fact, she asked me for mine."

"Not surprised."

"So, what happened in the Antwerp Building? Did you see the

Darth Vader of Manhattan?"

"I did. He's a piece of work. I think he would have loved to shove me down his stairs. No, wait. Hold on. That doesn't mean I know for sure that he's the one."

"What did you find out?"

"He's a callous fellow and is quick to dismiss anyone who crosses him. Brooklyn's picture is already off his rogue's gallery wall of models. The Gelly woman is, as far as he's concerned, no longer a viable talent."

"We know he's a boor, and if I had my choice, we'd find a way to shut him down. He exploits these folks, especially the women."

"I planted a seed that his little secret—his going both ways— is no longer a secret. Wouldn't be surprised if he feels threatened by that."

"Hey, I hope he doesn't turn any vengeance on you."

"Too obvious. If he is the culprit in Brooklyn's fall, he has to lie low. Any new violence will point the finger."

"Okay, Ms. Marple. So what next? What do we do now?"

"Do you know how to get to where the Gelly woman lives?"

"If I remember, she still has a day job in the Museum of Modern Art up on Fifty-Third Street. We have her contact info, but if you want to stop over there, it's only a few blocks."

"What kind of job?"

"Since she was only selected a few times for runway work, she had to hang on to some sort of income. Brook used to say she was probably the poorest docent at the museum and jokingly referred to her as the artists' worst enemy."

"So they were openly hostile, Brook and Corrine?"

"Not really. Brook never confronted her. It was a private observation since she knows Corrine's personality."

"Which is?"

"She's Miss Uncongeniality. Negativity personified. We often wondered who had wounded her in her childhood."

"Hmm. I've seen that a lot. Damaged goods. Okay, let's take a hike. It's good for the mild arthritis in my lower back."

"You mean you're not perfect?"

—

MOMA is the acronym by which New Yorkers know the museum. Charlotte is attracted to the displays they book and owns a reproduction of Picasso's black-and-white Guernica, a powerful anti-war painting. Their gift shop has been the source of several art pieces she has purchased for friends living in her village.

"If she's on a tour, we may not be able to talk with her," Broadway says. "But, I think she shares a little office somewhere in the complex. We'll have to ask."

"Is she partial to you? I mean, your presence won't stir resentment, will it?"

"Oh, no. In fact, she actually hit on me once when I was at one of the shows."

"Say, young fellow, you get hit on a lot."

Broadway blushes. "Damned if I know why."

"Really? I know why." She laughs, and he blushes more.

An information counter is in the lobby, and Broadway approaches a young woman dressed in a dark blue uniform. At different points in the large entry, there are posters on tripods promoting a showing of the current resident artist, Salvador Dali, emphasizing his eerie, oozing depictions.

"Can you tell us where Corrine Gelly's office is?"

The woman looks up at Broadway, for a moment seems startled, smiles broadly, and says, "Of course."

Charlotte repeats under her breath, "I know why."

The woman's badge notes that her name is Kelly Capello, and when she describes how to reach Corrine's office—up the ramp on the second floor—Broadway says, in a sweet, low voice, "Thank you, Kelly."

The door to the docents' office is open, and they enter but see no one. Broadway calls out, "Corrine, are you in there?"

From around a corner, they hear a voice, "Just a minute." Corrine enters, stands for a moment, a paper cup in her hand, perhaps surprised, perhaps annoyed.

"What are you doing here?"

"This is Charlotte Smart, a friend of my mother's, and we would like to speak with you."

She looks about, strides over to her desk, pushes a few papers around, and replies, "I'm pretty busy."

"Won't take long. Charlotte is curious about some things and cares about our family, so she asked if I would introduce you."

"I'm pleased to meet you," Charlotte says. "Saw you at the studio, but we didn't get to talk."

"That cad isn't interested in bringing me back on. He's a horse's ass."

Broadway says, "We may agree with you about that."

"We heard there was an opening now that Brooklyn is off his list."

"That's why I was there, but he's got his favorites." She stops, a look of contempt on her face, and adds, "I'm not one of them."

"I wonder if there is anything about Brooklyn's tumble that you could help us understand. I mean, she isn't a clumsy person, and it isn't likely that she would simply fall down stairs she is so familiar with."

Corrine stares at Charlotte as if to ask, *Who in the hell are you, and why are you asking me?* Aloud, she says, "Someone fell a year ago, a new girl named Phillipa. Broke an arm. They don't light the area well. It isn't hard to misstep."

"I'm not sure if anyone told you," Charlotte says, ambling over to the desk and leaning forward, "but Brooklyn says she was pushed. That it was no accident."

A fleeting look of terror crosses Corrine's face, gone in an instant as she replies, "That bastard!"

"Stout?" Broadway asks.

"Who else? Yes, he was—pardon my French—shtooping Brook, but I gathered she was fed up with him, as every other woman has been. He probably got pissed at her and decided to take his revenge."

"So," Charlotte says, "you believe Donald Stout deliberately tried to injure Brooklyn."

"There was some talk about Phillipa being helped down those stairs too. Nobody paid much attention to it, but we all knew she was on the outs with the big man."

"Cross him and he punishes you," Charlotte says, as if to herself.

"Never got to do it with me. Didn't think I had the look. Wasn't even interested in sleeping with me. Almost all the number ones, over the years, have been his mistresses. Well, Kyla is in the pole position now, but she already has a guy and so is off limits to Stout."

"Is that how it works? If he knows someone is off limits, he lays off?"

"Not necessarily. This guy that Kyla is hooked up with, Andy Burrus, is a special case."

"How so?" Broadway asks, instantly on the alert.

"It's supposed to be secret stuff, but I gather that the Burrus family has a lot of dough, and when Kyla was auditioning, the son, Andy, kind of a playboy type—too much money, no skills, nothing to do with his time—wanted her as his toy girl. So, his family—the father, I think—gave Stout a bundle, Kyla was hired and 'given' to Andy, and she's indebted to him. But, it also makes her immune to big Donald's usual agenda."

"She agreed to secure her career by going along with the 'deal' to be Andy's…uh, girlfriend? That's like blackmail," Broadway says, the disappointment in his tone apparent to Charlotte.

"Call it what you like. We all do that. It's hard to make it in the world of show and tell, and, of course, models have to show more than they tell."

"I don't mean to be critical, but you sound terribly bitter about all this," Charlotte says, moving away from the desk as if to give Corrine space.

"Shit!" Corrine explodes. "Who wouldn't be? Look at me. I'm not grotesque or anything. Maybe my boobs are too small, maybe my hair frizzes up, maybe my nose is a trifle too long, but I'm a presentable woman who is locked out of a profession I'm dying to enter. And that boor, Stout, is a prime reason."

"You have to go through him? Aren't there other agencies?"

"After his poison is spread? Good luck. It's like being blacklisted."

"You really hate that guy," Broadway says, nodding in agreement.

"You got it."

Charlotte leans back in and asks, "What would it take for him to reconsider? With Brooklyn no longer there, he does need another model, right?"

"I told you, I thought the same thing. Too bad about your sister," she says to Broadway, "but when it happened, I figured I'd reappear. Donald Duck Stout acted as if I were dead. Not even a hello. I'm not one of his stable mares."

Charlotte catches Broadway's eye, turns away from Corrine, and says, "Corrine, believe me, I'm sorry for your situation. Thank you for even listening to us. We won't trouble you any longer."

"If you can figure out a way to harpoon that Stout prick, more power to you!"

They descend the ramp and step out of the museum onto Fifty-Third, and Broadway asks, "Think she's a clever liar?"

"I have no doubt, but that doesn't mean she is the culprit with Brooklyn. Don't know if you noticed, but I took her paper cup very carefully and slid it into my purse. It would be nice to have her fingerprints. However, it is fascinating to learn about that Andy Burrus fellow and the hold he has on Kyla. Money speaks loudly and clearly."

Broadway looks forlorn and replies, "Yes, damn it, and it overpowers logic and honest love."

His pain is not lost on Charlotte.

"By the way," Charlotte tacks on, "Corrine's perfume. I recognize it. Something called 'Black Midnight.' Advertised as perfect for a man or a woman."

11

Brooklyn allows the therapist to manipulate her legs, one crossing the other and back again, slow movements, with no sudden twists, each ending in pressure to stretch a bit more than the last time.

When it is over and the husky woman has left, she lies in her oversized bed, flushed with the exercise yet beleaguered still by her dismal situation.

America Lobero, her round-the-clock aide, asks, "Missy, is there anything I can get for you, something to drink?"

She shakes her head.

"The doctor is due any minute."

A brief look resembling pleasure appears for an instant, and she replies, "Better than a poke in the eye with a sharp stick."

In her hand she holds a note, given to her sealed, which she now reads silently for the fourth time:

Brook, I am so sorry for your accident. We were quite a pair, but I know you had a different focus than I. Some time has passed and I realize that I still care deeply about you. When I get to my office, I will write out a check to you for five thousand dollars. It's not a bribe or anything, but it's to help you with your recovery. No strings attached. These flowers are a peace offering. Love to you, Aaron.

Seeing him does stir some old feelings, though she is not sure if they are resurrected love or simply familiarity. She lies here now, lips turned downward in a smirk, and actually says out loud, "A-B, when I kissed you off, you were enraged enough to want to kill me. I wouldn't have been surprised if you had decided to shove me down a flight of stairs. But, to reappear in my life like this—well, there's something phony about it."

As an afterthought, she mumbles, "And I don't need your blood money."

Her pondering is broken by the door-chime sounding, and shortly Dr. Bruce Landry saunters into her room, his unshaven face spread in a genial smile.

"Well beautiful woman, how goes it today?"

His mood tends to be contagious, and, right through her morose feelings, she gives him a welcoming smile back.

"A happy doctor. What a blast!"

"An appreciative patient. What a delight!"

"So, what new development brings you to my bedside? Am I terminal, or is there hope?"

"Let's hope your injury is terminal, and you'll soon be up and dancing in the rain."

"Is it raining?"

"Not today, but it will be. Snowing too."

"If no bad news, then what?"

"Wanted to visit with you, see how the physical therapy is going, ask some questions, and make some suggestions."

"Suggest away."

"A couple of questions first. Are you in any pain?"

"I'm not."

"Do you feel any numbness or any sensation in your lower limbs?"

She thinks for a moment and says, "Last night, I awoke about three and could swear my right leg was itching. When I touched it, no feeling."

Dr. Landry is silent for a time and says, "In spinal cases like this, I want you to know that the first sensation that seems to return is itching."

A light shines in Brooklyn's eyes—only briefly, but nonetheless there, and it is not lost on Bruce Landry.

Brooklyn murmurs, "So maybe there is hope."

"Look, attitude has a lot to do with healing. Some patients drag themselves down into a pit and can't climb out. What I want you to do is go back to a few weeks ago, to your healthy, exuberant, physically gifted self, remember the joy and the challenge, and understand that this is simply another challenge. Yes, it is a daunting one, but it is something you can and will conquer."

Now, at last, a full smile from Brooklyn. "With such an upbeat doc, how can I not do what you say?"

There is another silence. "And besides," Landry says, "I like you, and I want you vigorous and sound."

Softly, Brooklyn says, "Hey, I like you too."

"Uh, well, I also want you to begin a regimen of sitting up straight in bed and dangling your legs over the side, trying with all your might to see if you can get even a toe to wiggle."

Brooklyn cries.

"Sorry, I didn't mean…"

"It's not you. My legs have always been my pride. I was a runner in high school. I've had strong calves and thin, shapely ankles. Now I have to see if my toes can move…."

Almost in a whisper, Landry says, "To keep those beautiful legs shapely, there has to be exercise. Otherwise, they will atrophy. At this time, I know you can't force your limbs to bend and flex, but the therapist can help with that, and let's see if, in a few days, you can help the helper."

He takes her hand and squeezes.

A warmth passes through her and she squeezes back. *What in hell, am I developing some sort of 'thing' for my doctor?* Smart as she is, she tells herself, *I'm pretty sure he has some sort of thing for me. Wow! Who'd have thought it?*

She can't know that Charlotte had thought it when she saw them together in the hospital.

"I'm curious," Landry begins, "how a lithe and athletic person like you can take such a horrendous fall. Was there a slippery place at the top of the stairs? Did you trip on something?"

A sob catches in Brooklyn's throat.

It takes a moment for her to blurt out, "Somebody pushed me."

"What?"

"I was hit hard on my back."

"You're saying it was not an accident? Do the authorities know?"

"They know but won't do anything about it. No proof. My word against…well, against everybody else."

"Holy crap, Brooklyn. There has to be a way to find out."

"You saw that elderly woman with my family. She's like an amateur detective or something, and my brother engaged her to investigate. I have no idea what she can do."

"But who would want to hurt you?"

"There might be a few people around. Could be envious other models, or a spurned boyfriend, or…anyone with a secret grudge."

"Is there any reason for you to be afraid? I mean, if the culprit's real intent was to kill you, will there be another try? If so, you need protection."

"You want to protect me?"

A short laugh and he says, "Want to is one thing, but I can't give up my work to sit at your side day and night."

"America, my nurse, is here all the time. She's pretty cautious about letting people in, and she's also strong. You should see her lift me up to give me a sponge bath."

The image of Brooklyn, stripped naked, being bathed, stirs Landry, and he licks his lips in nervousness.

"Here's my card," he says, "with my private cell number. Call me if you need anything at all."

"What if I just need someone to talk to?"

"That too. And I'll check in on you again in a day or two."

He squeezes her hand again and turns to go.

"Do try the exercise I suggested, and let me know if you feel any sensations in your lower extremities."

"I like it when you visit. Try to make it tomorrow."

"I like it too. I will."

—

The sun fades as cool winds whip up fulminating clouds, and an ominous parachute mantles the city. In the late afternoon, a slanting rain splatters Manhattan's darkened canyons. Charlotte has called Shanna Cavanaugh and now asks Broadway to come with her to the Antwerp Building again since the detective has secured a court order to enter and examine the locale of the fall.

Always alert to weather, Charlotte carries the little, expandable umbrella in her shoulder bag as the two of them exit another yellow taxi and walk together under her butterfly-decorated canopy with its bird-beak handle.

"My little brother in California gave me this," she tells Broadway. "They don't have much use for umbrellas in Los Angeles, except in January and February."

"Only been there once. Had a small part at the Taper Theatre. Ran for three weeks. I liked it, but more opportunity for stage work here in the Big Apple."

Small rivulets slither along the curbs, and, in the colder air, breath is visible, like little puffs of exhaled smoke. Charlotte remembers being in the big city at Christmas time, some fifteen years earlier, during a monster snowstorm; the Manhattan traffic, cabs and all, had come to a grinding halt. It lasted for nearly two days, ruining her and her friend's theater weekend, and it took the snowplow crew nearly a week to restore normal commerce; many folks blamed the mayor for being indolent.

Not the same now. This rain is a minor nuisance but not critical.

They enter the old building and at once see the typical yellow tape sectioning off the stairs, while above them they can hear, unmistakably, Donald Stout's shouting voice.

"Who the fuck is responsible for this? How can I run a business if my entry is shut off?" A brief delay, then, "How long are you going to take?"

Another voice—calmer, female—recognized by Charlotte as Detective Cavanaugh's, responds, "Calm down, sir. It will take as long as it takes. We may have a crime scene here, and our CSI team will collect what it needs, then we'll be on our way."

"Yoo-hoo, Detective," Charlotte calls out.

"Ah, Ms. Smart. Duck under the tape and come on up."

She and Broadway climb the stairs, he surprised at the vigor in Charlotte's step as she ascends. Quite a specimen, this Charlotte Smart, quite a septuagenarian!

As they reach the top, Charlotte's cellphone buzzes.

"Excuse me one moment," she says, normally reluctant to show priority to a distant caller over a person in her presence. She sees who it is and steps away for a bit of privacy.

An agitated male voice says, "Sister, what in hell are you doing?

Almost seventy and you're gallivanting into New York to solve another mystery? What's gotten into you?"

"Oh, Greg, this is fascinating. I'm meeting the most interesting people, beautiful and talented, and, yes, suffering from an awful crime."

"But why you?"

She is whispering: "Well, 'til now, the police refused to see it as an act of violence. A lovely young woman was pushed down a flight of stairs. She is alive but badly hurt. Her mother and brother contacted me. I couldn't turn them down. So far, not much progress. But some...."

"Are you in any danger? Knowing you, I'll bet you are."

"I don't think so. Whoever did this won't want to call attention to another act, obviously deliberate. The brother of the victim is quite a doll, and he's my constant companion. A substitute for you, little brother."

Stout's agitated voice roars over her so that she misses Greg's comment.

"Should have known that old lady was behind this! Meddling old fool."

"Got to go," Charlotte says. "A possible suspect is berating me."

She hears: "Stay close to that guy, the brother. If you need me there, I'll come."

"Don't be silly. I'm fine."

She turns and steps toward the little pool of officers at the open custodian's door. Despite her bird-beak umbrella, drops of water glisten on her shoulders and arms.

Detective Cavanaugh says, "I see the two of you have already met."

"She thinks she's Hercule Poirot," Stout says. "None of you will find anything here. No crime occurred. Brooklyn fell, that's all."

"Wonderful. Then this little investigation will clear everything up," Cavanaugh says. "Now, please step back and let the team do its work."

Stout snarls at Charlotte, his posture as menacing as a curled rattler's, about to strike. He slowly backs against a sidewall, arms folded, head on a level, ironically, with a painting of a dancer, crouched on parquet, in tears.

Cavanaugh smiles at Broadway as Charlotte introduces them. Well, of course, every female smiles at Broadway. On his part, there is a brief moment of surprise at the detective's smooth and symmetrical face, the surprise that often comes with seeing a "pretty" police person.

"The brother of the victim," Cavanaugh says. "How is your sister doing?"

"About as well as can be expected. She has a caretaker; she can't walk, doesn't have feeling in her legs, and is pretty depressed."

"Brooklyn is quite determined," Charlotte says, "and my bet is she will fight to regain her mobility." She stares at Donald Stout as she says this.

The forensic crew has already moved the heavy container of floor wax from the closet, and one of the men says to Cavanaugh, "Dusted this baby for prints. Got a variety. At least three, maybe four different ones. We'll take 'em to the lab."

"Excuse me," Charlotte says, "but two things: one is that you will likely find my prints there since I tried to heft the canister the other day to see how heavy it was and didn't have my plastic gloves with me. And two, by chance, did you discover any loose hairs on the canister? Brooklyn has long, blonde hair, and if that was indeed used to strike her in the back, there might be some collected hairs."

The same man signals to a helper and points. The second fellow, wearing those plastic gloves Charlotte mentioned, the kind one sees on television, kneels and shines a blue light on the canister. After barely ten seconds, he says, "The lady is right. Not a lot, but a couple of strands."

"Ah," Cavanaugh says, smiling caustically at Stout, "a crime scene!"

Stout frowns and mutters, "Don't look at me."

12

At the bottom of the stairs, several models are collected, including Kyla Pino and Brent White, milling about, gabbing curiously, and, as Charlotte, Shanna, and Broadway descend, the group falls silent.

"The tapes will be removed in a couple of minutes," the detective says. "Wanted to look around."

Still a silence, so Broadway says, "NYC detective. It has to do with Brook's fall."

"I visited with her only an hour ago," Kyla says. "Beautiful as ever, but really bitter."

"Yes," Broadway says. "I'd be too if my whole career suddenly exploded."

"Her doctor was just leaving. He told me he was optimistic."

"Glad to hear it. He likes Brook, and I think he's eager to help."

"I agree," Charlotte says. "He certainly likes Brooklyn."

Brent steps over close to the detective and says, "If you're here, it has to mean some treachery occurred. Can you tell us, or is it a secret?"

True to form, officers rarely answer questions, and Cavanaugh says, "What do you think happened?"

"Me? I don't know. I mean, she fell; we all know that, but that wouldn't be cause for a police investigation."

"Smart fellow," Cavanaugh says. "It might be a good idea for all of you to know that your friend and fellow model, the victim in this case, was likely propelled down these stairs by force. It was not an accident."

A few may have known this, but a whooshing intake of breath from the others, if not heard, can be felt as they absorb the stunning information that a serious crime has been committed.

The forensics team begins to work their way down the stairs, collecting and balling up the yellow tape. "All finished," one of them says.

"You're free to go on up," Cavanaugh announces. And, as an afterthought, tacks on, "Watch your backs. Don't go close to any deep cliffs."

The several models ascend, except for Brent White, who lingers.

In a moment, he sidles up to the little trio of Charlotte, Broadway, and the detective and, in a soft voice, says, "I was here that day."

—

The rain persists, and they stand in the entryway to the Antwerp Building, gazing out at the waterlogged traffic and the scurrying pedestrians, either pushed by or struggling against the blustery wind.

"Stout asked to see me, so I had been in his office. I went out into the studio room to exercise and Brook was there. She only spent a few minutes and then left."

"So," the detective says, "tell us your point."

"I didn't actually see anyone else, but I heard some muffled noises, then a short scream. By the time I got out there, Kyla was tending to Brook at the bottom."

"You were no longer with Stout when you heard the scream?"

"No. I had left his office and, as I said, was doing some stretching in the studio."

"And Stout, where was he at that time?"

"I'm not sure."

"Is there another door to his office besides the one into the studio?" Charlotte asks.

"Oh, yes. There is also another entrance to the building, in the back. His other door leads to that stairway."

"And does his other door also include a hallway that comes around to the front staircase?" Cavanaugh asks.

"Right. The back hall, we call it. None of us ever uses it. It's his private passage in and out when he wants to bypass people in the studio."

"You didn't see Stout any more after that?"

"No. He didn't show up where Brook had fallen, so I assumed he had gone out the back way."

Charlotte asks, "And you saw no one else?"

"Kyla had just arrived, and after a few minutes, two or three other models came in. The emergency team was here in about ten minutes."

Charlotte can see that Broadway has become agitated, and she touches his arm.

"Some sick person had to sneak in and do this. Either he or she knew how to get out the back way as well or had to climb down and step over my sister to get out."

"Good point, Broadway," Charlotte says. "And we also have to realize that an outsider would not likely know about the closet with the container that seems to have been the weapon."

Cavanaugh smiles. Amateur detective but pretty damned good. "Thanks," she says to Brent. "It's okay. You can go. Keep what you know to yourself. Perps become desperate when they think the noose is closing in on them."

When he is gone, Charlotte says to the detective, "I lifted the wax can to see how heavy it was, and, since I could handle it, I presume whoever used it to pummel Brook could have been a male or a female."

Definitely pretty damned good, Cavanaugh thinks.

—

In the studio, Donald Stout collects his selected invitees into a circle and says, "Listen up, you stars. The half dozen of you are the ones who will carry us, and I have some wonderful news to report."

He hesitates and asks, "Where's Brent?"

"Downstairs," Kyla says. "He's talking with the group that was checking out the stair area. He'll be right up."

Stout's eyes narrow, and an almost imperceptible sneer forms on his lips, which he discards at once as he says, "Okay, I know there is discomfort about what happened to Brooklyn. We all love her, but now we have to get on with our work.

"You remember we were bidding on a grand show of assorted wear at the Sheraton ballroom coming up very soon. It apparently came down to the Obregon Agency over near the East River and us. Well, I'm happy to report that they accepted our bid. We have less than a week to prepare. It isn't like a theater production where we have to learn lines and all, but we do need to practice—and at least view the new creations in advance, so I can decide on your assignments."

A model named Julia, tall, thin, sweet-looking, skin white as alabaster, asks, "I forget if you told us; is it Pierre Cardin, Wang, or what?"

"No, no, no, sweetheart. No forgetting is allowed. A good memory is critical in this business. It's Christian Dior, top of the line." He scowls at Julia, who shrinks away.

There is a moment of absolute silence as the team absorbs Stout's criticism, one of his traits they have learned to expect.

"That's probably the oldest one," Kyla says, adjusting the mood.

"Dior was Normandy-born and founded the House of Christian Dior in nineteen forty-seven. When he died in nineteen fifty-seven, Yves Saint Laurent succeeded him. Then, in nineteen ninety-six, John Galliano took over. He's the one with whom we negotiated."

Brent enters, softly says, "Sorry," and steps into the group of fellow models.

Stout ignores him and continues, "This is a most profitable venture for us, and it means bonuses for each of you if we pull it off. Dior created what was known as the New Look, and, believe it or not, much of it has lingered till today. These Dior fashions will be marketed throughout the world."

He stops to see if any one of his little band has a question. Kyla, now his number one runway model, says, "When will you have the artists' renderings? I mean, so we can see the various styles?"

"I have them now." He points to the long table at the far end of the studio, and the assembly can see fifty or more sheets of glossy paper spread out, covering the entire top.

"Tentatively, I have listed your names, sometimes more than one, by each creation. That is, of course, flexible, so don't think of it as a done deal. Your input is needed as well. Now, if there are no more questions, I suggest you peruse the entire collection and we'll see where it takes us."

When he finishes, the young and beautiful people move to the table, as Stout says, "I'd like to see you in my office, Brent."

When the two men have exited, Julia, red-faced and pouting, says, "Well, excuse me. I don't think he ever told us, so how was I supposed to know it was Dior?"

"Don't let him get to you," Kyla says. "We all have to absorb his periodic tirades. That's just who he is."

Andrea, a five-foot-ten-inch, long-legged, tan-skinned woman with deep charcoal eyes, says, "He's a horse's ass. We shouldn't have to take his crap. This is a cooperative business. If I had any kind of nest egg, I'd quit this hole and hit the pavements for a new agency."

"Me too," Deanna says, shorter than Andrea but with the same ebony eyes, her pretty face distorted by a frown.

"Well, look at it this way," Kyla says. "He does get important gigs, so we have exposure."

Glancing about first to be sure the office door is closed, Andrea says, "You know, I wouldn't be surprised if he had something to do with Brook's fall. She kissed him off, and he's a piss-poor loser."

"Ooh," Julia squeals, "look at these gowns. Aren't we going to dress up!"

"Yeah, with these outfits, we will definitely kick ass," Andrea says with a little laugh.

"As long as Donald Duck doesn't mix and match us with the wrong pieces," Kyla adds.

The other models laugh, a sense of relief at humor following the boss's not-surprising censure of one of their members.

The door opens and Brent enters, his dark face somber as the outside weather, Donald Stout behind him a couple of steps.

The big man, glowering at his ensemble, mutters, "All of you, I decided to call off today's run-through. You've seen the drawings, and I want you and the others here tomorrow at eleven o'clock. Spread the word. And no fucking grumbling about the decisions I make. It's my show."

—

After assuring Charlotte and Broadway that she would let them know as soon as the forensics folks come up with anything, Detective Cavanaugh has driven off in the slushy afternoon.

Under Charlotte's umbrella, she and her handsome young companion are about to part as well.

"I have a meeting with my agent. Might be a part in a new musical."

"Before you go, I have a question or two."

"Yep."

"It seems that your sister said no to two men in the past year, and one decided to show up at her apartment, while the other wants to dismiss her fall as an accident. I know the latter and have some thoughts about his crass attitude, but I don't know much about the former. I believe you said his name is Batchelor."

"Aaron Batchelor, Mr. Money. My mother does well, but that guy is a true wheeler and dealer. What do you want to know about him?"

"First, how could he have found out about Brooklyn's situation if they are not in touch, and second, what is his motive for revisiting her life now?"

"I'm not sure where he could have read about it since it wasn't considered a crime, and the *Times* or the *Daily News* wouldn't cover an accidental fall. The man has an attitude when it comes to women. She finally figured him out. As to why he showed up, well, he never has given up on Brook. He's like a forlorn ex-lover, even though she hasn't shown him any reason to hang on."

"Curious," Charlotte says. "Perhaps he has some inside source giving him information."

Broadway looks at her with admiration; he hadn't thought about any of that.

"Have fun with your agent," Charlotte says. "I hope whatever musical it is will be a smash for you."

He smiles warmly at this little, gray-haired sleuth of a lady. "Glad I took voice lessons. I'm a baritone, the guy who gets dumped. The lead part will go to a tenor."

"You're the lead guy in my book."

—

Mark Angel is a no-nonsense agent. His tiny office is off Fifty-Eighth Street and Fifth Avenue, in a twenty-story building, rather new and quite elegant. He has occupied the same office for fourteen years, got in before the rents skyrocketed, and is listed under rent control. He greets Broadway with a quick hug, not his most successful client, yet a personable young man with high potential.

"Hey, the guy who is about to become a star. Have we got a role for you!"

Broadway has never liked the inclusive "we" people use when they mean "I." Servers in restaurants do it all the time: "How are we today?" He has begun replying, "I don't know about them, but I'm okay." Angel seems to relish the impersonal.

"Tell me about it, Mark," Broadway says as he sits across from his agent's untidy desk, strewn with papers and what appear to be manuscripts.

"Yes. Everybody knows the *Sleepless* story. Caught the whole world in its tender web. Well, a couple of brilliant music guys bargained for the rights to make it into a Broadway show. Now, I ask you, what better actor to be in it than a man named Broadway? And not just any man but a gorgeous hunk like you. The only thing I worry about is if they think you are too good-looking to be dumped and would outshine the guy who plays the Tom Hanks role."

"So when do I audition? And have any of the parts been cast yet?"

"They've inked Ira Tenant for the part Hanks played, Sam Baldwin. Tenant had the lead in the revival of *Brigadoon* a few years ago. And, they've jacked up the role of Hanks's Seattle girlfriend—the one his son doesn't care for—to make her a more significant character who can sing and dance. That part is already given to a cute and feisty young thing named China Olivier."

"What?"

"Are we having trouble hearing?"

"No, we aren't, but by chance, I just met that woman yesterday."

"Oh, well, in the original screenplay, your character and hers never meet. My guess is it will be the same on stage. But, I hope you're on good terms with her since you'll rehearse together."

"No problem. So tell me when."

"That's why I called you in. You're to be at the theater by two o'clock tomorrow. Does that work for you?"

"I'll be there. Any suggestions?"

"Bring your voice—and, of course, that Barrymore

countenance."

"I'm too young to know what that means."

13

Charlotte, perhaps eccentric, maybe only in love with all aspects of nature—wind, sun, surf, rain—ambles about in the damp Times Square area for an hour, eying the people, peering in at the touristy shops. In a recent TV ad, she had seen a phrase: *Times Square: Where Energies Collide.*

When about to enter the Sheraton hotel, she hears the buzz of her cellphone, steps under an eave near the automatic doors, digs out the little plastic device, grins again at the wonder of technology, and says, "Greetings."

"Shanna Cavanaugh here. Thought you'd like to know that we processed the prints on the floor-wax container. Yep, your prints are on it, and so is the second-floor custodian's. We know him because he had one arrest as a teenager for possession; otherwise clean, and, according to the building super, a family man, and would hardly have a reason to hurt your client. There are two other sets of prints, but they aren't in our system. Could belong to any of the models there, or that nasty boss, or even someone from the outside. Because of civil liberties, we can't just go in and fingerprint people, so we are kind of at an impasse."

"I understand. And the hair strands? Do you know if they belong to Brooklyn?"

"We're working on the DNA, and there is no reason to believe they are anyone else's. As soon as we find a match, we'll let you know."

"I can't tell you how much I appreciate you doing this. I know it isn't a big-news murder or anything, but it is so important to this lovely family to track down this…well, this culprit."

"Hey, Charlotte, a crime is a crime. We don't dismiss cases because of a severity clause. I'm indebted to you for alerting us to this little baby."

"Thank you, Shanna. I'm about to go to my hotel room for half an hour of rest. I think the rain is letting up, so it may be a lovely night."

Detective Cavanaugh giggles. "You are something else."

They click off, and Charlotte takes the elevator, all glass on one side, open to the panorama of the hotel's interior, with its hanging green gardens and dramatic architecture, to the eighteenth floor.

Different from Broadway's and Shanna's conjectures that she is indefatigable, Charlotte does need downtime, not, however, from physical exhaustion, but from emotional overload. It has been her habit, when stress rises to mountainous dimensions, to get off by herself, commune with her quiet side, and gently re-order her priorities.

As her brother knows, and as she has revealed to others in her previous investigations, she is an astronomy buff, reads whatever she can find in the *Science News* magazine, and sometimes enjoys passing the newest discoveries on to others. It gives her a sense of power, odd in some ways, to learn of a new exoplanet orbiting a distant star; in fact, one was recently found that experts believe was "captured" billions of years ago from another passing galaxy. Grasping the vastness of the cosmos is beyond her capacity to understand, though she takes comfort in knowing it's the same for most folks.

In her eighteenth-floor room, looking out on the towers of New York City at a sky streaked a vivid blue but with ominous clouds still part of the canvas, she turns inward, closes her eyes, and breathes deeply.

For several minutes she stays in this posture when again her phone, this time the hotel landline, rings jarringly, shattering her mood.

"Yes?" she says with a slight irritation in her voice.

A male voice, hoarse and scratchy, says, "Another ballsy woman. Stay out of things. You could get hurt."

"Who is this?"

"Wouldn't you like to know."

Click. The connection is broken.

Charlotte sits on her bed, not frightened but surprised that, by warning her openly, someone would reveal a kind of desperation about being apprehended. Changes the energy of the case. Cavanaugh needs to know this. The voice was male, but maybe there is a bad-guys' partnership going on, maybe some sort of conspiracy.

We'll see what develops.

Her eyes turn toward the digital clock blinking on the bedside table, and she notes the time as five forty-five; she lies back on her pillow and, in a moment, is asleep. When she awakens, there is only the black night, illuminated by the window lights of the neighboring buildings. Again, a glance at the digital clock: *Nine-fifteen, too late for any more investigative work tonight. Call Cavanaugh in the morning. Find out how Brooklyn is doing and what she thinks of her ex-boyfriend's visit. Would like to spend a few minutes with that Andy boy, to catch his point of view.*

She snaps on the small light near her bed, jots a few notes on the Sheraton pad, smiles at her own presumption that she is some sort of crafty detective, and goes about doing her evening ablutions before retiring for the night.

In one of her previous two investigative adventures, she was threatened with crazy notes pasted together from the *New York Times'* printed letters. When her brother fretted about her safety, she assured him that, at her age, physical aggression was not a big worry—and besides, in that caper, the perp was not a professional but a wounded entrepreneur out for vengeance. In some ways, this seems like a similar situation: an angry, spurned, envious, or insulted civilian rather than a hardened, vicious criminal.

—

Morning daylight fills the corners of her elegant bedroom, and, as is her custom, she rises and begins a routine of stretching and bending. After showering and caring for her teeth, she attends to her skin with a white aloe-based Eucerene calming cream, which she had read was beneficial, perusing her arms, hands, and face for any dark spots. The old folks at Bigelow Village often have a swarm of sun-caused blotches on their hands or foreheads, consequences, Charlotte believes, of neglected skin care.

She descends in the swift and silent elevator to the street level, exits onto Broadway, and heads for a deli on Seventh Avenue.

It is rare for her to indulge in heavy breakfast food, but this morning, a morning when the full sun has returned and is creasing through the high-rise Manhattan towers, she orders a ham and cheese omelet, orange juice, and green tea.

"Broadway," she says into her cellphone, "How can I reach Andy Burrus? I'd like to have a conversation with him. Call me when you get this message."

She doesn't notice a burly man seated a few tables away, watching her every move.

—

At eleven-thirty, Charlotte is in the fourth-floor open area of the Sheraton, where there are stylish shops, a lounge, and a high-priced café, crowded with early lunchtime tourists. Near the entrance to the food court, there is a ledge where several folks sit, waiting for others or watching the foot traffic pass, most dressed in trendy clothing, comfortable in the opulent environs. Her phone buzzes, but since she is in the process of diagramming a visual aid, a lot like a sociogram, with several possible suspects printed in at different intersections, she allows it to go to her voice mail.

A smile crosses her lips at the parade of affluence—feeling amazed again at what she is doing in this luxurious setting—and, after a few minutes, makes a final entry in her notebook, nods to herself, and says aloud, "Yes, a distinct possibility," then punches in her retrieval code and hears a frantic Broadway's voice exploding on her cellphone. "Charlotte, call me as soon as you get this message! There's been a nasty development."

"What?" she asks when he answers, herself flushed with what might be ugly news.

"Kyla called me a few minutes ago. Seems they were all supposed to meet with Stout at eleven o'clock to begin rehearsing for an important gig. When he wasn't there, which never happens—he's absolutely strict about being on time—the whole group began to wonder what was wrong. The models don't go out the back, the stairs on the other side of his office, which is kind of Stout's private passage. But Kyla and another model named Phillipa, the girl who once fell down the front stairs, decided to look in back."

He hesitates, out of breath.

"And?" Charlotte asks.

"They found Donald Stout."

"So?"

"He was lying in a heap at the bottom of the stairs. Dead."

PART 2
Someone's Been Murdered on the Great White Way

14

The Stout Modeling Agency friction has profoundly captured the attention of New York City's finest—and, since she had already been at the site, the primary investigator assigned to the case is Detective Shanna Cavanaugh.

Broadway and Charlotte stand beside the detective in the back hall, at the bottom of the long flight of stairs, where a forensics officer hovers over a white sheet covering the crumpled body of the once feisty, and doggedly intolerable, Donald Stout.

Who mourns such a man? Once a child, an infant, a mother's shining star, with grand potential, impressive promise—what wounds altered his life direction? How does one turn sour, take on the persona of a tyrant with a hedonistic bent, ambitious to a fault, in psychological terms, suffering from narcissistic personality disorder?

Off to the side, in a corner, several models are gathered. Of the little assembly, only Brent White shows sadness, his dark cheeks wet with tears.

"Well," Broadway says to his companions, "all these folks may be out of a job. Stout ran a one-person operation. With him gone, I have no idea who will take over his agency."

"Hmm," Charlotte lets escape, and quickly adds on, "but of prime importance to the detective here, and your family as well, is the confusion this creates in the search for the person who shoved Brooklyn—and the very angry person who decided to punish Stout."

Cavanaugh, with a short laugh, says, "Yes, Charlotte, good thinking. And my guess at this moment is that we have two different culprits. Motive becomes a critical element."

As she says this, from the top of the stairs, Sarah Farivar appears, an expression of disdain on her sallow-looking face.

"The nasty man got paid back," she mutters, staring at the white heap on the old but polished, brown linoleum floor.

"This is my mother," Broadway says to the detective.

"Uh-huh."

"Mother, this is the detective assigned to these two cases."

"So do we know if this Stout genius is the one who broke my daughter's back?"

"We know somebody tried to hurt her; we don't know that it was Stout."

"Yes, well of course someone tried to hurt her. She's not a liar. She knows she was pitched off those stairs."

"Come on in, Mother, but down the front stairs and around to the back door."

The female forensics officer in a khaki-green uniform has been bending over the inert form of Donald Stout, examining his upper torso closely, seemingly focused on the back of his skull. She rises and nods to Cavanaugh, who steps over to her.

"Shanna, this guy fell down the stairs, true, but there is a severe hematoma in the back of his head, on the left side, that was surely a blow from some sort of heavy weapon. I don't see how he could have gotten such a wound from the fall—especially since all his other bruises are on the right side and more superficial. The whack on the skull likely killed him before the tumble."

"Thanks, Rachel. Any idea about what sort of weapon?'

"I'll have to do an X-ray to gauge the depth and angle of the contusion. Should know in a few hours."

The group of models has been conversing quietly all this time, and now Kyla moves over to Broadway, Charlotte, Sarah, and Shanna.

"What I'm about to ask may be poor timing," she says, "but we have an important show coming up, and it's already contracted. Donald could have had some kind of trust fund or even a will, but for now, we need to carry through with our immediate plans. What I'm saying is that we need a leader, someone respected and appreciated by all of us."

She stops, and her audience waits; what is she getting at? Why is she telling us this?

"I'm talking about Brooklyn," Kyla says, arms splayed out to the side as if to say, *How can you be so obtuse?* "She's the logical one to steer us through this project."

Broadway beams, Sarah scowls, and Charlotte tilts her head slightly to one side. Finally, Broadway breaks the curious silence.

"Wow! Kyla, are you sure? I mean, this would lift her spirits to the moon. What a way to chase away her awful pessimism."

"The six or seven of us all agree, and I'm sure the other half dozen would go along with us. We need decisions to be made about assignments, and the changing room has to be supplied with makeup artists, costumers, a timekeeper, and an emergency maven. Donald did all those things."

"You want a crippled girl in a wheelchair to run a modeling show?" Sarah states blandly.

"That doesn't matter," Kyla responds. "She knows the routine. She doesn't have to walk down the runway herself."

A voice from the doorway interrupts their dialogue.

"Hey, Kyla, what's happening? Heard the owner guy got wiped out."

"Who are you?" Detective Cavanaugh calls back.

"They all know me. I'm Andy."

"Well, Andy, this yellow tape means these stairs are off limits, so if you want to join us, come on in, but stay away from the staircase."

"I dig. A Hollywood crime scene. Heavy stuff."

Broadway mutters, just loud enough for Charlotte to hear, "You're the heavy. I wouldn't be surprised if you did it."

To Rachel, Cavanaugh asks, "Estimated time of death?"

"Rigor has already faded, so it has to be at least a few hours. Again, I may know more after an autopsy."

"Okay, everyone"—Cavanaugh raises her voice—"time to vacate. We need to mop up here, remove the body, finish dusting for prints, all that."

Andy Burrus stands near Kyla, inappropriately grinning for such a tragic event, and says, "People keep falling down stairs."

A look of disdain crosses Kyla's face, and she waggles her hand as if to say to her boyfriend, "Jam it, Andy."

Broadway wants to shout, "Yes, the idiot needs to be monitored!" He looks at Charlotte and notices she wears a frown. On her part, she is deep in thought about several developments: the detective's comment about motive, the troupe's desire for Brooklyn to lead, the spontaneous appearances of Sarah Farivar and Andy Burrus.

She steps over to Andy and, almost in a whisper, says, "Say, young man, could I speak with you in private for a couple of minutes?"

Broadway watches with interest as Charlotte consults with his rival, the "idiot," and, true to her request, she takes only two or three minutes with Andy, smiles at him, and turns back to the others.

—

Dr. Landry is standing at the side of the couch in Brooklyn's apartment, and he shakes his head. "You can do this, Brook. I think it will give you a wonderful focus, help your healing."

"Are they out of their minds? I'm supposed to organize a runway show with these limp legs. It's crazy."

Nurse America Lobero, in the doorway to the kitchen, says, "You been getting out of bed and I been wheeling you out here. That's progress."

"Progress, sure. I can almost wiggle my toes. And how in hell would I get up all those stairs to the studio? Someone going to carry me?"

"Did you know there's a freight elevator in the Antwerp Building?" Broadway says. "Passengers rarely use it, but it's available, so we can get you to the second floor."

Brooklyn begins to cry. "Those absolutely stunning women want a…broken body guiding them through this event. What a contrast! What a sick joke that would be on me."

Charlotte, quiet until now, says, "I must say, Brooklyn, that it is no joke. You might be breaking new ground here, opening up new vistas."

The room is hushed for a moment, and Dr. Landry says, "Wouldn't that be lovely, to open up new vistas."

"Hah! A view from the bridge—a vista from the wheelchair."

"Sitting in a wheelchair doesn't dull your senses," her brother says. "You are the most alert member of the company, and they all know it. That's why they want you to lead."

More tears.

America says, "I could go with you. Could take care if you need something. Besides, make my day to see all that glamour."

"It may be the ramblings of an old lady, but you really would be a pioneer," Charlotte says. "In my next life, I plan to be a pioneer in the discovery of exoplanets that are the proper distance from their stars to support earthlike existence. You can be one without waiting for the next life."

Tears turn to a quick laugh. "Brooklyn Farivar, first person in history to coordinate a designer showcase from a wheelchair!"

"Why not?" Broadway says. "I've got news for you: the headline could very well read, 'First person to be triumphant in leading a….' Well, you know the rest."

Again, a silence.

Dr. Landry's hand settling on Brooklyn's shoulder is not missed by Charlotte.

In the long moment of stillness, only a vagrant horn from a tense driver on the street far below can be heard; it is as if the small group is united in sending noiseless energy to Brooklyn to acquiesce.

Her voice timid, unsure, she finally whispers, "I guess…I'll do it."

15

"Hello, Greg. Well, what started out to be a family investigative issue, where this young girl was apparently shoved down a flight of stairs, has now turned into a full-fledged murder. Aren't you excited? My third murder mystery. I know you worry about me, little brother, so I'm trying to keep you tuned into what I'm doing. What makes this case unusual is that the person killed was the prime suspect in the attempt to injure the woman, Brooklyn Farivar by name. Now that he's gone, everyone has to adjust to the new possibilities, including, of course, a lovely female detective with whom I have a solid connection. Lots of envy operating here, and resentment and hurt feelings. It will take some doing to sort it all out.

"In my *Science News* magazine, I read about oceanographers who were trying to map the sea floor of Antarctica to help understand previously unknown underwater channels that allow warm water to flow toward fragile ice shelves. You know what they did? They outfitted fifty-seven elephant seals with electronic tags on their heads since the seals often dive all the way to the bottom. It has been working. They call it bathymetry.

"I know you get impatient when I try to reason metaphorically, so let me get to the point. Sometimes it takes unusual measures to uncover unusual mysteries. I'll keep you posted on my…uh, unorthodox measures, my human equivalent to bathymetry.

"That's all for now. Love to Meredith.

Hope all is well. Love you."

—

"You'd think," Broadway says to Kyla—he has managed to escort his sister up the old elevator and into the studio, assuring America that she would not be needed—"that all people have some sense of remorse for dastardly deeds. Whoever shoved Brook and whoever bludgeoned Donald Stout, by their silence, are saying, 'Screw the world, I'm comfortable with what I did.'"

Kyla nods in agreement. "Sociopaths have no conscience. Their nastiness is shrugged off like light rain."

"I guess. It means they've lost the capacity to put themselves into their victim's position. Seems to me, if I look at the world through the sufferer's eyes, I'd be a lot more likely to stop hurting him."

"That's you." She pauses and says, "That's why I like you."

Her last sentence brings him up short. *Why did she say that? So, she likes me. What will she do about it? That rich adolescent from the blackmailing family still holds power over her. Or…with Stout's demise, maybe not.*

"I can't stay, Kyla. Help Brook as much as you can. I have…well, it's an audition."

"For what? Tell me."

"Later. Might not like it, or they might not like me. I'll let you know."

Leaving his sister in this moment, which she looks at as an ordeal, causes Broadway great angst, yet she knows of his opportunity and has insisted he goes.

As part of life's mysterious interweaving, this brother and sister, whom Sarah once proclaimed would be famous, are now thrust into the spotlight of quite different but equally imposing new life challenges.

China Olivier could well be one of the models at the Stout Agency. She stands five feet eight inches, has a hint of red in her hair, and her face is a Technicolor display, with a band of light freckles on her nose. Her first name is a product of her parents being government emissaries in the Far East. When she sees Broadway appear on stage, she squeals.

"My hero!"

The producers' eyebrows go up, and one, a woman named Geraldine Falk, asks, "Do you know each other?"

"My accident. He pulled me from the car."

"Well, well, a hero, in fact. Come up here, young man."

The team that conducts the auditions, in this case, comprised of the dramaturge, the on-stage director, and two producers, appear to examine Broadway, up and down and sideways, before handing him a script and asking him to read a page, cold.

Duck soup. His past experiences have given him the confidence to read any lines with passion and insight, even if he has never seen them before. His one trepidation is that he may not have the proper singing voice for the part his agent told him might be his.

Thank goodness they do not ask him to sing a song from this musical since he would have to sight-read it, and he didn't feel he could do the lyrics justice. Instead, they ask him to sing "On the Street Where You Live" from *My Fair Lady*, a song he has done before. A pianist plays the intro.

As he wends his way through the charming words—"People stop and stare, they don't bother me; for there's nowhere else on Earth that I would rather be"—he tries to avoid looking at China Olivier. No need for other emotions to get in the way. He finishes with a flourish, "Let the time go by, I won't care if I, can be here on the street where you live."

In *My Fair Lady*, Freddy Eynsford-Hill is Eliza's suitor, who, as we know, loses out to Professor Henry Higgins, and, as such, is a parallel with the character in *Sleepless*, Walter, who loses out to Sam Baldwin, the little boy's father.

Applause all around, though Broadway is aware that the bigwigs applaud everyone who auditions.

Geraldine Falk winks at China, turns to Broadway, and says, "I have only one worry. You and China are both gorgeous, so why would the two principals dump each of you for each other?"

The dramaturge, a man named Charlton, says, "Hey, I'd take our chances on that. Beautiful people fill up the theater, and besides, looks aren't the only element in love."

The director, Jamison Brown, is beaming as he adds, "I agree with Charlie. For my money, we've found the perfect foils for our Tom Hanks and Meg Ryan characters."

Broadway is bubbling with excitement but keeps a straight face, a professional countenance, as if to communicate, "It's important to me, but I'm a busy actor, and if this doesn't work out, something else will."

"We've had six others read for this part," Ms. Falk says. "In fairness, we'll need to review all our notes and be in touch with everyone. As you have heard, we like you, Broadway, but it isn't a closed deal yet."

"I understand," he says. "Any idea when I might find out?"

"Tomorrow," Jamison Brown says, as if trumping anyone else's opinion. "Leave all your contact information with Tony over there."

As Broadway heads off the stage and up the aisle, China Olivier scurries after him.

"Are you free later? Maybe six o'clock for dinner?"

He notices the bruise on her face, the only remnant, as far as he can tell, from the accident, and he also notices the green eyes, freckled nose, perfect teeth, and eager smile. He flashes on Kyla. His heart is racing. Why does he feel, suddenly and profoundly, as if he is about to cheat?

"Uh…depends. I have a critical commitment with my sister. But maybe you'd like to come to her session. It's a modeling agency, and she's coordinating a big show. I expect they will be rehearsing this evening."

"Tell me where."

What a foolish gesture! Okay, so Kyla has made no real move toward me, but she has dropped hints. Now, is it wise to have a new woman march onto the scene? On the other hand (when he conjures up that phrase, he thinks of Tevya in *Fiddler on the Roof*), *having two stunning women as possibilities could well stir each of them, especially Kyla, to be more forthcoming.*

His thoughts flit from finding fault to wanting to celebrate this mind-blowing opportunity, rare among New York's massive cadre of frustrated would-be thespians and performers.

Man, what a blast to hook into such an amazing role! Brooklyn has to know—and my mother, of course, even if her approbation is not a necessity.

He hustles back to the modeling studio and, as he enters, sees the entire troupe clad in makeshift outfits as facsimiles of the real creations they will be wearing next week. His sister is speaking in a voice slightly elevated yet soothing in its tone. His thought: *What a contrast to that poor, dead, pompous Donald Stout!*

He spies Charlotte sitting in a hard-backed chair in the far corner, smiling with pleasure, and approaches her.

"How did your audition go?" she asks.

"I won't know for a day or so, but it feels good. One of them seemed to imply that I had the inside track."

"I'll be surprised if you don't get the part." Another smile. "Who could resist you, Broadway?"

"Ah, they have to see if I fit. That's always the case. Talent has to be there, but the role must be a solid match." He pauses and asks, "How is Brook doing?"

"She is rare. I see how the others respond to her. Respect. Lots of love flowing back and forth. She knows which of them walk in a given way, which have a look that melds with certain apparel, and she is so good at gently insisting on certain facial and mood expressions."

"That's the key, as I remember. One gown necessitates a somber look and walk, another requires assertiveness, and still, others range from gleeful to slinky to contemptuous. Brook was a master at compatibility with her attire."

"Have you noticed something a bit surprising out there on the floor?"

"Like what?"

"Like a person."

He gazes about the dozen assembled models. "Holy shit, Corrine Gelly is out there."

"Yes, and notice how Brooklyn has arranged a large portable board at the edge of the parquet and how there are maybe fifty or sixty photos plastered there, each one of a different designer outfit. She has them numbered and has names attached to just about every one."

"So each model knows her wardrobe."

"Well, I heard her say to Corrine a while ago that number twenty-seven and number thirty-two will be hers. Twenty-seven is a jumpsuit, and thirty-two is a two-piece pantsuit. She told Corrine she would do great justice to those two designs."

"Reaching out. Donald had canned her, and Brook's brought her back."

"There will be enough creations for most models to prance about with five or six different ones, except for Phillipa, who seemed okay with three, and Corrine, who had no complaints about her two. What I liked was that Brooklyn consulted with each person before clinching her or his assignment."

"I'm curious, Charlotte, if anything going on now is influencing your thinking about the culprits in the two crimes."

"As a friend of mine from Minnesota used to say, you betcha.

However, I must admit that just because everyone here is cooperating and seeming to be on the same page with Brooklyn doesn't mean that one or more of them didn't do the ugly deeds. Clever people do a lot of innocent things to camouflage their trespasses."

To the surprise of both Charlotte and Broadway, Dr. Bruce Landry enters the studio. Brooklyn sees him and, not lost on Charlotte's keen eye, seems to blush.

Landry skirts the parquet and sidles up to join the two other guests.

"She seem to be handling this okay?"

"Like a pro," Broadway replies. "Watch and learn."

From her wheelchair, Brooklyn is referring to photos, one at a time, using a long pool stick as a pointer. Her accompanying words are such as: "This is a diaphanous type gown, and requires fluid movements made with a flourish. Perfect for you, Julia. Here is a more formal outfit, to be modeled with dignity, a straight face, and even a look of power—the accomplished businesswoman. Right up your alley, Andrea. See this playful creation with bright colors and eye-catching sparseness, a sexy piece designed for fun. Deanna, you will fly in this one. Brent, it would be cool if you act bold and aggressive, especially with the two Jamaican-type sporty creations; more wholesome with the tennis outfit."

Of the dozen models, only two are male: Brent and another rather introverted fellow named Antoine—taller, thinner, perfect for designs that focus less on masculinity and more on aesthetic fluidity. Brooklyn seems, remarkably, to know which man would do which piece of clothing best.

"A genius at work," Charlotte says. In a softer voice, she asks Broadway, "Who would ever want to hurt that scintillating young woman?"

"That's the mystery."

"Yes, and the other mystery is who, then, would be upset enough to want to—as the gangsters say—off the boss?"

Dr. Landry catches at least part of the exchange and inserts, "Brooklyn is going to heal. Mark my words. She is a fighter. Muscles need to firm up to compensate for nerve damage, but my best guess is she will walk again—if not even be able to dance or play tennis."

"You're an optimist, Doc," Broadway says. "But I'm pulling for your guesses to be accurate."

At this point, another guest enters the studio. Those who know him are shocked to see, striding vigorously toward them, a smiling Aaron Batchelor.

16

Charlotte has never been to the United Nations building on the East River, and though she is not financially employed by the Farivars, she is hesitant to take time away from her verbal commitment. After all, they are putting her up at a luxurious hotel, paying for most of her food, and have the expectation that she will devote her energies to solving the riddle of Brooklyn's fall.

Well, there will be another opportunity, even if her active years may be limited. Perhaps, if she can track down the culprits in the Brooklyn and Stout cases in a reasonable amount of time, she can still squeeze in the U.N. before returning to Bigelow Village.

A lot depends on what she can learn from several key players—and, of course, on Shanna Cavanaugh's expert input.

Aaron Batchelor showing up raises eyebrows. In keeping with his burnished Wall Street image, he is clad in a wintry camel-hair coat, a matching wool scarf wound around his neck, and elegant leather gloves. Broadway seems perturbed, Dr. Landry uncertain, and Charlotte—well, she is not surprised. The man has an agenda, and his presence offers an opportunity to find out what it is.

Brooklyn decides to take a fifteen-minute water and restroom break and slowly wheels herself over to where the visitors are standing.

"Not sure I'm pulling this off," she says in a self-deprecating voice.

"Brilliantly, Sis," her brother responds.

"Might not want to overdo it," Landry puts in. "Stamina may

be missing."

"Oh, I don't feel tired. Too much adrenaline, I think. I'm jazzed by the whole challenge."

Batchelor, who has joined them, says with a bit too much joviality, "You are a wonder, Brook, as I remember you, as you always were. On top of your game."

"Isn't this kind of like slumming for you?" Broadway snaps.

Any tone of resentment missing, Batchelor responds, "Love the ambiance. New York is replete with appealing little tucked-away locales. Anyway, I've been here before. Brook knows. It was my hangout for a time."

"Yes," Broadway says, enmity in his manner obvious, "until my sister dumped you."

"Come now, big brother, it wasn't like that. And anyway, that's teenage language. We had our differences, but also a lot of good chemistry. Right, Brook? For a while there, we rocked."

Dr. Landry, clearly uncomfortable, says, "Not good to get Brooklyn emotionally upset, so if there is some old business that needs airing between you two, I suggest you remove yourselves and attend to it."

"Who's this?" Batchelor asks.

"I'm Dr. Bruce Landry, Brook's post-op physician."

Charlotte watches the two men keenly, the former beau and the present likely suitor, the one no longer a desired influence in Brooklyn's life, the other not yet an intimate one. Jealousy, she remembers hearing, is fear of loss, yet neither of these men possesses this remarkable young woman, so what else might be in play here?

"Look," Brooklyn interrupts, "I'm in the middle of an important run-through and can't deal with any other concern. I hope you all understand."

"Yes, dear," Charlotte says, "quite astute of you. There are priorities, and perhaps those of you who have different ones would be willing to discuss them with me? Somewhere else. Away from Brooklyn."

No takers. Dr. Landry reaches over, commandeers the wheelchair, and rolls Brooklyn back to where the models are reassembling. Broadway frowns at Aaron Batchelor and turns away. Batchelor cocks his head, shrugs, and sits in a hard-backed chair on the periphery of the parquet.

A complication. At this moment, another person appears in the doorway to the studio, unsure, peering about, a mixed look of concern and expectation on her pretty face. Dressed in a reddish, thigh-length dress, her head topped with a red woolen beret, and with a smart, green jacket slung over her arm, China Olivier catches Broadway's eye and prances into the room.

He blushes—not missed by Charlotte—and steps forward to greet her. A brief hug, the standard showbiz greeting, and they move together to the row of visitor chairs.

"Uh, China Olivier, this is Charlotte Smart, a friend of our family. Charlotte, I believe you may have seen China sitting in the street after her accident."

"I did, and I am delighted you are all in one piece. Too many beautiful young women lately have been injured. It's an epidemic."

The scene is not novel to China, though the characters are. She peruses the room and says, "I only have a couple of bruises, nothing serious. Car is pretty useless, though." She looks directly at Broadway. "Which one is your sister?"

"That's what Charlotte was talking about. Brook had a fall, and she's the one in the wheelchair."

"Oh, I'm so sorry." For a moment, she hesitates, then says, "She's a real beauty."

"She is," Broadway responds, "and the troupe sort of anointed her to run the show for a gig next week at the Sheraton Ballroom."

The entrance of another stunning female tweaks the sullen Aaron Batchelor's interest, and he ambles back to the trio.

"I'm Aaron, and you are…?"

"A friend of mine," Broadway inserts.

Pause, as China catches the lay of the land and says simply, "China."

"Ah, I've been there," Aaron says. "Promising country. We could learn a thing or two about their labor policies."

"It's called exploitation." Broadway's voice is a hard bite.

"American bleeding hearts can't tolerate the living conditions, but oh, how we love their cheap products."

"Opposite sides of the fence," China puts in. "But, I assure you, I have no connection to the country, China, except that my parents were assigned there and handed me this moniker."

Their caustic discourse is interrupted by Brooklyn's mellow

tones, saying, "We are going to knock them dead. Let's move on to the next series of designs, and we'll try to establish each one's mood."

In the following few moments, the visitors hear phrases such as, "Better with one hand on your hip," "Faster pace, as if late for an appointment," and "A pouting look; it stirs the male buyers." After a time, she pauses, looks back at her visiting friends, and says, "Hold on a minute."

She wheels herself over, close to China, and puts out her hand. "I'm Brook, and though I don't know you, I wonder if I could borrow your beret for a few minutes."

China's smile says there is an instant connection between the two, and she hands her red topper over to Brooklyn, tossing her head vigorously to adjust her disturbed hairdo.

Charlotte, in her alertness, sees a curious and perhaps concerned Kyla Pino staring hard at where Brooklyn has gone—at this new, attractive woman seated beside Broadway. *Relationships,* she almost says aloud. *The games begin.*

Brooklyn takes the crimson beret and rolls back to Andrea, her tallest model. "With the third piece you are wearing, I would love for you to add a cap like this. Do you have one? Whether the Dior people would like it, I don't know, but the design is rather autumnal and seems to be begging for a bonnet of some kind."

"Your sister is a jewel," China whispers. "I've done some modeling. She has a keen eye."

If it comes to it, Broadway will have, Charlotte thinks, *a hell of a time settling on one of these stunning beauties.* Kyla is his sister's good friend, and he knows her better; China, Charlotte has already decided, is a sensitive young woman and partnered with Broadway in her professional work. This handsome young man has obviously loved a great deal in his life: he loves his sister, previous girlfriends, maybe a dog or cat, perhaps his father, and, in a stilted way, his mother, Sarah. As with all of us, experience in love is helpful, but when courting, the uniqueness of the current love-person is nonetheless a massive challenge.

As she ponders the scene, Charlotte lands on an insight that perhaps the culprit, or culprits, who committed acts of violence are in this room—except for the adolescent-like Andy Burrus. It is always good to review periodically what has transpired, and she runs through each event in her mind, even though the modeling rehearsal is a distraction; it is why she knows she needs to get off by herself at some point, as she has done in her previous ventures, to quiet her thoughts and escape external stimuli.

Brooklyn's voice is soothing in its soft intensity: "Deanna, you look breathtaking in that dark piece; it accents your lovely dark eyes. You see, everyone, how Julia's pale skin brings out the vivid colors in that sapphire gown? Marvelous! Phillipa, your look is perfect for that two-toned flowery creation, and Kyla, I love the look on your face with that skimpy green outfit, as if you know you are being risqué, but so what!"

Almost as if an answer to a wish, the impassive Andy Burrus saunters into the studio—trusty Blackberry in one hand, the other brushing back his straggly locks. It takes him a moment to catch the scene, and finally he trudges toward the little cadre of guests.

"What's up?" he asks as if it isn't obvious.

With Aaron Batchelor and Andy Burrus now present, two men he can't tolerate, Broadway snaps, "The sky is up, the stars are up, the ceiling is up."

"Ha-ha."

There is a stretched moment of silence from the visiting group, only Brooklyn's gentle words breaking the room's stillness.

"Now that the guy is dead, what's going to happen?" Andy asks, ignoring the group's attention to the rehearsal.

His question, in turn, is ignored as the visitors hear Brooklyn say, "Brent, it wouldn't hurt for you to show a spot of anger as you move down the runway. Of course, not all men are angry, but imagine yourself at the beach and being ignored by people or in a café when eyes pass over you. It's the bane of the different and the elderly that they seem to be invisible." She looks at Charlotte with a smile.

"I'm not elderly," Charlotte whispers to Broadway. "I'm mature."

"That you are," he responds.

China hears their soft exchange and grins, showing a gleaming row of perfect, white teeth. Already, she captures the alignments in this new ensemble of folks—the hostility, especially between the men, the crass language and harsh stares, and, with each comment, a bite, the only warm connection between Broadway and Charlotte. Has to be some jealousy involved; has to be a frustrated attraction somewhere.

No one seems to have noticed on the door to what was Stout's private office, an envelope attached with Scotch Tape. No one, that is, except Charlotte, whose eyes constantly sweep the area for anomalies. Slowly she rises, skirts the parquet, and, surprisingly to Broadway, produces from her slit-of-a-pocket a pair of rubber gloves, which she slips on.

As if it were an old habit, as if she had been doing it all her life, she carefully removes the envelope and returns to her seat.

<h1 style="text-align:center">17</h1>

In large printed letters, on a sheet of plain, folded white paper, are the words *DYKE STILL OUT.*

"But what in hell does that mean?" Broadway asks no one in particular.

They are standing in the dark of night on the entry stoop to the Antwerp Building, Charlotte, Broadway, and China; Brooklyn is seated in her wheelchair beside them. In the early evening, traffic is like a toyshop at Christmas, autos and buses of all colors and sizes wheeling about as if on display. The agency models are in the process of accessing either their parked vehicles or taxis; Kyla is a hundred feet away with Andy Burrus, about to enter his sleek sports car, looking over her shoulder at Broadway. Aaron Batchelor, after obsequiously congratulating Brooklyn on a "spirited" session, has slid silently away to hail a cab.

Assuming the question is aimed at her, Charlotte is quiet for a moment, studying the cutout newsprint letters.

"Ah," she says at last, "it's an anagram. How brazen can someone get?"

"What?" Brooklyn asks.

"Juggle the letters, and the message, though with perhaps a purposeful misspelling, reads: 'I KYLLED STOUT.'"

China looks bewildered, and Broadway touches her arm. "We've had some strange goings-on. After Brook had her fall, the boss of the agency, Donald Stout, was clubbed to death. I wouldn't blame you if you decide to get the hell away from here."

After a pause to assimilate the information, with a light in her eye, China replies, "It's like *Masterpiece Mystery* theater on television. A real-life whodunit. Seems as if Charlotte here is the point person."

"Oh no, my dear. The family asked me to look into Brooklyn's tumble. The death of Stout has been a bonus conundrum. I'll need to be in touch with Detective Cavanaugh about this deliberately veiled confession."

"But I wonder what is meant by Dyke Still Out?" Broadway says.

"Dyke is a slang word for lesbian," Charlotte replies. "That in itself is something to ponder."

"Charlotte, in your opinion, what in hell is Batchelor hanging around for? Brook has given him no reason to think he can get back into her life. Right, Sis?"

"Of course not. He told me he was feeling remorse about our split-up, and all I said was that things change and people move on."

"I might ask," Charlotte begins, "if you think he still carries a grudge about you…uh, dumping him."

"It's been over a year. I can't imagine he hasn't found another babe. He likes to impress women with his wealth, with gaudy little gifts. As far as I knew, he put me away a long time ago."

"Well," Charlotte goes on, "I ask because he seems obsessed with you. Maybe feeling rather guilty, too, as I understand he offered you some money for your medical expenses."

"I told him to keep his money." She stops and, in a tone laced with contempt, says, "My mother has plenty of money."

"Brook, are you up for getting a bite to eat? I'll be happy to take us all out to the deli down the block." Broadway looks at Charlotte and adds, "It's a world-famous New York deli. The Carnegie on Seventh near Fifty-Fifth."

Brooklyn inhales deeply and says, "Let's do it."

—

There is no place quite like New York City at night. It stirs a memory again for Charlotte of the ad she saw on television, which declares that Times Square is "where everything collides for attention." If the buzz of that incessant motion isn't enough, the garish and devilishly hypnotic glare of rainbow lights stuns the senses. It causes

Charlotte to go away in her mind to more idyllic scenes: the wild geese in the rain-ponds near her retirement village, the tranquil view from her apartment window of a serpentine creek with its cattails, and the sharp, crisp gurgle of water tumbling over rocks.

It is an easy walk—and wheelchair ride—for two blocks to their eatery, the New York veterans experienced at the game of tolerating the ambient commotion, and Charlotte blissful as a child in her reverie.

"My parents are from around Binghamton, in Upstate New York," China tells her new friends, "and I grew up in the little town called Johnson City. It's actually a tri-city area, the third little hamlet, Endicott, named for the big Endicott Johnson Shoe Company there. They had a minor league baseball team, the Binghamton Triplets, owned by the Yankees. I used to go to the games as a child. Saw several raw-boned kids who went on to become Big Leaguers. Periodically, my father would be sent to the Far East as an emissary for the State Department. He was a professor at the college in Binghamton and a specialist in Far Eastern Studies."

"Hence, the name China," Broadway adds.

The atmosphere in the Carnegie Deli is frenetic, even though it is well past the usual dinner hour. Noise is part of the package, an artifact of the desired mood. Servers, and certainly their server, are wizened, no-nonsense women, cynically terse, like old-time Catskills comedians. With their draw, the name tag reads *Millie*, and, thankfully, she has a sense of humor.

"Ya want the hot-sweet mustard or the standard yellow with that sandwich? Whaddya want in the soup, rice, noodles, or a matzo ball? Tell you what: if you want noodles, I'll ask them to put in an extra noodle. Yeah, I get that it's too late for caffeine, so do you want decaf or some other kind of poison?"

Orders taken, China resumes, "As a teenager, I studied voice, was in *Hello, Dolly!* and played Marian the Librarian in *The Music Man.* Then I was lucky to get a scholarship to Julliard for dance. Been in New York seven years now. Hectic, but quite a trip!"

Charlotte says, "About your accident, you were fortunate, and wasn't it good that Broadway was there when it happened? With Brooklyn, at first it was thought to be an accidental fall, but she set us all straight. It was a deliberate act, and we're waiting for some fingerprint data to see who the culprit might be."

"But why are people being hurt at that agency? I mean you, Brooklyn, and also that Stout fellow. Who is so angry or…desperate?"

"That's why we're asking Charlotte to help us. She has experience in ferreting out the bad guys," Broadway inserts.

"I hope your young life is free of vengeance and other venomous motives, but something nasty is operating here," Charlotte says. "It seems as if one person decided that Brooklyn was in the way and tried to hurt her, and another person hated the boss so much—or thought he was the culprit—as to club him to death. Not a pleasant way to go."

As she finishes these words, her cellphone vibrates, and she smiles at the intrusion, again hating that the distant person has priority over folks right in front of her. But since she is hoping for a call from Cavanaugh, she decides to excuse herself and answer.

"Ah, yes, Shanna, so what's the good word?

"…Really? I understand—I never leap to conclusions. …Well, of course, you didn't need permission to get his fingerprints once he was dead. …So, no question they were his. …Sure, in fact, it is likely that cleaning supplies would go through his office first, and that could explain his prints. …Who? …Yes, I did tell you about that threatening call. …A man? Assigned to watch out for me?"

She lifts her eyes and peers about the bustling eatery. "…Okay, I don't know who that is, but I won't worry. …No, I don't see anyone suspicious. …Thanks for the overkill, ha-ha. …Well, I have something to show you, too, a note someone tacked onto Stout's office door. …Fine. Talk to you in the morning."

When she returns to her friends, Broadway is laying out some bills to pay for the repast, China thanking him—appreciation a learned product of her precarious economic state.

"My mother's car is in a lot a couple of blocks from here. I'll be glad to drive all of you to your destinations. Where do you live, China?"

"I have a small flat on Forty-Fourth near Fifth Avenue."

"Mind if I take Brook uptown first? She's near the park."

"I can walk if you don't want to make three stops," Charlotte says. With a rather sheepish smile, she adds, "The detective has some sort of surveillance on me—for protection, you know—so I feel pretty safe."

"Madame," Broadway says imperiously, "I shall deposit you at your doorstep. Not a problem."

Charlotte first, then Brooklyn; he unfolds the wheelchair, lifts her in his arms, sets her carefully in it, and rolls it into her complex. He has already cell-phoned America, and she is waiting at the elevator.

None of this is missed by China; nice man, loves his sister, is a doting brother, kind, helpful to everyone.

At her apartment, they sit in the car for a few minutes, Broadway painfully aware of Kyla's awkward situation, her obvious curiosity over this new, stunning woman with him, her own negotiated pact with Stout no longer a necessity. China is a jewel, a heady compliment to his persona, her interest in him also apparent. How in the hell does he handle this relationship surfeit?

"Your sister is quite a woman," China says. "It's refreshing to see how the two of you care for each other."

"Our mother, kind of sour in some ways, always promoted family loyalty. She's an immigrant herself and a survivor. Brooklyn and I tried to take the good things from her and ignore the oppressive."

"My parents were doing, but I was the middle one of three and sometimes felt sandwiched in. My older brother is a lawyer, and my younger sister is in medical school. I'm the oddball, the aesthete, though I admit my folks were proud of my Julliard achievement."

"I would hope so."

Broadway realizes their conversation is at the cliché level: where are you from, what's your family all about, who's your favorite singer, what foods do you like, in general, what's your daily routine? Cutesy stuff but also calculated to deflect the me-you agenda just below the surface.

"This may be forward of me," China begins, "but I know we'll be working together for maybe a long time, and I'd like to know more about you."

"I'm an open book. Be as forward as you like."

"Well, I gather you aren't married, but, considering all your, uh… assets, I presume you are involved with someone…."

He can't hold back a little smile. This dazzling woman wants to map out the territory, grasp his eligibility, careful not to intrude on a prior commitment, but eager to know what her chances are with him.

"Okay, in the interest of fairness, I'll tell you my romantic history if you tell me yours."

She grins. "Deal!"

He briefly describes his relationship tour with Monica, how and why it ended, and, after a pause, says, "I'm attracted to one of the models—Brooklyn's best friend, Kyla—but, up to now, she's been hooked in with someone."

"I'll bet I know which one it is. I could see the most appealing woman on the parquet glancing over at you—more than once."

"She's appealing all right, but…"

China interrupts, "I was almost married once, about four years ago, but my parents thought I was too young and that it would stifle my career. He was a football coach, former pro player. Big guy, lots of muscles, but, as I think back on it, not many muscles upstairs."

"We're both still young, but not rookies when it comes to tries at emotional bonding. No clicks, though. At least not yet."

At that, she leans over and kisses him, long and lusciously on the mouth. He does not resist.

18

On her hotel room door, just as on Donald Stout's office door, there is a taped envelope. Again she dons her rubber gloves before removing it and entering her luxurious residence.

On her well-matched, luxurious bed, she opens the missive and reads: *EXIT SHOWN?* It takes her only a couple of seconds to decode the anagram: *WHO IS NEXT?*

In the morning, a chill settles in on the Big Apple, not unusual for November, but borne on a dry, cold Norther that cuts to the bone. Shanna Cavanaugh is greeted and admitted into room 1840, shivering off the outside weather.

"What a spot, lady Charlotte! Warm and cozy and fit for a queen."

"In here, I feel like a queen. Not my normal surroundings, I'll tell you. A simple bedroom would have been enough, but this elegant parlor comes with it. My apartment in the retirement village is tidy and comfy but not lavish."

"Got to wear a heavy coat when you go out today. Canada and the Great Lakes have sent us a present. Brr."

"And I will have to go out. A couple of folks I'd like to talk to."

"You have some messages of some kind you want to show me."

"I do."

She hands Shanna the two envelopes, careful to warn her first about fingerprints. The detective laughs as she dons her own ultrathin plastic gloves.

"So, you have deciphered both these notes to mean what?"

"They are both anagrams, and the first one is *I KYLLED STOUT*, and the second is *WHO IS NEXT?* Pretty brazen killer, if you ask me."

"And a warning call as well. The second note could mean you. Graziano, who has been tailing you, will have to be on extra alert."

"Haven't noticed any Graziano or anyone on my tail. I'll take your word for it. I suppose it does make me feel a little less vulnerable."

"The prints on the canister from the closet are the custodian's, yours, and Stout's. There is one other set, but it belongs to someone not in our system."

"Hmm, and I suppose none of the models would be in your system unless arrested for some crime?"

"True, none of the models, none of the boyfriends, and no family members. Kind of leaves a plentiful planet of possibilities."

"Ah, Shanna, you're like me—like to speak with alliteration."

Though she isn't positive about what that means, Shanna nods and smiles.

"Who do you want to speak with today? Which of the pipeline of beautiful people need to be plumbed?"

"I spoke…briefly with Andy Burrus, Kyla's odd young boyfriend. He's likely to do anything, but not crafty enough either to be writing anagrammatic notes or to plot a murder." She stops for a moment, gets one of her faraway looks, and says softly, "At least by himself."

"A conspiracy!" Shanna says and stomps her foot.

"Maybe. What I don't know is, of all the people in this bizarre scenario, which ones are connected to each other, connected enough so that the benefits are there for more than one of them."

"Has to be a payoff for everyone involved."

"Yes," Charlotte says pensively, "and the payoff could be access to a job, a person, or even to financial gain."

"Seems as if the models would all qualify for wanting financial gain. That Burrus kid supposedly comes from a wealthy family, so money might not be his motive. The Farivar mother doesn't need money, but she certainly would want to avenge her daughter's fall. There are a couple of other outsiders you've mentioned; one is the model that Stout got rid of but Brooklyn reinstated, and the other is

Brooklyn's ex. Each could have motives for hurting Brooklyn, the woman to remove her from the number one spot, and the man to pay her back for dumping him. As to the Stout murder, again, the Gelly woman had good reason to polish him off, but I don't see that the former boyfriend did."

"Wonderful summary, Shanna. As we both know, there still may be hidden motives we know nothing about. In good time, though; in good time."

"We're certainly not ready for any arrests right now, but I want to caution you to move about with care. Some idiot doesn't like you puttering about in this soup."

"Hard to putter in soup. And yes, I shall be careful. Your Graziano guy is darned good; haven't picked up on him yet."

"A thickset guy, dark hair, usually needs combing, but you're right, he's skilled at his job. I'll text him about the letters, and I know it will even sharpen his attention on you."

"Thanks, Shanna."

"Need a ride anyplace?"

"In fact, I might. I'd like to visit the Burrus family—and I understand their home is uptown, near the park, actually on Park Avenue. A pricey part of town."

"It is. My car is downstairs. Glad to be your chauffeur."

What a thrill to zip through Manhattan in an unmarked police car, knowing that any fudging on traffic rules will not be penalized! All of this—in fact, the whole caper—is quite a thrill.

—

Central Park runs about six miles north and south, is close to a mile wide, and is probably the most famous park in America. Halfway up its Park Avenue length, it is lined by luxury apartments and condos. President Nixon had one there. So did several movie stars. Beyond it, to the north, is the Bronx, including the once-venerable Yankee Stadium, now torn down and rebuilt, as with so many deteriorating arenas. Columbia University is near 125th Street, and Harlem stretches from the East River to the Hudson River along 155th and into Washington Heights. A Tony award-winning musical, *In the Heights*, was focused on the diverse Latino populations living there. The contrast (which Cavanaugh knows and Charlotte has heard and which may soon become an issue in the sticky cases they are pursuing) between Harlem-Washington Heights and the Park Avenue residences is stark.

The building the Burrus family calls home is a polished, seven-story edifice with an eight-foot-high door and a twelve-hour-a-day doorman. It is secured at all times and only announced visitors are admitted. Shanna Cavanaugh knows that Charlotte will have a hard time getting in unless, of course, an identified officer of the law requests entry.

"I know you didn't ask, but I'll accompany you. Might be the only way they'll let you in."

"Oh, Shanna, I was hoping you would. I am not a lone wolf, and your insights are critical."

The doorman, a tall, lean man not in a special uniform but wearing a cap that looks as if it belongs at an Army-Navy football game, gives them close scrutiny as they approach.

"The Burrus family," Shanna says in her official voice. "Police business."

Upon the appearance of a badge, the doorman, the name *P. Cardella* stamped on his chest badge, punches in a code on the wall monitor, mutters several words, turns back, and announces, "Apartment seven twenty-two. The elevator is on your right."

When the door opens, they hear, "So, what has the little shit done now?"

The man, bald on top but with ample hair on each side, is dressed in a gold-hued silk shirt, short-sleeved and unbuttoned for several inches in front, showing curly, dark chest hair. He is of moderate height, a bit paunchy in the middle, yet still vigorous, and with broad shoulders. He might have been a football player in his younger years. There is the putrid odor of cigarette smoke on his clothes. He steps aside to allow the two women to enter his apartment, though one might debate whether to call it that; it would be more accurate to label it an extravagant abode, drawing the sort of reaction Julia Roberts had when first entering Richard Gere's place in *Pretty Woman.* Charlotte, in fact, though she rarely uses such language, is tempted to say, "Holy crap, what a palace!"

Objets d'art in proliferation, an original Chagall on one wall, what appears to be a Van Gogh on another, sculpted busts of children on two pedestals, and a long table in the room they enter, made of solid Philippine Mahogany: Charlie Burrus seems to be the only person in the rooms.

"Well, sir, this is Ms. Charlotte Smart, and I am Detective Shanna Cavanaugh. We are interviewing folks about the issues at the Stout Modeling Agency. Your son's name came up and we thought we should get a little background."

"He's not in trouble?"

"As you know, he has been seeing Kyla Pino," Charlotte says, "and she is Brooklyn Farivar's close friend. Brooklyn had a terrible fall down the stairs at the agency building, and the cause is under investigation. Then, I'm not sure if you know that Donald Stout, the owner, was killed just a day or so ago."

"Read about it. Awful stuff. I met the man once."

"We understand you donated some money to his enterprise," Charlotte says softly, without accusation in her voice.

"Hell, I guess I did. The boy asked me to. He's a burden, my Andy. Can't seem to find direction."

"May I ask what business you are in, Mr. Burrus?" Shanna puts in.

"Investments. You know, let the money do the work, not the person." He laughs at his own attempt at humor.

"And does Andy have a specialty? Did he go to college, get some training, or what?" Charlotte asks.

"That's the problem. His specialty is laziness, and his training's been how to seduce women. He looks for the shortcuts. Never saw him work hard at anything."

"We can check this out, but has he ever been arrested or convicted of some…crime?" Shanna asks.

"Petty theft when he was fifteen, and possession of weed when he was seventeen. No convictions. It's only a matter of time."

Burrus saunters over to a buffet where several bottles and glasses are stationed. "Like a drink? Scotch, bourbon, or maybe a French red wine?"

"No thanks. On the job, you know."

As Burrus pours a half glass of dark liquid—scotch, most likely—Charlotte also declines, moves slowly about the large room, staring at the artifacts, and finally says, "You aren't happy with the direction your son's life has taken. I would imagine he doesn't heed advice from you."

He laughs, takes a gulp of the brown liquid, and replies, "The only one Andy would pay any attention to was his mother, and she bailed out six years ago."

"Bailed out?"

"Left a sinking ship—or at least she thought it was sinking. I had a run of bad luck, and she found a different sugar daddy. The joke, ultimately, was on her since my fortunes were reversed, and I'm doing nicely now, thank you. And her new man? Well, he had racehorses and made some sloppy choices. His mares got stuck in the mud."

"So she is no longer with him?"

"Right. Hops around a lot, does Jenny—Jennifer Sue, actually. Now? Not sure who she's with."

"You say your son sometimes listened to her, but he doesn't see her anymore?"

"I doubt it. Wouldn't tell me if he did. He only needs me if he gets desperate for the green stuff."

"So," Charlotte summarizes, "Andy doesn't consult with you, goes his own way, gets into trouble, and every so often hits on you for a bailout."

"I guess you could put it that way. I'd like to see him fly right, get his act in order, but for the life of me, I don't see how."

"Did you ever meet Kyla Pino, the model he's been dating?"

"Nah. Know she's a model, but I steer clear of his tawdry doings. They would pull me down. I only met one of his babes, pretty little thing, a spick twerp he latched on to when he was eighteen. From Washington Heights up in the Bronx. Imagine, hooking up with a greaser. I think he saw her as an alternate source for his addictions. You know, all those slimy street pushers."

"Yet," Shanna says, "you were willing to bankroll him with Stout to get the woman he wanted."

"Hey, that Stout guy seemed talented, so I thought maybe Andy would connect with him. You know, a role model. The money wasn't a fortune, but it made Andy happy for the time. And that babe was head and shoulders better than the brown-skinned trash. I could see him being sucked in with all those immigrant losers. Uh, is he still with the new honey?"

Charlotte waggles her hand back and forth. "Kind of. The deal you made with Stout sort of died with him."

"I bet you were an athlete in your younger years, probably

football," Shanna says.

"Yeah. It's a shame we have to grow older. I was a pretty good center on my college team."

"And professional?"

"Nah. Played on Saturday but not on Sunday. Not big enough. After a big meal, I was only two hundred pounds. Nowadays they grow 'em two-eighty to three-twenty."

There is an awkward silence, and at last, Burrus says, "Seems to me you think Andy did something pretty nasty."

"No accusations," Shanna says. "Just checking everything out."

"Okay. I wouldn't like to see him end up in the middle of the East River on Rikers Island."

"Let us hope not," Charlotte says. "Anyway, we want to thank you for answering our questions."

"By the way, Mr. Burrus, what's the name of the investment company you either own or work with?" Shanna asks.

"Oh, it's kind of a limited partnership. We gave it a funny name, like those Hollywood production companies. It's registered under the title 'Bright Boys.' My colleague is a Wall Street maven named Batchelor."

19

"What a first-class bullshitter, " Shanna says as they walk to her car, buttoned up against the wind. "A racist pig if there ever was one."

"Yet, I catch that he is concerned about his son."

"Yep, though in a limited way. Concerned and uninvolved at the same time. No wonder the boy has no compass. He is sort of tossed out in a stormy sea with no direction."

"Good image, Shanna, but Daddy may be more dedicated to junior's activities than he lets on. Don't want to dismiss him as a person of interest in whatever benefits little Andy. Thinks his child is a mess, yet might not want to see the family name sullied."

"The connection with Batchelor can't be coincidence. The kid obviously knows him. There's the twosome you were guessing about."

"Could very well be. Andy would need someone brighter and more sophisticated to do the ugly things we've been looking at."

Their conversation is interrupted by a drone on Shanna's cellphone.

"Cavanaugh. …Okay. Any more specific than that? Great… Thanks. Be in touch."

Charlotte gives her a quizzical look.

"Forensics. They're pretty sure the weapon used to club Stout was a heavy metal object, left an almost perfect circle where it met the skull. They say it had to be a hammer of some kind, with a rounded head."

"Ah, so of all the people in this sordid little escapade, who is a builder or construction worker—or, who knew where to get hold of a round-head hammer?"

"Almost anyone on the last part. And I don't think any of them is a carpenter or woodworker."

"The practice room at the agency has a walkway-riser that had to be built by someone—maybe Stout himself. And, in his office is what looks to be a small-scale model of some architectural design, which he likely constructed. That would mean he might have a stash of tools somewhere—that someone knew about."

"Okay, we'll search his office and also his apartment—or wherever he lived."

In Cavanaugh's car, Charlotte is pensive for a time, then asks, "Shanna, do you have a family in New York?"

Shanna smiles and replies, "Hey, cops do have private lives. I was married once when I was nineteen. Lasted two years. I entered the police training academy, and my partner bailed. Said my life would be too iffy and he couldn't take that chance. He's still in the New York area, out on Long Island. Sells real estate. Now get this: he married a long-legged, illicit entertainer. Quite a transition, from policewoman to porn star."

"Mom and dad? Brothers or sisters?"

"Mom's alive, about your age, lives in Fort Lauderdale, Florida. Dad passed six or seven years ago; pancreatic cancer. No cure. Gone in three months. Ugly way to die. I have one sister, four years older, moved to the mountains of Colorado. She had two kids; one died as an infant, a boy. I've never seen the other." She stops, a memory shimmering. "Still think about the little guy, that he'll never learn to ride a bike, never kiss a girl."

Charlotte sneaks a look at her tough companion, sees the glow of moisture in her eyes.

"Funny how no one thinks of police as people. They're badges, roles, interchangeable, one with another." She hesitates and shifts focus. "Since I've gotten involved in a few mysteries, I can understand the allure of being a police officer. When I was younger, every time I saw someone break a traffic rule, I wished I had been a cop. Even now, though I don't drive very much, I get furious when folks flout the law."

"Where can I take you, Charlotte?"

"Back to my hotel. I have some marks to put on my suspect

chart."

—

China Olivier versus Kyla Pino. *What in hell do I do with that?* is Broadway's conundrum. He knows Kyla will become available, especially now that Stout is gone and that dumb adolescent Andy Burrus no longer has a hold on her. *But, damn it, China doesn't fool around! Delicious! A brassy babe with haunting allure. Have to move delicately, not too fast or too slow, or could be out in the cold with both of them.*

"Broadway Farivar here. Kyla! Just thinking about you. Are you okay? What's up? …Well, I'm going to meet Charlotte in a couple of hours. …At her hotel, the Sheraton, in Times Square. …You want to join us? …Sure. Four o'clock. Room 1840. See you there."

Hmm. Interesting development. Wonder what she has in mind.

Ruminations are interrupted by another call.

"Hey beautiful, Mark Angel. Guess what? You got the part. I just heard from Geraldine Falk, the producer. They want you for the role of Walter, the boyfriend. Need to sign papers."

"Yes! What a bonus! Life is good; life is great. Just tell me when."

Curious man, this Mark Angel, Broadway ponders. *Falls in love with his clients, calls us beautiful, compliments us sickeningly, yet, in all fairness, and, as far as I know, has never laid a hand on any of them. Well—certainly discreet, surely ultracautious. More accurate to say, never laid a hand on me.*

Got the part! A break, at last. China probably knows. Kyla ought to know. Brooklyn has to know. My mom—well, of course.

Angel tells him that the first script run-through will be in three days, that this production team likes promptness and endurance, often rehearsing for six hours straight. Opening night is still a few months away, but time sneaks up, and it's better to be prepared than sorry.

The good with the bad—Brooklyn's fall, the killing of Stout, the models asking Brook to lead them, Kyla showing interest, China really showing interest, landing this hallmark part....

Charlotte wants to see me, and Kyla will be there. A breakthrough? New evidence?

He is walking down his namesake, munching a blueberry muffin, all the New York people, the pretty with the petty, affluent and poor, looking suddenly delicious. A wispy blonde passes him, hair wet as if just washed, face scrubbed, ready for a commercial, two suits scurry by, late for a mandated board meeting, an exasperated mother scolds a tot for picking up dropped candy from the 'filthy' sidewalk.

He wanders by the Shubert Theater, eyes drifting upward to the banner above the entrance: *New Musical: Coming Soon.* A reprise of the Berlin musical, *Annie Get Your Gun,* has just ended a six-month run, well received, but not a mega-hit. Will *Sleepless in Seattle* be the next bold billboard draped across the building's face, repeated a hundred times all over New York, reviewed from Boston to San Francisco, blurbs in playbills, ads in the *Theatre News* in every hotel in the city?

My career, he muses, *has been steady and unspectacular. Could this be my personal mega-hit? It's not the lead but a meaty part that will give me a chance to flaunt my talent.*

He smiles at his own brassy attitude as he says aloud, "I am going to shine!"

—

"Marvelous news, Broadway," a beaming Charlotte says and spontaneously hugs him. "I love that story. It ought to lend itself well to a musical score."

"The words-and-music team is highly respected, so I presume they will step up."

"Your sister producing an important fashion show and you landing a great part; the Farivar kids are riding a comet!"

A knock on the door tells them Kyla has arrived.

"Come in, sweetheart. Happy to have you join us. We'll make this a social event and a fact-finding session."

She pours three glasses of red wine. "Don't know for sure who donated this bubbly, but it was on my table when I got here this afternoon. A note said something about 'compliments of the house.' Does that mean you, Broadway?"

"No, but it could mean my mother. Every now and then she does something generous like this."

"Here are some famous New York roasted cashews from a corner vendor, or at least that's what the sign said. I was also tempted to indulge in some of their aromatic sausages, but my good sense told me to spare my arteries."

"I'm not sure what you mean by fact-finding," Kyla says. "Unless you're on the trail of some facts I don't know."

"We are on the trail of a lot of facts, though, in situations like this, some are red herrings, deliberate distortions to confound an investigation."

Sweet music frames their conversation, a station Charlotte found on her bedside radio devoted to retro songs from the fifties and sixties—Sinatra, Sammy Davis, Dean Martin, Sarah Vaughn, Lena Horne, Streisand.

"Kyla, you had some reason for wanting to join us," Brooklyn says, his voice rising at the end as if expecting an answer.

"I'm…confused. We talked about my relationship with Andy and I sort of left the reasons up in the air." She turns to Charlotte. "Sorry for bringing this up in front of you. I know you have other things to discuss."

"My dear, you are welcome to bring anything up. I am a most discrete person, and nothing you say will be repeated."

"Look, Kyla, we already know that Andy's family donated to Stout's agency as sort of a deal—if you would go along with him being your boyfriend. The only thing that was hard to understand was why you had to do that. You are a jewel. Stout would have taken you anyway. Brook and you are…were…his most promising models."

Tears cloud her eyes as she responds, "Stupid of me. I have no feelings for Andy. He's a crude little boy. But Donald made it clear that if I wanted access to the prime fashions, the favored spots, I had better go along. With Donald gone, I feel suddenly airy, unburdened."

She stops and cries hard. Charlotte embraces her.

After a moment, Kyla says softly, "I saw you with that beautiful woman."

Charlotte nods at Broadway, a cue for him to speak up, and when he hesitates, she cocks her head and purses her lips.

"Well, here's the story. Her name is China, and she and I are both cast in a new Broadway musical called *Sleepless in Seattle*. I've only known her two days. She's a singer-dancer. I'm excited about the part, but when it comes to China, I…don't know what to say."

Again softly, Kyla murmurs, "Brook always wanted me to hook up with you. I was trapped in that awful deal. Now that it's over, I'm afraid it's too late."

The music is the only sound for a time, and Charlotte is the first to speak. "It's really none of my business, but I have strong feelings that if people want something to happen, they have to work at it. I don't believe in destiny. Destiny is a matter of choice, not chance."

Broadway reaches for Kyla's hand. "You know, I'm not some kind of in-demand guy who has this awesome power to pick and choose any woman out of the world's inventory. Kyla"—he lowers his voice—"you know I've been drawn toward you for a long time. That Andy fellow kept me away. Let's…see what happens. And no, it's not too late."

Again, Charlotte breaks a brief silence. "May I change the subject? My role here is not as a mediator or matchmaker. Once we can get these terrible crimes solved, I'll be on my way back to my quiet life in Pennsylvania."

"Sorry, Charlotte," Broadway says. "It's your show. Go ahead."

"Well, the detective and I paid a visit to the…uh, little boy's father in the high-rent district of Park Avenue. He's what the kids today would call a 'trip.' Wealthy as Trump, or close to it, but also harsh and, in many ways, crude. He thinks of his son as a failure, yet, up to recently, plies him with funds hoping to straighten him out. Now, Kyla, you may not have known this, but Andy had a Puerto Rican girlfriend from Washington Heights about a year ago—gave the father nightmares since he is as prejudiced as they come. Somehow that connection seemed to give the boy access to the drugs he was using. Andy has a couple of minor arrests but nothing that stuck. My guess is his father bought his way out each time, then, six months ago, bought his way in with you."

"I never asked him about other girls. I didn't care, one way or the other."

"So, what happened to her? Is there some story to that?" Broadway asks.

"My guess is that good old Charlie Burrus may have paid her off too. He couldn't have anyone with his name hooked in with a minority, and especially a brown-skinned one."

She pauses and asks Kyla, "I presume Andy thinks you and he are still an item?"

"I haven't said anything to him, but I intend to."

"Well, I must tell you that I believe he is a possible suspect in Brooklyn's fall. With her out of the way, his 'girlfriend,' meaning you, would have the number one spot. I doubt he would kill off Stout—you know, bite the hand that feeds him."

"He doesn't think in those terms. I mean, he wouldn't care about me having a prime position with Stout. He hardly thought of me at all except to decorate his arm when he went someplace."

Charlotte is aware that Kyla avoids any reference to the physical relationship she had with Andy. Just as well. Broadway doesn't need that as part of his equation.

"Since you are hypothetically still on his arm, maybe you can play detective. I would love to know—though there was no mention of it—if he got that Washington Heights girl pregnant. You see, if he did, I would lay odds that Daddy Burrus took care of it and then wrote his son off—no more bailouts, no more financial subsidies. At least not after he paid Stout for you."

"You mean little Andy, the texting aficionado, is running on empty? What about that sleek passion pit he drives?" Broadway asks.

"You know," Kyla says, "last night he was muttering about how expensive gasoline is now. Never did that before."

"As you said it, Broadway, he could be running on empty— unless someone else jumped in to take Daddy's place."

Dinah Washington is singing "These Foolish Things" in the background; for Broadway, the lyrics are some of the most memorable ever written: "The winds of March that made my heart a dancer, a telephone that rings but who's to answer? Oh, how the ghost of you clings, these foolish things remind me of you."

"Like who?" Broadway asks.

"Like I don't know yet," Charlotte replies.

"How can I play detective?" Kyla looks puzzled.

"I'd love to know if the old girlfriend had been pregnant, if she gave birth or aborted, and if Burrus senior, as sort of a final gesture of rescue, paid her off. I may ask the detective to try to find the young woman. We'd learn a lot if we can do that."

"What would we learn?"

"Well, my handsome young friend, we would learn if Daddy is telling the truth, if Junior became desperate, and if he had motive to do something shady for a monetary reward. I intend to—as the law-enforcement people put it—grill the boy as soon as I can, but he'd likely tell Kyla more than he would me."

"Not sure if I'm up to it, but I'll try," Kyla says.

"Not the end of the world if you don't."

Broadway hugs her.

Charlotte pats her on the shoulder.

20

In the Manhattan Precinct Stationhouse at 306 West 54th Street, Shanna Cavanaugh is eating a banana. Charlotte is seated beside her in an interrogation room with three walls painted khaki green and the fourth a full-length mirror—actually a one-way viewing glass.

It is quiet as a churchyard, except for Charlotte softly drumming her fingers on an ugly green-top Formica table.

In a moment, a uniformed officer opens a khaki-green door and allows Andy Burrus into the room.

"Great," Shanna says. "I'm so glad you were willing to come in. It's likely you can be a big help to us with the case we're working on."

"Don't know anything. It's a waste of time."

"Maybe so, but let's give it a shot. See, there is a lot of sadness here. That beautiful young woman, Brooklyn, is in a wheelchair, and her boss, the agency owner, is dead."

"Boo-hoo," Andy says.

"You're not sad?" Charlotte asks.

"Hardly knew either one. Saw Stout a few times. Not my type. The girl, well, other than the fact I would have loved to get into her pants…"

"Yes, yes, I get it," Charlotte says.

"Young fellow"—Shanna looks at him through narrowed eyes—"since you've been dating Kyla, one of the other models, we believe you know a good deal more than you are saying. Did you see any friction between the owner and any of his people?"

127

"Yeah. Lots. The guy would come down hard on them. Big man in town. Had to run the show."

Taking a calculated risk, Charlotte says, "Like your father."

"What?"

"Big man, like your father."

A stretched silence and Andy replies, "My old man is a prick. Sorry if I offend your womanly feelings, but he's off my list."

"Because he cut off the green?" Shanna asks.

"Look, I don't know how you're getting all this, but Charlie Burrus cut me off a long time ago. He's one sorry asshole. The money part was just the latest shit."

"Who's your best friend?" Charlotte looks him steadily in the eye, making him squirm.

"I...I'm a loner," he mutters.

"So Stout and his models had friction. Can you name names?" Shanna asks.

"I don't know. That little Gelly bitch was on the outs with him. And the Black guy, Brent, seemed to have a love-hate thing going."

"Andy, we know more about you than you think. I'm going to ask you something very personal, and Detective Cavanaugh and I want a candid answer. The young Puerto Rican girl you had a fling with, the one from Washington Heights—we could track her down and ask her, but it would be a lot smoother if you can tell us—did you get her pregnant?"

As if absorbing the color of the room, Andy's face takes on a pale green hue, the stubble on his chin a darker forest green.

All he says is, "Shit."

Patiently, the two women wait, and, as if the realization filters in that he is out of choices, in a guttural voice, he murmurs, "Yeah. She didn't know from protection. Told me she wanted to get married. As if I'd marry her."

Following up, Shanna says, "And your, uh, old man—how did he react?"

"Typical. Chewed me up one side, down the other. Told me he was through. I was on my own. As if I wasn't already."

"Ah, but that time it meant no more bailouts."

"Well, he agreed to give Stout some cash to help me hook up with Kyla. I think he was relieved I had a gorgeous new babe who was white and American. But then, he wrote me a note—email and text, both—that he was washing his hands of me."

"Okay," Shanna says, pacing the small room, "so now, tell us how you're getting the bread to fuel your gas guzzler, eat out, pay rent. All that."

"Hey, what is this? I thought you wanted help from me. Why are you digging up my stuff?"

"There was a crime, young fellow. In fact, two of them, and we need to look at everyone. Including you." Shanna actually pokes him in the chest with her forefinger.

"I…I know people. They help me out."

Charlotte cocks her head to one side. "I thought you said you were a loner."

"Yeah, but…"

"My guess," Shanna says in a tone laced with accusation, "is that you do favors for people and they reward you. Am I right?"

"Uh, sometimes."

"And what kind of favors?" Charlotte asks.

"I don't know. Take 'em places. Shop for 'em."

"Hurt someone they don't like," Shanna inserts.

"What? What do you mean?"

"If people had a grudge against, say, Brooklyn Farivar and wanted to punish her, they might pay you for carrying out the deed. Like pushing her down a flight of stairs."

"Hey, man, get off my case. I didn't push the broad anywhere."

"But you might have been paid off for an exchange of information," Charlotte puts in. "That person might have needed to know where to hide out, like the custodian's closet, and what time Brooklyn would be leaving. Those things. Money for information— makes him a co-conspirator, right, Detective?"

"You bet. A long vacation in Rikers…unless…"

He looks confused, a struggle between admitting something that could still be conjecture and possibly saving his own skin, as his eyes flit back and forth across the barren room.

Finally, with a grunt, he stands and blurts out, "I'm out of here. You got nothing on me."

"Yet," Shanna says.

—

Most of the time, doctors are anonymous creatures, diagnosing and prescribing while keeping their own lives private. Bruce Landry is no exception, though; with Brooklyn Farivar, his manner combines the professional with the personal. Affairs of the heart are mysterious, often ascribed to chemistry, and, with Landry, that chemistry is bubbling like a Yellowstone geyser about to erupt.

In her neatly kept apartment, Brooklyn is seated on her couch, a dark blue, puffy affair with a pattern of lighter blue fleur-de-lis throughout. Her most-attentive physician is seated beside her, grinning widely.

"Brooklyn, I am delighted! Try it again."

A brave smile spreads on Brooklyn's pretty face as she wills her energy downward, past her left thigh, past her calf, below her ankle to the tips of her toes, and voila, they stir and bend!

"A breakthrough," Landry says. "Sensation is returning. It's a super sign."

"I don't know what it means since I can touch my toes and not feel anything."

"It's a slow process; movement first, feelings next."

She laughs. " I have lots of feelings, but not in my legs."

He looks at her with a penetrating gaze, deciphering oblique messages not his strong point. "Uh…what kind of feelings?"

In the kitchen, her ear tuned in to their conversation, America Lobero grins. Perhaps it is her own peculiar superstition, but the fingers on both her hands are crossed.

"Well, I have lots of feelings concerning the agency and the show I'm trying to direct. I have strong feelings about my lousy physical condition. And…I have feelings…about you."

"Me?"

"Yep. But I can't expect you to be interested in me in a…well, in a man-woman way. Why would you want to hook up with a handicapped person—with a cripple?"

Landry's thoughts race back in time some thirty years, painful thoughts long ago shoved into a sheltered corner, of a mother driving home in a furious storm, a big rig swerving to avoid a too-late-seen pedestrian, sideswiping her car, sending it careening into a massive elm tree. This passed on to him from a devastated father, heard but hardly absorbed by six-year-old Bruce.

For four years she survived, unable to leave her bed, by then Bruce knowing her as the mother everyone else had to take care of.

Oh yes, he knew about living with someone disabled, immobile.

"Listen to me, Brook. Having a disability alters the way you move about in your world; it doesn't change who you are."

He pauses. "Uh…who you are is—well, it is remarkable! And yes, I'm drawn toward you and afraid you'll be reluctant to take a risk for just that reason: a negative view of your future."

America, in the adjoining room, nods vigorously.

"My future," Brooklyn says tentatively, "was always tied to my pushy mother's expectations. My bro and I were only good enough for her if we became stars. This…this injury blasts all of it to pieces. I've already had to revise what that means."

"Believe me, Brook, you are a star—as a person, a woman, and as a professional in the modeling business. I saw you at work. Brilliant!"

"A detour, never again as a model, myself—a miniature, though hopefully, less tyrannical, Donald Stout, behind the camera, not in front. Quite an adjustment. I'm going to need time to come to terms with that new future."

"A mixed bag, as you see it. But keep in mind, there is still hope your injury will turn around. I think it will. In time, you'll walk again and, if you choose, model again."

"And if I don't? I bet that'll send you running for the hills."

"Hey, I'm your doctor, and if you'll let me, I'll…I'll be your boyfriend. What do you say? You gonna let me in?"

A glint of excitement lights up her now-flushed pink face.

Landry can't stand it and leans in. For a moment, time freezes like a mountain lake in winter; then, as if responding to a spring thaw, Brooklyn leans in as well.

A bit too loudly, America calls out, "Si, si!"

21

It is tempting to compare the teeming New York metropolis with the more laid-back, extended city of Los Angeles. Charlotte remembers the days when she still enjoyed flying, visiting her brother in California and being treated to a Jane Fonda theater event. The exquisite Lipschitz sculpture between the Mark Taper and the Dorothy Chandler Pavilion, set in a cascade of water geysers erupting every few seconds, stirred her aesthetic juices. "Nowhere in the world," she recalls telling her brother, Greg, "is there a sight to match this"—and, all the while, the countenance of Placido Domingo gazed down at them from the façade of the Chandler auditorium. A perfect spot to enjoy theater or music.

The magnificent New York boroughs, specifically Manhattan, have their superb venues as well, magnetic attractions that pull thousands of visitors a day into Times Square, an area the politicians are proud to say is elegantly safe for tourists. Police are often seen patrolling the streets until well after midnight, and now and then one may see an officer on horseback.

Some of the city's grand attractions have fled the coop, the Giants migrating to San Francisco and the Dodgers abandoning Brooklyn for Los Angeles.

Though she is not a sports fan, Charlotte is aware that New Yorkers have the Yankees in the Bronx, the Mets in Flushing, and, of course, the New York Knicks are the basketball favorites of millions of Big Apple residents.

The Metropolitan Opera is a world-class operation, and

Carnegie Hall's music enchants thousands each year. Entertainment galore for all sorts of tastes.

But perhaps the most alluring aspect of Manhattan is its unmatched live theater scene.

Broadway's adventure in a major production on *The Great White Way* is about to begin.

Brooklyn's adventure as coordinator of a world-class modeling event is only a few days off.

Her investigation of ugly criminal acts is like a gauntlet thrown down for Charlotte; with no apparent eyewitnesses and meager forensics evidence, the challenge is hefty.

Detective Cavanaugh tells her, "I would like to interview the Farivar family. I've never met the daughter who was injured, and I think it might reveal a lot to watch the three of them interact."

"I agree. Momma, as you may have picked up, is crusty and highly judgmental. She is the mother bear defending her brood, and who knows what that may have triggered. Broadway and Brooklyn are devoted to each other, and, though each has an independent personality, would not let any other relationship, potential or realized, trump theirs."

She stops and, as an afterthought, tags on, "You know, Shanna, it might be a wise idea to get that troubled young lad, Andy Burrus, with his pompous father, Charles, together in a room. A lot is gained from observing how clashing family members interact."

First things first: Broadway arranges a meeting in Brooklyn's apartment with Mother Sarah, a sullen attendee; her disconnect from the New York police has made her attitude toward them abrasive.

"So, what do you need to see us about? You people need to be out there finding the sick person who hurt my Brook."

"Mrs. Farivar, you'd be surprised at what's been going on," Charlotte replies. "Detective Cavanaugh's people have discovered some important clues."

"Yes? Like what?"

Shanna smiles and addresses herself directly to Sarah as if the others don't need to know. "Fingerprints are important data. On the canister that was used to vault Brooklyn down those stairs were several prints. One set was the custodian's, another was Charlotte's—since she lifted the container to assess its weight—and a third set was Donald Stout's. Unfortunately, that does not tell us for sure that he was the perp since deliveries are made to his office and he may have handled the can earlier."

"No excuses for that pervert," Sarah says with venom. "If he wasn't killed, you could squeeze him 'til he confessed."

"There is a fourth set of prints, but they belong to no one in our system, and we cannot invade people's privacy by demanding they give us access to theirs."

Broadway adds, "So they could be anyone's—I mean anyone in the modeling troupe or anyone who knew Brook, though he—or she—would also have had to know about the storage room and Brook's schedule."

"Yes," Charlotte says. "It's an open field, but we may be able to narrow it down. Brooklyn, only you know who, of all the folks at your agency, would even dream of wanting to injure you. We can go down the list and eliminate a lot of them pretty fast."

"Oh, I have no idea. There are only two men, and Brent is, well, like a friend. The other male model is rather distant. Of the women, Kyla is my pal, and Andrea, Deanna, and Julia have always cared about me. Corrine and I have had our issues, but I don't think it was personal; most of it was because Donald wasn't impressed with her, and she became frustrated. There are maybe five or so others, but we had no problems between us and I can't imagine them wanting to harm me."

"All right. That's a start," Charlotte says. "And then there are also Andy Burrus, who is a sad little fellow likely to do almost anything to maintain his monetary lifestyle, and your former boyfriend, Aaron Batchelor, who suddenly popped back into your life for no apparent reason."

"That one," Sarah puts in, "that Wall Street big shot, thinks his excrement has no odor."

Charlotte smiles at the gentler way of expressing a nasty judgment; Mother Sarah is a clever old duck yet cannot camouflage her ruthless bent.

A dozen ruby-red roses were delivered to Brooklyn's apartment, and America has set them, perky and lustrous, in a deep, purple-tinted vase. Charlotte can catch the almost narcotic effect of their timeless perfume and, as she does, marvels once again at how, as children, her mother filled her and her brother with precious aesthetic values: art, music, literature, an awareness of beauty, of aromas, the sensuality of touch, and most of all, curiosity.

Broadway says, "You went away there for a minute, Charlotte."

"The roses. Wonder who sent them?"

Brooklyn blushes. "My…uh, doctor. He's a most doting physician, I have to say."

Laughter from Broadway: "And a lot more."

It is not Charlotte's style to reveal developing information before it is codified, at least enough for her to think of it as factual. She and Shanna know the connection between Charles Burrus and Aaron Batchelor—a connection that could be compelling in unmasking the culprits in the two crimes—yet it would not be prudent to divulge this, as well as other information, prematurely. If she were alone with Broadway, she might consider including him since he is smart and an incisive thinker and might add to the story.

She sees, however, something that stirs her heart, not perceived by the others who are more used to such a thing as routine. What she sees, not even Brooklyn has realized.

"My dear," she says softly, directly to Brooklyn, "are you aware when you said those words, '…a most doting physician,' that you slid your right foot at least two inches toward your left?"

—

Awareness is the key to all behavior; Broadway remembers his basic psychology professor at NYU telling the class that little jewel. It stayed with him for several years, and sometimes, when a person he encounters invades his space, blocks an aisle, rattles popcorn containers during a movie, blurts out a non-sequitur, interrupts, or generally ignores others' presence, he mutters—not loud enough for the offender to hear—"Awareness."

No one had noticed Brooklyn's foot movement other than Charlotte; however, once she verbalized it, the reaction was electric.

"Hey, Sis, you rock," Broadway says. "Let the healing begin."

"I told you," Sarah adds, "a Farivar doesn't give up."

For Brooklyn, the recognition brings tears.

America Lobero, standing several feet away, says in a soft voice, "I see that before. Not sure I see right. But I watch her move the toes."

The mood of the room is palpably lighter, the roses redder,

their fragrance a heady complement to the ambiance. The Farivar family, for the first time in a couple of weeks, senses a return to the way it was before—well, before the fall.

It is time, Charlotte thinks, *to ask a penetrating question.*

"Brooklyn, I want you to think back and see if you can come up with the answer to what I'm going to ask. When you and Batchelor broke up—or, if it is more accurate, when you dumped him—how did he take it? You mentioned that Stout became almost threatening, but how about Aaron Batchelor?"

She is silent for a moment and finally says, in a monotone, "He asked me to marry him. At first, I thought something like that might work. He is a successful man, attractive physically, and was clear about his affection for me. But his narrow spectrum of availability to another person simply turned me off. I could tell him something, and ten minutes later he would ask me a question about what I had just said. He was always somewhere else. Not sure why he wanted me, except maybe for a trophy on his arm when he was with his millionaire pals.

"I realized he was in love with an image, not a person, so I bit the bullet and kissed him off. How did he react? Different from Stout, he wasn't openly menacing, but since I knew him well, I could read the narrowing of the eyes, the tight, straight line of the mouth, and I knew he was filing away something for the future.

"When he showed up in my hospital room, I became instantly on the alert. Even though a year had passed, I had no idea if he now was engaged in payback."

She stops but adds, "I wouldn't be surprised if he was. If he is."

Cavanaugh says, "Motive. The driving force in any crime."

Charlotte says, "A long memory. Holds on to a grudge."

Broadway says, "A money monster; on the gold standard. I never much liked him."

Before they leave, Charlotte sidles up to America and says, almost in a whisper, "If that Batchelor fellow comes to visit Brooklyn again, offer him some refreshments. When he's through, take his glass into the kitchen, careful to hold it on the bottom, and save it for us."

22

Next on the agenda, get the two Burrus men together, the haughty and clearly pompous father with the resentful and petulant son. Not a simple task. Though Kyla's help in finding out if Andy's Washington Heights girlfriend had been pregnant is no longer a need, Shanna wonders if it might work by getting Kyla involved in this meeting; if not already, she will shortly tell Burrus, the younger, that they are no longer a couple. Maybe Burrus, the elder, who was thankful his son had latched on to an acceptable woman, would like to intervene since, at one time, he tried to help the boy hold on to Kyla with bribe money to Donald Stout.

Sure enough, with Kyla's inclusion, a meeting is arranged at the Stout Modeling Studio, though, to insure compliance, the Burrus men were not told the other one would be there. The message went something like: "We are eager to pursue the investigation of the crimes that were committed and need your presence. Kyla Pino will be there, along with the detective and Ms. Charlotte Smart—and possibly Broadway Farivar, the brother of the woman who was injured on the stairs."

Ego, and a compelling drive to be around beauty, stirred Charlie Burrus to reply in the affirmative. Andy Burrus said, "More crap. Okay, I'll come."

"What the shit is he doing here?" Andy blurts out.

"Greetings, boy," Charlie says. "Hope this mess isn't one you're tied up in."

Kyla breaks the Burrus conflict with, "I want to tell you that for the past several months, I have felt trapped. Donald needed a cash flow, Andy needed a new babe, and you, the daddy, wanted to see your kid with someone other than a girl from the Heights. Well, with Stout gone, I feel free. Free as a bird. And, as of this moment, I am officially flying away from the sick deal made for me. My declaration of independence."

"You dumping me?" from Andy.

"Already did," from Kyla.

They are seated in pulled-up folding chairs, available for modeling events; in his attempt at aesthetics, Donald Stout had them painted red, blue, yellow, green.

Charlotte intervenes: "We need to clear a few things up. Your son, Andy, hooked up with a woman from Washington Heights, and you didn't like her. Didn't meet your standards of someone to grace the Burrus family. It seems the breakup wasn't going to be clean. Apparently, the young woman was pregnant with Andy's child. So, you paid her off—for what, an abortion, to have the baby and then disappear, or…tell us?"

Andy stares at his father with a look that could wither anyone, particularly a family member, but Charlie Burrus breaks into laughter.

"The little beaner was all bluff. Told her I'd give her nothing unless she went to this gynecologist I know. Said she wouldn't, so I said I wouldn't. Disappeared like fog in the wind. Never heard from her again. I wouldn't be surprised if Andy, here, is shooting blanks."

"Yeah, you'd like that. No grandkid to grace your fucking old age."

"Now, don't get nasty, son. I'd love a grandson to carry on the Burrus name—provided it was with an acceptable female." He pauses and adds, "This dish is spectacular. If she don't want you anymore, maybe she'll go for someone more mature."

Kyla blanches and, with a grimace, replies, "In your dreams."

"We're not here to discuss romance, Mr. Burrus," Charlotte says. "Despite your disdain for your son and his choices, you seem to want to support him—or, at least did until recently. The question is, to what lengths would you go to make him into a person acceptable to you?"

"What the hell is that supposed to mean?" Burrus clouds up, his manner, all at once, hostile.

"Back off," Shanna says. "We're talking here, not threatening.

Ms. Smart wants what the police want: answers to questions about crimes that occurred in this building."

"Not my game. Don't know a thing about all that."

"We'll see," Charlotte replies. "Meanwhile, the Burrus men, pals or not, had every reason to gain from what happened."

"How did I gain?" Andy shouts. "My old man disowns me, and my girlfriend dumps me!"

"Really, Andy," Charlotte continues, "we already know that you picked up with others to keep your sports car and your lifestyle percolating. And, as for your girlfriend, you had no idea at the time that she would want out."

"Picked up with others? You get some drug dealer from Harlem to finance you?" Charlie challenges.

"Wouldn't you like to know!"

"Whether your father would like to know is not the issue, but we definitely would," Charlotte says. "Your bankroller is an important piece of our complex puzzle. If you continue, young man, to act as if this whole affair is a game, you may find yourself the number one suspect."

An animal cry—not one of distress, but of fury, like a mother lion aware of a threat to her cub—explodes out of Charlie Burrus: "What in the hell do you mean, number one suspect? My son may be an underachiever, and he sure is an immature parasite, but he ain't no murderer!"

Shanna again intervenes, "No accusations yet, Mr. Burrus. But the fingers are beginning to point."

Andy pivots his head back and forth like a metronome—a click, in fact, coming from his throat with each twist.

"Okay. You want it, here it is. You"—he nods at his father—"shit all over me and cut me off. But your sweet little partner in crime—that fat cat Wall Streeter, Aaron Batchelor—must have had some reason to double deal you and stepped in to help. Yeah, he's been feeding me. Not sure what he gets out of it, except I think he's still carrying the torch for that Brooklyn babe."

"And?" Charlotte inserts.

"And what?"

"What else did he ask of you for his generosity?"

"Nothing. Well, he asked questions about Stout's Agency, its schedule and all that. And I promised him I wouldn't tell anyone, so now, I'm sure he's gonna be pissed."

"You're a dumb little fucker," Daddy Burrus says, and realizing the presence of Kyla, adds quickly, " Uh, sorry for my language. Son, Aaron Batchelor is my investment partner. He's not a wellspring for a freeloader. And he don't do something for nothing. I know him well. Payback time will come if it hasn't already."

Shanna Cavanaugh stares hard at both the father and son and says evenly, with grim determination, "You two are playing word games here, and that's fine, but you're getting awfully close to spilling the ingredients of this nasty crime stew. One or two more ingredients and we may be ready to put on the cuffs."

Aware that Shanna's comment has some mixed metaphors, Charlotte smiles and adds, "Andy, you're young enough to still make your life work. The things your father said that did make sense are that he'd like for you to find an appropriate woman, and he did not believe you are a murderer. So, even if Daddy will no longer ply you with undeserved funds, I gather he wants the best for you."

Her analysis seems to stun Andy, and he bolts out of his red-painted chair and begins to pace. At last, he mutters, "A father shouldn't disown a son."

Charlie Burrus rises from his green-painted chair and mutters back, "A son shouldn't dishonor a father."

Broadway, who has been rather silent throughout, places his hand on Kyla's forearm and says to no one in particular, "It's important for everyone to get the message this woman put out a moment ago. Her relationship with you, Andy, bought with nothing less than a monetary bribe, is officially over."

He faces Kyla and tacks on, "Yes, you are free as a bird. And that makes you wonderfully available."

Kyla stares at Broadway. "Available for whom?"

Charlotte grins widely. Murder mystery or not, isn't it heavenly when young love blooms?

"Don't leave town," Shanna says to the Burrus pair.

23

Rehearsal time. *Sleepless in Seattle* will become *The Great White Way* musical. Broadway Farivar and China Olivier, along with the other principals, are asked in for a first-read run-through.

The blooming of young love may be premature since Broadway's affections are agonizingly divided, especially now, here, in the close confines of a half dozen folks sharing loving as well as alienating words from pristine scripts. China reads with passion and, even more, with stimulating touches and ingratiating smiles, inhibitions discarded, displays of affection permissible in the make-believe role of a fictitious character.

Not that her closeness is resented, seen as gratuitous or forward; Broadway is pulled like a wave to the shore by this elegant and luscious young woman.

"But I can see your little boy resents me," China emotes to Sam Baldwin, Jonah's father.

Broadway catches the interchange, waiting for his turn, and, in his role as Walter, says to Annie, "For two people engaged to be married, we're about as connected as players on opposite teams. What's going on?"

The principals playing Annie and Sam are seasoned actors, and Broadway respects their perspicuity; reading with them is more than an exercise.

After nearly two hours, with the director and producer hovering yet saying almost nothing, Geraldine Falk says, "Enough for today. There will likely be some editing in the script, but learn your parts. We meet again in two days, same time, same place.”

China grabs Broadway’s arm and says, “Whew, time for a glass of wine. Whaddya say?”

“Uh…sure. The Sheraton’s only two blocks away. They have a pleasant lounge.”

“I wouldn’t care if it were an unpleasant lounge.”

—

“So, tell me what’s happening with your sister’s fall and that Stout fellow’s death. Any new developments?”

It is late afternoon, the time when many bars and pubs offer their wares at discounts, hoping to entice the pre-dinner crowd. This lounge is in the high-rent category, and no bargains are to be had. Wine is nine dollars a glass, and mixed cocktails are up to twelve dollars a drink. Broadway, still the recipient of his mother’s largess, is not concerned about the cost. The tables are set apart at respectable distances to allow guests optimum privacy; tranquil music hovers like a soothing mist; a panel of high and broad windows allows the light in from Seventh Avenue, though the interior hue is soft and tastefully subdued.

“We know Brooklyn was struck from behind, though the culprit is still a mystery. Some folks think it was Stout who did it in a lather about getting dumped, but others say he would have been stupid to hurt his best model. Still, someone may have considered him the perp and decided to get even. He was hit on the back of the head with a heavy object, maybe a hammer, and sent down the back stairs. Even our elderly friend, Charlotte, who is quite the sleuth, is finding these mountains hard to climb.”

There is a long quiet moment as they both take in the relaxing ambiance. Finally, China says, “I love the way you read. Great interpretation, especially since it was all cold.”

“How about you? You’re spectacular. Sam Baldwin has to be nuts to turn you down for anybody else.”

“But, as the dialogue notes, the little guy, Sam’s son, Jonah, finds my character boring. Well, after a while, Sam does too.”

“The leads are good, aren’t they.”

“Mm. Yep. Especially Ian Tenant. I saw him do Brigadoon. Great tenor voice. But we’re good too. It’s a solid cast.”

Broadway is aware that, as in a previous moment, they are skirting anything to do with them and their incipient connection. Already having experienced China's intrepid nature, he doesn't expect this deferment to last long.

He is correct.

She places her smooth hand on his. "I'm sure you think of me as a pushy broad, but...well, I really like you. In this town, it's hard to find the genuine article; I meet lots of men, but too many on the make, with inflated egos."

"The center of the entertainment world. Guys, and girls too, come here to get discovered. Makes for competition. Actors—and other performers—become skilled at self-promotion since they learn pretty fast no one will do it for them."

"How come you're not like that? I wouldn't call you shy, but you're one of the least self-absorbed men I've ever met."

"Thanks for the compliment. My mother used to berate my sis and me if we showed any signs of being vain. She was always vain herself, so I think she decided her kids ought not to be."

Another silence. At last, China says, "That girl in the studio, I think her name is Kyla, has a thing for you, doesn't she."

This abrupt reference to Kyla tips Broadway off balance; he blocks for a moment, then says, "She's my sister's best friend. I...I like her. She's been involved with someone."

"Doesn't answer my question."

"Uh...I'm not sure. Maybe."

"And do you have a thing for her?"

"Come on, China, that isn't fair. You and I are brand new, and we're colleagues. I'm sure we'll get to know each other very well in the weeks to come."

She shrugs, her lips in a pout, the lower lip over the upper; she tilts her head to the side and says, "Hey, just trying to gauge my chances. Nice to know the competition, don't you think?"

A voice from over his shoulder startles Broadway, and he turns to see a smiling Charlotte.

"Well, well, imagine running into you two here. You may find it a stretch, but I came down to indulge in a glass of red wine before dinner. Had no idea I'd find you beautiful people."

"Charlotte is staying in this hotel," Broadway says.

"Yes," Charlotte says. "I won't presume to invade your

privacy, but since we are together, let me ask you a question. Do you think Andy Burrus has the smarts—and, of course, the motives—to have pulled off either of these crimes we're investigating?"

"If you're asking my opinion, I'd say he's a messenger type. He wouldn't think up anything, but he might obey orders."

"Ah. One other quick question. Brooklyn has been very nice to Corrine Gelly. Would you think Corrine might be the culprit in either incident, and if so, would you expect her to be remorseful because of your sister's benevolence?"

"I catch your implication; if she is remorseful about having done something dreadful, the proper questioning could get her to spill it all."

"Smart lad. Exactly what I was wondering."

"Corrine could have done either—pushed Brooklyn out of petty envy and/or later polished off Stout because he still refused to bring her back into the fold."

"I agree. Well, I'll leave you two alone." She pauses and tacks on, "Though I can't be sure, I think Detective Cavanaugh's assigned bodyguard for me is standing over there, pretending to read a newspaper."

"You're too clever, Charlotte. Makes it hard to sneak up on you about anything."

"The only reason one would want to sneak up on me would be if he or she thought the noose was tightening."

"Is it?"

"It's tighter than it was a few days ago."

China says, "This really is a Sherlock Holmes whodunit."

"Would you settle for Ms. Marple?" Charlotte asks.

When she leaves Broadway and China, instead of steering toward the bar, Charlotte takes a sharp right and approaches the man she suspects of guarding her.

"Graziano," she says softly.

The man fumbles with his newspaper, nearly trips as he steps forward and nods his head.

"Sorry, ma'am, clumsy of me."

"Not at all. I so appreciate the fine job you are doing. Makes me feel quite safe."

"Ain't supposed to reveal myself. I messed up."

"Well, I won't tell anyone. Meanwhile, thank you. I hope your services are only needed for surveillance and not intervention."

Graziano looks confused for an instant, smiles, and replies. "Yeah, me too."

She turns and heads back into the lounge area, sidles up to the bar, and settles on a high stool, feeling flushed that, at her age, she can act like a barfly.

24

"What the hell, you prick! Why are you messing with my son?"

"Don't spring a leak, Charlie. Along with another local, he did me a favor, so I greased his palm."

"What kind of favor?"

"My ex is the one who took a tumble down the stairs. Since Andy was involved with one of the models, I had asked him and another model to clue me in about her agency. I guess I'm still stuck on Brooklyn."

"What did you need to know about that agency, except that a lot of foxy babes hang out there?"

"Oh, I asked them about their schedule so I could drop in on Brooklyn one day. Didn't much like that Stout fellow. A pretender. My investment colleagues told me he was a phony, wanting inside tips without any assets to back them up."

"From what I knew of him, he was a petty dictator but with a bit of talent. I tried to help Andy by giving the guy a donation because of the broad he had a thing for; last time for me. In fact, Stout was unappreciative. Took the dough as if he earned it. Andy's a screwed-up kid, so I think you giving him bills keeps him from doing stuff on his own."

"He told me you cut him off."

"Not exactly. I just want him to grow up."

They are in a polished and extravagant office in lower Manhattan, only two blocks from the Twin Towers tragedy. Batchelor is seated behind a rectangular oak desk, clean on top except for a state-of-the-art computer and a cradled black-and-silver phone. Aside from the desk, the room is cluttered, as if the man hung on to every record and every receipt he ever negotiated. Perhaps surprisingly, there are also no bookshelves—therefore, no books. A cabinet on the left wall, metallic and sturdy, has a combination lock.

After a silence, Charlie Burrus says, "Cops have been questioning me. They got a detective and—for some reason—an old lady looking into the events at that place."

Batchelor, for a brief moment, seems to tense up, shrugs slightly, and says, "Routine, I'm sure. When there is a murder, everybody needs to be interviewed. Surprised they haven't figured out my connection there, slight as it is."

"They'll get to you. That broad I said Andy was hot for, well she's dumped him now. Kind of leaves him hanging. Hope he doesn't do anything really stupid."

"Like what?"

"Like try to get even with her, the way somebody did with the one you've been after."

"Terrible. Ruined a promising career. Still beautiful, though."

"Yeah, a beautiful cripple."

"Uh, what did the detective want to know?"

"I think they're trying to pin the girl's fall on Andy. Don't know about Stout's murder. Likely not the same person."

"I agree. The first one was a jealousy move, the second revenge."

Burrus looks at his partner oddly and says, "You seem to know a lot about it."

"Tell me how the runway show is coming," Charlotte asks Broadway. They are about to enter the Antwerp Building to watch a final run-through.

"Brook is amazing in so many ways. She's had to intervene in some bickering—not about her, but between a couple models."

"Who and what?"

"The two men. Brent was favored by Stout, and Antoine resented it. He was always getting the shit jobs. Now that Donald is gone, he wants equal treatment."

"What kind of…shit jobs?"

"His garb was never quite as glamorous as Brent's, or so he

thought. And Stout made him the monitor for keeping the roll sheet."

"Roll sheet?"

"All the models sign in every day. Stout was strict about time and all. It was like public employees punching a clock."

Charlotte purses her lips and looks away, leaving the room for a moment, considering a new possibility, but only for a moment, as she turns back to Broadway and asks, "You said your sister is amazing, which I already know. But in what other ways did you mean?"

"Well, she asked Antoine to assemble the music for the show on a single disc and, when he is not on the runway, to key in the selections. He was delighted and feels more a part of things."

"Tell me about the music."

"Another way Brook is amazing. She's picked out background music for each sequential part of the show: for evening and formal wear she chose Beethoven and Tchaikovsky; for morning and outdoor attire, "New York, New York," "We'll Have Manhattan" by Ella Fitzgerald, and "Give My Regards to Broadway"; for the third part, Sinatra singing "I Did It My Way," and "Climb Every Mountain" from *The Sound of Music*."

"My, my, what a potpourri. Tunes for every taste."

They reach the top of the stairs and turn toward the studio; the sound of angry voices echoes down the hall.

Antoine—tall, blonde, almost gaunt—is pointing a finger into Brent's burly chest; the contrast between the two men is startling to Charlotte. Brent is smaller, dark-skinned, a man who cultivates a muscular look. Their differences are a blow to gay-straight stereotypes.

"Well, my muscle-bound little friend, with that idiot gone, the odds have changed. You're not the automatic favorite anymore."

"Oh, yeah? Skinny white-bread guys are out of style. Makes no difference who runs the show. And besides, no talent is no talent."

"Looked in the mirror lately? Big pecs don't make the man. Sensitivity does. I got it, you don't."

"The only thing you got is blonde hair, and that won't get you shit in this business. Most guys are bald now, anyway."

Andrea, another darker-skinned model, tall and shapely, says, "Cut it out, you two. We've a show to do and we don't need bickering. If you want to chew each other up, do it outside when our work is over."

Brooklyn comes rolling in, Dr. Bruce Landry guiding her

wheelchair. At once, she senses the tension and calls out, "Okay, beautiful people, we are a family. Lots of family things to do to close this gig out—a final run-through, music and all—so Antoine, how about if you key up the disc, and everyone else, find your places. Everything as if it's the real show except the actual designs."

Her personality magnetic, her persona revered by the entire ensemble, Brooklyn's instructions subdue the group, and an immediate activity begins to develop. To Charlotte, the "family" tag was a clever pacifier, and her respect for young Brooklyn Farivar takes another leap forward. Softly, to Broadway, she says, "I'd like to see those roll sheets. Do you know where they'd be stashed?"

As might be expected, the police have combed through everything in Donald Stout's office, though, as Charlotte knows, they would have no solid reason to confiscate the models' roll sheets. Several models had been questioned—about their whereabouts, schedules, and relationships with Stout—their collective testimony revealing nothing incriminating. Roll sheets only show attendance during rehearsals. Yet, to Charlotte, they may be revealing something the officers have overlooked.

Broadway whispers something to Antoine, Stout's official roll-keeper, and is directed to a cabinet near the door to his private office.

Charlotte strolls over, opens the cabinet, and at once sees a thick heap of yellow-pad-lined paper. Perusing the pile quickly, she corrals the stack and files them away in her large purse. Time enough later, in private, to examine each list, especially those on the dates when the two stair events took place.

As she returns to her companions, another stirring breakthrough occurs, which upstages anything the troupe is doing.

Calling out to Julia—a tall, creamy-skinned woman, too thin, really, to look healthy, yet a stellar runway performer—Brooklyn's words are, "Julia, as you parade down the path, better if you cross your feet over so they are in a straight line." Without any conscious awareness of what she is doing, as she finishes her advice, Brooklyn crosses her right foot over in front of her left.

Broadway points, Charlotte gasps, and Kyla, who had been standing by their side, her turn coming up shortly, screeches. The reactions from her supporters startles Brooklyn and she twists her head about in confusion.

"Sorry, Sis," Broadway says. "But do you know what you just

did?"

"What? What did I do?"

"You took your own advice," Charlotte says.

Looking down, Brooklyn sees her feet, one in front of the other, and begins to cry.

Landry, who had not seen the movement, grins widely and pats Brooklyn's shoulder. "It's starting. Your recovery!"

To everyone's surprise, the entire ensemble, frozen for an instant, now begins to applaud.

25

It could have been an oversight, possibly deliberate, and certainly, had Stout checked, a reason for one of his patented temper fits, but neither of the male models had signed the roll sheet the day Brooklyn was injured. In most situations, such an omission would hardly be cause for alarm, and a simple question or two could verify if the two men had, in fact, been present.

For Charlotte, it takes only a few seconds to check with Brooklyn if she recalls her two male colleagues being absent on that day—the day she was attacked.

They are in the studio room, all models having departed, and Shanna Cavanaugh on her way to pick Charlotte up, though all Charlotte had told her was it would be to visit a new candidate.

"I remember we had a short rehearsal that day, and I checked the wall clock when I went in right afterwards to tell Donald our relationship was over. I thought nobody was missing, but my memory sort of went blank after the attack. Brent and Antoine had been quarreling a day or two earlier, and later, when I was leaving, Brent was around, in and out of Stout's office."

"How often do folks forget to sign in on the roll sheet?"

"With Donald's attitude, never."

"And, since Antoine was the keeper of the roll, he surely would have been diligent about his own signature."

"Sure."

"When you say quarreling, did you witness it, or hear it, or what?"

"They are always at each other. I think Antoine resented Brent's personal connection with Donald, though I didn't find out about that until later."

"This may not be something you know, but are they both gay?"

"I must be naïve, but I never tuned into those things. Now I know that Brent is, and I can take an educated guess that Antoine is too, or at least bisexual."

"What makes you say that?"

"Well, he was also hitting on Andrea, a tall, brown-skinned model."

"Ah, so could jealousy be an issue?"

"I guess, but I can't imagine Brent being jealous because of Andrea—unless he was protective of her because she's a sister."

"Antoine was jealous, then, of Brent and Stout?"

"Maybe. If not jealousy, then envy over Brent getting preferential treatment."

"Going back to the day of your injury, if the two of them were, indeed, absent for the rehearsal, one might presume Donald Stout would be upset. One might also presume that the two men were doing something together."

"As I said, Brent was there later, after all the group had gone, and I was leaving Donald's office. I don't know if he and Antoine were together before that."

"Looks as if I may need to enlist Detective Cavanaugh to interview those two men. But, one more thing: since Corrine Gelly had been…dismissed by Stout, she would not have been around the studio that day?"

"Oh, definitely not. Donald had disdain for her. It was sad. She's not the most likable person, but he really crapped on her."

"Yes. And she would have been quite wounded by that attitude."

"One thing," Brooklyn adds, "that seems a little odd to me. You know I asked Corrine to join us again; well, that wasn't my brainchild."

"Oh? What do you mean?" Charlotte asks.

"Aaron, my ex, at first wanted to give me money for my medical costs, but then, later, he suggested I create a different climate than Donald had, and the first step ought to be to reinstate Corrine and get Antoine more involved. How he knew about them and their situations was a surprise to me."

"Indeed," Charlotte says.

"So, who's the new suspect you want me to interrogate? Or, is this one of your marvelous hunches—which often prove to be correct?"

They are in Shanna's police vehicle, an unmarked eight-year-old Chevy, Charlotte dictating an address offered up by Brooklyn. The usual Manhattan traffic makes the going slow, yet there is comfort in knowing at any time they can display flashing lights and maneuver around gridlocks. Since she had begun doing "detective" work a year or two ago with Augie Hartunian in Pennsylvania, Charlotte is aware of an umbrella of security around her whenever she is accompanied by an official officer. At her age, she has told her brother, danger calls up a transient emotion, not a stimulus for terror, though, in all truth, she would like to enjoy the amazing rewards of life on planet Earth for another twenty or more years. No unnecessary risks is her motto: she won't go sky-diving or bungee jumping, and knowing that Officer Graziano has been trailing her sends off warm feelings of safety.

Nothing, however, can be guaranteed.

"You may know that there are two male models at the agency, one sturdy and muscular, the other lean and aesthetic-looking. They have issues. Brent, the burly one, had been favored by Donald Stout, and in no small measure because they sometimes…well, slept together. The other one, Antoine, has been resentful. They have been loud and accusatory, and the whole ensemble knows about it."

Her attention divided between the tale and the traffic, Shanna says softly, "And this is important to our investigation because…?"

"I checked the sign-in roll sheet for the day when Brooklyn was hurt, and neither of those men was on it. By itself, that doesn't say much, but Brook told me that, after the whole group had dispersed, she saw Brent hanging around, in and out of Stout's office. The possibilities are, he and Antoine could have been off somewhere, maybe feuding—or it could be that one was threatening the other to…well, do something."

"Still not clear to me."

"Only a hypothetical scenario, but what if Stout, in his fury over Brooklyn dumping him, commanded his male…uh, lover, to punish her? But since Brent was known to be friendly with Brook, could he have struck a deal with Antoine that if he did the dirty deed,

Brent would try to influence Stout to be more generous with Antoine's career?"

"Pretty sick. How could a guy be friendly with someone and want another guy to catapult her down a flight of stairs? Doesn't make sense."

"I agree it stretches the imagination. But what I think we need to do is track down this Antoine fellow, whom I have never talked to, and get his story about that day. I don't see him as the culprit in Stout's murder, but he could be—like that gullible Andy child—a tool of someone else's scheme."

"I can hear the plea now: my mother, father, brother, buddy, uncle, or some other acquaintance, made me do it. The universal courtroom excuse: someone else is responsible."

"You see, Shanna, it's quite possible that Stout, enraged with disappointment over his top model and girlfriend…well, dumping him, wanted to show Brooklyn who was boss. No intent to cripple her, but certainly to hurt her. And he likely would have made that clear to his lackey, in this case, Brent, all the time knowing that Brent cared about Brook. A test, if you will, of Brent's devotion to him."

"But Brent couldn't see himself hurting his pal, so you think he may have tried to bribe the other male model, one he had issues with, to do that rotten deed?"

"I wouldn't be surprised if Antoine's prints are the ones yet to be identified on that canister. According to what I could gather, Antoine is one frustrated model, and this may have been the only way he could see himself getting into favor with his boss."

"Hmm. Sort of a twisted state of affairs. This Antoine character has to be desperate about his career to agree to a trade-off that ruins someone else's. And then, the whole thing explodes in his face when the boss, who—if he believed that Brent guy—could grant him favors, gets polished off and replaced by the person he tried to injure."

"Quite a nice synopsis, Shanna. And yes, I believe that is what the two men are feuding about now. I can hear Antoine's argument: 'You promised me, and I did the thing you wanted to Brooklyn, and now look where we are!' And I can hear Brent's reply: 'I didn't expect you to cripple her. And who would know that Donald would buy the store?' I imagine Brent must feel deep remorse about Brooklyn since, indeed, they had been friends."

"Stout wanted his revenge, Brent wanted not to be the instrument for it, while Antoine wanted more of an inside track. Brooklyn got her back broken and the three men ended up in deep shit. Then somebody took care of Stout, and now we have to deal with the other two patsies."

"I might not phrase it exactly like that, but my guess is you got it right."

Another police vehicle, lights flashing, sirens squealing, looms up behind them as a gaping hole opens up in the traffic ahead. Shanna has pulled over as well, respectful of her colleagues' emergency, and when the black and white is gone, says to Charlotte, "Big city, always something going wrong. Folks don't appreciate the massive task we police officers have."

"I'm always amazed at how people get so twisted as to want to break the rules—and, even worse, harm other people."

"Yep. There are millions of Americans who would never think of committing a crime, and thousands who would."

They are approaching the Village, where Antoine's digs are; Brooklyn had alerted Charlotte that, if it were the sixties, he would be considered a hippie, probably living with a group of others and certainly unconcerned about elegant surroundings.

They wheel along a curb painted white for loading only, and Shanna places a flashing light on the roof of her car.

From the address, Antoine's building looks to be a walk-up, though no names appear anywhere below. In the entryway, there is one large mailbox, also with no names on it. The hall is dark, cruddy, Charlotte thinks, and there is a flight of some dozen stairs leading to more darkness above.

On the landing is a narrow hall seeming to lead only to a large, closed window, and on the opposite side, a plain wooden door, spray-painted with bright acrylic colors and abstract designs.

"A commune," Shanna says.

"I'd bet the Russian communes were more ordered than this. An autocracy can demand conformity."

"Let's see what it's like inside."

She raps forcefully three times.

After a long minute, the door slides open a few inches, and a tall, dreary-eyed man peers down at them. His dress is less than casual, as if it were the middle of the night and he had just been disturbed from a deep sleep.

"What is it?"

"I presume you are Antoine Bontemps? Sorry to disturb your rest. I'm Detective Cavanaugh, and this is Ms. Charlotte Smart. We'd like to ask you a few questions."

"About what?"

"Brooklyn Farivar's fall—and all the things leading up to it."

A quick look of surprise, maybe terror, then a shrug. "I'm afraid I don't know much about that."

He stops and makes as if to slide the door shut.

Shanna places her hand between the door and its frame. "Only take a few minutes. We'd like to come in."

A beat, then, "Oh, what the hell. Come on."

He steps aside and the two women enter what can be seen at once as a phantasmagoric cornucopia of colors and shapes. Music from an exotic Far-Eastern instrument, perhaps a sitar, floats softly in the air, scented by sweet fragrances—too sweet, really—stemming from a row of flower bouquets on the lowest shelf of an oak armoire.

Antoine picks magazines and newspapers off a pair of bright blue chairs, which, when naked, can be seen to be in good shape, without tears or stains. He points to the chairs for the women to be seated and props himself up against the armoire.

Charlotte smiles at the contrasts: the ambiance an obvious attempt by the residents to be radically unique, yet, to her, the essence of conventionality, although an allegiance to a fringe sort of orthodoxy.

"You're one of two male models in the Stout Agency," Shanna says, "and we understand that you have been feuding with the other one."

It is apparent that Antoine does not speak abruptly, a long moment of silence following the question, as if the answer is a ponderous conundrum. When, however, he finally answers, it is concise, even terse.

"Not feuding. We don't feud."

"I'm curious," Charlotte says in her gentle voice, "what you call it, then, when others in your group report elevated voices and angry confrontations."

"Brent is a bit of a bully. Every now and then, I take him on."

"What seems odd to some of us," Charlotte goes on, "is that Brent pressured you into doing something. Something that was nasty and punitive, ordered from the big boss, himself."

This information pierces Antoine's taciturn armor, and he blurts out, "That is a bald-faced lie. Yes, the little vermin was given an assignment—an odious one, to be sure—and he tried to slough it off on me. I refused. End of story."

Shanna scowls as if to say, *Convince me.*

"Are you saying, Mr. Bontemps, to be coldly frank, that you did not propel Brooklyn Farivar down the front stairs in the Agency's building?"

"You bet your ass that's what I'm saying. The little muscle-bound fag tried to blackmail me to do it. I gave him the finger."

"So, then did Brent White do the deed?" Charlotte asks.

Another beat, Antoine's reticent pace restored, as he says with a subdued tone, "I wasn't there that afternoon. Neither was Brent at first, and some people think we were together. Well, we weren't. But I gather from the others that he came in after rehearsal. I have no idea if he did it."

"Tell us," Charlotte says, "if you were to do what he asked, what was Brent offering?"

"He was Donald's little boy toy and got all the good gigs. I got the leftovers. Tried to tell me he would talk Stout into putting me on prime time. I didn't buy it."

"You're saying he was ordered by Stout to hurt Brooklyn, that he wanted you to do it instead, but you refused," Shanna summarizes.

"It's what he told me. Anyway, it turned out all wrong."

"Why," Charlotte asks, "do you think he wanted you to do it?"

A moment of silence, and, "That child had two passionate connections. Stout was his bed buddy and Brooklyn his modeling mentor. He was supposed to obey one but probably couldn't imagine betraying the other."

"So, obviously, he was pissed at you for saying no?" Shanna puts out as a question.

"He gets pissed all the time. I shine him on."

As he says this, the door to the apartment swings open and a young girl, three pieces of silver in each ear—to Charlotte, very likely a wannabe copycat of Lizbeth, the hippie hacker from *The Girl With the Dragon Tattoo*—saunters in, sees the guests, and grumbles, "Shit. And I was in the mood to screw."

"Uh, this is Toby, my roommate. These are cops."

"Oh, I'm not a cop, just an interested party."

"But I'm a detective. We've been conversing with your boyfriend."

"He's not my boyfriend. He's my fuck-friend."

"Hey, Toby, they don't need the gory details."

"Whatever."

"Okay, if you have to know, ladies, Toby is why I missed the meeting that day. She was having an abortion and needed my help."

After a moment, Shanna says, "All right. We'll check with this Brent fellow as well. This ugly situation has to be resolved."

"Yes," Charlotte adds, "and you know, Antoine, sometimes stories don't match, and then the detectives have to find out who is…well, lying."

"Hah! It's not me, that's for sure."

"Antoine doesn't lie," Toby says with a wide grin, showing perfect, snow-white teeth. "He messes up a lot, but no lies."

"Good to know," Shanna says.

26

The music for *Sleepless in Seattle* is introduced to the cast. Broadway and China receive their songs, as do the entire ensemble, and all are given several minutes to peruse the lead sheets and get a feel for their parts.

More than she needs to, China touches Broadway, a tap on the forearm, a playful pat on the shoulder, once a brief hug when he sings a phrase aloud. Each of her contacts flushes him, stirs his passions, yet, he responds almost not at all: a smile, a nod, his reticence a product of torn emotions. Kyla's presence is with him, in fact, consumes him, so that China's allure, vibrant as it is, becomes diluted, less robust, he is aware, than it deserves.

Jamison Brown, the play's director, asks each actor to sing through one song, a-cappella since there is no orchestra present. Sight-reading, then, becomes mandatory—a skill that Broadway, thankfully, has cultivated. To his delight, China, too, has no problem with her song, a piece titled "If Only You Could See Me," a plea to the lead character, Sam Baldwin, whose son, Jonah, favors the unseen Annie for his father.

Damn, but this woman is remarkable! The soft freckles, magnetic smile, colorful hair, and eyes are a feast for anyone observing her—and then, the talent; yet, Kyla, lithe and lovely as well; two delicious flavors, different yet equally appealing.

When Ian Tenant, who plays Sam, finishes his song, the rest of the cast applauds, his voice dazzling in its purity, comparable to Placido Domingo of the Three Tenors fame, a true operatic tenor.

What Broadway doesn't miss is that, while singing, Tenant's eyes peruse and even devour China's face. No ownership, of course, yet a twinge of jealousy. If it came to that, how in the hell could he compete with this icon of the Broadway scene?

The three-hour rehearsal ends as Brown says, in a stentorian voice confirming his own history as a thespian—a voice that carries to the back of the theater—"We rock! This cast is phenomenal. It will be a pleasure to work with all of you. Now, go home and learn all your lines and songs so that at our next meeting we can do a run-through from start to finish. Oh, and keep in mind that our playwright is still making adjustments, and so will you."

"The M.E. picked up a couple of metal fibers embedded in Stout's hair. No question about it, the blow was from a round-head hammer," Shanna says.

"M.E.," Charlotte repeats.

"Medical Examiner."

"Ah, and we know that Stout had been building a model of some kind in his office area—Broadway mentioned that he had an ambition to construct his own state-of-the-art studio."

"Okay. So who else knew about that and would have access to his tools?"

"Brooklyn was in his office quite a bit—after all, she was his girlfriend—and Brent, his secret amour, was also admitted in and would be aware of the mock-up and required implements."

"So, Stout was an artist of sorts, or at least an amateur architect."

Charlotte pouts for an instant. "Sad, isn't it. A man with many talents, yet terribly narcissistic and even brutal in his treatment of others."

"But this Brent fellow would have little to gain in killing off his own boss—his meal ticket, so to speak."

"I agree. Whoever might have pilfered a hammer from Stout's office must have sneaked in—provided, of course, that it was Stout's own hammer that did him in."

"We don't yet have the murder weapon, but I think we need to examine that office more carefully now that we know what we're looking for."

"Yes," Charlotte adds, "even if a round-head hammer is not found—or any hammer, for that matter—it is significant evidence in its absence."

"Good point."

"Also, Shanna, keep in mind that someone had to have been in the studio at an odd time, when no one else was there, to tape that note on Stout's door. That could have been almost anyone, though the message, DYKE STILL OUT, translated into I KYLLED STOUT, would tilt the writer toward the masculine."

"Never thought of that. Makes sense."

"Has to be an ego thing for someone to broadcast the deed like that. But, it also implies, without confirming, that the suspect in Brooklyn's fall was likely a woman—and maybe a lesbian. I'm not aware of any of the female models being lesbians."

"What concerns me is that the guy, if it is a man, knows where you are staying, and his second message, WHO IS NEXT, has got to be a threat. Oh, and by the way, neither of those notes had any prints on them. The person was smart enough to wear gloves."

"Not surprised. As to the threat to me, thank you for Graziano. I did finally spot him. Seems like a dedicated…uh, bodyguard."

"A good man. Used to be a professional bowler, then went to the police academy. Likes undercover work. Never married, no kids, but a longtime girlfriend who frets like hell about him."

This exchange is going on in Shanna's old, unmarked Chevy, the session with Antoine and his roommate, Toby, only a few minutes past.

"Well," Charlotte had said, "you know more about this than I, but it would seem to me that the next move is to query Brent White to see if his rendition of events matches or contradicts Antoine's."

Shanna had answered her, "Right on. I'll text my office to send me his contact information. We can head right over there and hope we catch him in."

Brent's domestic situation is rather different than Antoine's. He lives in an upscale apartment, walking distance from the Stout Agency, not as elegant as Charlie Burrus's Park Avenue digs, but in a modern, four-story building with a lobby like a hotel and a smoothly running elevator that sounds a shrill bell tone as it passes each floor.

The doorbell chime gives off a melodic rendition of "Torn Between Two Lovers," the first phrase repeated three times before the door is opened.

"Well, I recognize you folks. What's up?"

"Okay if we come in, Mr. White?"

"Sure. Want some coffee or maybe a glass of wine?"

"Thank you, no," Charlotte answers, as Shanna shakes her head.

"So, how's the investigation going?"

He is wearing a tight see-through vest showing his muscular build, an attribute to be flaunted.

"Steadily progressing," Shanna says. "We do, however, need to ask you a few more questions."

"Fire away."

Charlotte speaks first: "We just left your buddy, Antoine."

At that, Brent frowns, rotates his head around as if stretching out a stiff neck. He says nothing but is clearly on the alert.

"…And he tells a story that is chilling if true. And, sorry to say, it indicts you."

"That pale pervert is a chronic liar," Brent blurts out. "Whatever he says is pure pig poop."

"Hmm. Colorful language," Shanna inserts.

"Well, I don't know what he told you, but he's a jealous son-of-a-bitch, completely talentless and desperate to point the finger."

"Yes. And he pointed it at you," Charlotte says.

"Not surprised. What does he think I did?"

Shanna looks at Charlotte, who nods to her, giving her the go-first sign.

The interior of Brent's apartment is neat as a pin, Charlotte wondering if he hires a house cleaner or does it himself. Colors proliferate: the walls appointed with modern art, red and blue dominating, a couch all red except for butterfly shapes spattered about, and throw cushions everywhere, multicolored, some clashing with the blue-red theme.

Shanna asks, "Is it not true that Donald Stout was disposed to punish Brooklyn Farivar for dumping him and asked you to do the job?"

A long pause punctuates the tension in the room, and, at last, Brent replies, "He was pissed, for sure, and told me that Brook needed to have her comeuppance. It was, like, he wanted to plant a seed with me. Not a direct command or anything. He knew I cherished Brook, and, sick as he was, it would be poetic justice for him if he could intimidate me into hurting someone I cared about."

"So?" Charlotte interjects.

"So nothing. I wouldn't hurt Brook. Antoine and I had already discussed Donald's tyrannical style—and I let slip that he would love it if someone taught her a lesson. Antoine, the loser that he is, tossed out that Donald and I were vengeful bastards, and he stalked away. As to what happened to Brook, I don't have a clue. I think I was the last one to see her in the studio, and then she was found at the bottom of the stairs."

"As far as you know, Antoine did not push her to try to make it look as if you did it?" Shanna asks.

"Look, I didn't see anyone else around at that time, so, for all I know, Donald sneaked out of his office and did the deed himself."

"Mr. White," Charlotte says, looking him directly in the eye, "why would Detective Cavanaugh and I be disposed to believe you? Donald Stout had control over you and your career, and it makes sense that he could pressure you into doing what he wanted."

"Wrong. Donald was a confused guy, liked to dominate his flawless female models, and…well, me or anyone else. I'd never betray my friend, and what happened to Brook devastated me."

"Let me ask you another question," Charlotte says, switching gears. "As far as you know, which, if any, of the models are lesbians?"

"I don't know of any, though I have my suspicions. Phillipa, who fell down some stairs a year ago, and Corrine, who is an off-and-on part of our team, could be, but they haven't come out. A big dark secret. There's externalized homophobia, which straight people practice, and there's internalized homophobia, which gays take on as a form of self-loathing. I hate that. It shows shame and dishonesty."

"Summary time," Shanna says, "Your story is that you turned Stout down when he tried to influence you to harm Brooklyn, and, in addition, your sometimes pal, Antoine, wasn't interested in any sort of vengeance. As to who, in your troupe, could be gay, you have suspicions about two of the women but no certainty about them."

Brent shrugs. "Yeah. That's pretty much it." He pauses and adds, "Though I don't know why that last part's important to you."

Not disposed to answer questions, Shanna says, "Okay. We have your story now. Let's hope it all checks out."

Charlotte adds, "I catch your affection for Brooklyn. She is a remarkable woman, and I hope your loyalty to her continues."

At the bottom of the stairs, Shanna says, "Which of these

losers do you believe?"

"There is a difference," Charlotte answers, "between believing and trusting. Think of this young fellow, Brent, giving his body to Donald Stout, someone he clearly has disdain for, to ensure his status in the modeling troupe. And think of Antoine feeling left out and desperate to be as appreciated as the other male model, obviously his rival. After hearing both their stories, I am inclined to believe a lot of what they said, but I wouldn't trust either one of them to deliver a glass of water with goodwill."

Shanna's laugh echoes in the lobby area as she replies, "Well put. I doubt either of these marginal guys is a murderer or Brooklyn's attacker."

"Okay—but as I often told my brother last year, don't close anything out, and no one learns much from conclusions. Safer to say maybe, or not likely."

27

In the lobby of the Sheraton, Charlotte pauses at the elevator, looks about, fails to see Graziano, and pushes the "up" button. At the eighteenth floor, she exits and walks with her usual sturdy stride down the hall to 1840.

"I'm firing you," a voice from behind her declares.

She turns to see Sarah Farivar treading heavily toward her. Her first thought is, *She must have been waiting here for me.*

Considering her talents, Sarah's attire is stylish, colors compatible, design fashionable; she wears a broad white hat with matching gloves, though her rather squat shape fails to show off her creations to their best advantage.

Charlotte tilts her head, smiles, and says, "Sarah, something's troubling you."

"You bet. My Brooklyn was tossed down a flight of stairs, broke her back, ruined her career—and nobody, including you, can find the scum who did it."

"Come into my room," Charlotte says, holding the door open.

She sees her bedside phone message light blinking, files that away for later, and points to a soft chair near a small writing table. Sarah ignores the gesture, stands stolidly, feet set widely so that she looks like an Adams family character, and says, "Why should we keep you here when you can't solve this disgusting crime?"

"You know, I appreciate your generosity in putting me up at this posh hotel, and, believe me, I do understand your frustration. Criminal behavior is tough to solve, and here we have two ugly trespasses. There is some progress, but it's slow going. I'm glad you came to see me, so I can fill you in."

"You see, that's all people do is talk about it. Nothing gets done."

There is a moment of silence. Charlotte sees an uneasiness about Sarah Farivar, eyes restless as a trapped animal, anger there, certainly, at the lack of resolution, but something else as well.

"The police call that interrogation. It's the way they gather information. Detective Cavanaugh and I have been doing a lot of it. Action has to wait until leads are confirmed. No one intends to keep secrets from you."

"So…do you have leads on who killed that vermin, Stout?"

"There are some clues, but nothing final. The same with your daughter's fall."

Another silence and Sarah says, her voice subdued, "The fashion show—right here in this hotel—will be this Saturday. From what I hear, Brook has her girls ready. Instead of her prancing down the runway as the lead model, she will be anchored in her wheelchair, observing and cheering them on."

The pain in her voice resonates with Charlotte, and she catches the magnitude of Sarah's disappointment: her perfect daughter, with such perfect promise, now immobilized, her future compromised.

"Yes, and quite a tribute to Brooklyn's mettle. The whole assembly loves her, and she is a brilliant organizer. Really gets the best out of them."

"Not the whole assembly. Someone didn't love her, and that sick person is enjoying her—or his—mobility while my daughter hopes she can walk again." She stops and, after a toss of her head, says, "Unless that dead boss, who got what was coming to him, is the one who did it. I still think he is."

"You may be right, but whether he deserved it or not, killing him was not the way to get justice for Brooklyn. Whichever person or persons did that took the law into their own hands."

This brings Sarah up short; she frowns and, with a near snarl, responds, "Persons? You mean it could have been more than one?"

"No proof, but there might have been a conspiracy. People teaming up to get some kind of advantage."

Now Charlotte pauses, looks hard at Sarah, and adds, "What do you think of that?"

"Well…I don't know. A lot of people had reason to dislike Donald Stout."

"Including you."

"Look, lady, I had nothing to gain from—how do they say it?—offing Stout. Yes, he was a bastard, and for sure I wanted him to be punished if he, indeed, hurt my daughter. She was pretty foolish in the beginning for ever hooking up with him in a personal way."

"What is needed, Sarah, is a grand finale. I know that's corny, but I've seen it twice before. When you get everybody together in a room and go over all the evidence step-by-step, amazing disclosures seem to come. It's remarkable how defensive people get when in the presence of others they have issues with."

"Everybody? Who is everybody? You mean all the models, the boyfriends and girlfriends, present and past? And how about fathers of boyfriends? And partners of fathers of boyfriends?"

"Oh my, you certainly know a lot about the characters in this plot. Well, of course, I'm sure Broadway has been keeping you up on things. There are a lot of folks who could be culprits in these particular events. Some you know, some you don't. We're not too far away from scheduling some climactic gathering. Of course, you'll be invited."

Sarah's eyes narrow, and her breath appears shallow and rapid as she turns on her heels and makes for the door. Without looking back, she says over her shoulder. "Okay, you can stay on."

—

When Sarah exits, Charlotte smiles.

A self-made woman, proud as a peacock, ambitious for her kids, crushed by her daughter's mishap, indignant about any suggestion she might have been vengeful, yet, in an odd way, I kind of like her—her energy and total devotion to her kids' welfare. A mixed bag.

She turns her attention to the blinking light, touches the appropriate button, and hears: "Charlotte, Shanna here. Found a toolbox in Stout's office closet. Lots of stuff in there, but no hammer. Had to be one at some time. The perp obviously took it away after the deed. Could have dumped it in the East River. Does lend credence to someone who knew where to look for a weapon. The good news? There are prints on the toolbox and other parts of the room. We'll see what matches we can come up with. Talk soon."

Charlotte jots down a few notes in her modified sociogram—a personal record of suspects, prospects, folks with attitudes, others with defensive postures, and a few with stars next to their names, prime candidates for one of the two nasty deeds.

"Nap time," she says aloud, and adds, "Tomorrow is Friday, and Saturday is the big fashion show in the ballroom below."

She props her bed pillows up, lies back, and, before closing her eyes, says, again aloud, "Wonder if I could sponsor a post-show reception here in my lovely suite?"

Her rest lasts less than an hour as urgent knocking pulls her from bed and to the door. She peers through the peephole and sees Broadway.

"My, my, what's the commotion all about?"

He strides in, both hands rolled into fists, eyes fiery as if astonished by some terrible revelation, paces for a moment, then flops down in the soft chair next to the table.

"It's like the ghost of Stout has come back to torture us," he says at last.

"Ghost?"

"Four of the group, Brent and Antoine, who supposedly can't stand each other, and Phillipa and Corrine, the two least appealing female models, have declared to Brook that they are not satisfied with their assignments—and all that only one day before the show. How can Brook deal with that? It isn't fair."

Charlotte's mind instantly goes to sabotage. One, or all, of those balking might want to see Brooklyn's first directing gig go down--but why, and which ones?

Her brother, in California, always chides her for waxing philosophical in critical moments, yet her bent is to apply new information in her environment to whatever current worldly discoveries she has made. Broadway already knows this about her.

After a moment, she says, "The mystery in any investigation can boggle the mind unless there are innovative ways of studying it. Until the last few months, astronomers had identified some five hundred exoplanets, meaning planets revolving about stars other than our sun. Only recently, because of a new telescope on a satellite that can measure ultraviolet light emissions and detect slight wobbles in stars, they now are aware of some twenty-five hundred more planets. Amazing what new technology can accomplish."

Broadway looks at her quizzically, his fire not yet extinguished, the burden his sister must absorb screaming out at him as a travesty of justice.

Charlotte catches his look.

"Oh—well, what I'm getting at is that the police now have ways to compare DNA samples and to match prints that were unheard of a generation ago. These rebels are likely not part of a conspiracy since they are so disparate in their needs. But one or possibly two of them would have something to gain from your sister's maiden coordinating enterprise hitting a snag. We are still unsure about the final prints on the heavy canister used to hurt Brooklyn, but my hunch is we will be able to correct that in a day or so."

"So you think the person who attacked Brook is likely one of these complaining models?"

"I can't be sure, of course, but if we match the forensics, we will know more."

"Uh…well, this issue with the fashion show is primary…." He stops, as if changing topics would shortchange his sister's issue, but, after a pause, his voice modified from defiant to imploring, begins again, "I wonder if I could ask you about something else. It's something I wouldn't think of discussing with my mother."

"Certainly. My hunch is it's an affair of the heart—and I can easily see that a mother might not be the one to consult."

"You're too smart," he says with a shy grin. "Yep. I have a real dilemma, and maybe you would have some insight."

Never having had children of her own, Charlotte casts about for tales she has read and events she has witnessed over her nearly seventy years that could offer her wisdom for the story Broadway is about to reveal. Good listener that she is, no pre-judgment is formed. Her internal message is: *Hear the young man out and see how he leans.*

"For a year I've had a thing for Kyla, even when all the evidence showed she was unavailable. After all, Brook and she are best friends, and I was privy to a lot of insights about her. Now that the little Andy-dandy is out of the picture, the path seems clear for me to try to hook up with her. But, damn it, along comes China, who is more forward, and who has openly declared her interest in me. I'll be thrown in with her for the next year or so, and maybe longer if the new musical is a hit."

Respectfully listening, Charlotte waits for a pause, and when it comes, she says softly, "Instead of it being a crucible of riches—I mean, after all, two absolutely stunning and bright young women—you see the situation as a terrible predicament."

"I do. So, what I've done so far is put up a stop sign to both women, when my heart cries out to bite the bullet, grab for the gold ring, make a decision and fly with it."

"It's quite a catch-22 to have more than one gold ring. Which one do you grab?"

"Exactly. I'm flattered as hell that even one of these incredible women is interested in me. I've never been good at final decisions. Guess that's why I'm still single and without a solid relationship."

"You know, Broadway, pickles like the one you're in can seem overwhelming without any clear resolution. But, what I've experienced is that life tends to unravel its ball of string in such ways that decisions sometimes make themselves."

"What does that mean? Are you saying the two women will somehow winnow the problem down—that I won't have to make a choice?"

"No way to predict; however, that is what could happen."

He thinks for a moment and says, "It will only take one of them to do that."

"Yes, it takes two people to say yes to a relationship, but only one to say no."

As a final word, spoken with deflated tones, he replies, "Makes me feel kind of helpless, like my life will be decided by someone else."

"Or," Charlotte tacks on, "the choice becomes crystal clear to you."

28

"Getting close to crunch time," Shanna says. "And guess what? Naturally, there were Stout's prints on the toolbox, but there was also someone else's. We weren't clear yet who they belonged to, but after you gave me that paper cup the Gelly woman had, we finally came up with a perfect match to the prints on the canister that propelled Brooklyn down the stairs. Kind of zeros in on her as the assailant—at least for Brooklyn's attack. But we also know that they are not the same prints as the extra ones on the toolbox. Two separate perps, though it doesn't rule out a conspiracy."

"Ah, excellent news, Shanna," Charlotte replies.

"Also, and I'm not yet sure how this will play out, but our people finished the autopsy on Stout and found that he had engaged in sexual activity not long before his death."

"My, my. They can determine that?"

"Yes, but we also found no semen or other recent fluids on Stout or on the couch in his office. Kind of odd not to have any residue."

"Well, now, I may be an elderly woman with old-fashioned sexual mores, but I must say that what you have been saying has brought up some rather vivid images."

"Oh? How so?"

"I won't go into it now. Maybe on Saturday if we can get our little corps of suspects together."

She is still in her hotel room, Broadway long since departed, and is about to take the fancy elevator to the ballroom floor to peruse the layout of the fashion event coming up on Saturday.

"Remember," she says, "that Aaron Batchelor touted Corrine and Antoine to Brooklyn, suggesting they be given richer roles. So, those recommendations could have been payoff for carrying out a revenge act for Batchelor. "

"Say, that's a good point. Wouldn't be surprised if Batchelor, the dumped ex-boyfriend, is behind all of this."

"A distinct possibility—but not yet provable. My guess is that, by Saturday, we will be able to piece all of this together."

"You go, girl,"

Cigarette smoking has long bothered her, and Charlotte, as is true with many older folks who no longer fear being bold, will confront a trespasser, not with vitriol, but firmness.

She is in the ballroom of the Sheraton, a giant hall with ornate crystal chandeliers hanging on sturdy bars from high ceilings, some decorator's conception of artwork on the walls—though Charlotte sees it as garish, scenes of satyrs and wild dogs—and a recently assembled elevated platform running the length of the room. On either side of the runway are dozens of comfortable chairs, five rows in depth, allowing for approximately three hundred guests to view the event.

At the command of a supervisor standing at the entrance end of the ramp, four or five workmen are still puttering about, adjusting and rearranging, while one of the workers has a cigarette dangling from his clenched lips.

"Say," Charlotte says to him, "I hope you know there is no smoking in this entire hotel."

"Yeah, so?"

"Young man, I did not put that out as a question. You are to extinguish your cigarette at once."

He looks at her, a look she can only read as scorn, realizes her age, perhaps governed by some ancient parental admonition to respect the elderly, mutters a muffled word that sounds like "shit," and throws his cigarette butt on the parquet floor.

"Well, now. Whom do you think will follow you around picking up your discarded poison pellet? That gesture is as odious as smoking itself. No one is your servant, and littering that way only increases your thoughtless behavior."

"What the hell you talking about?"

"I'm talking about being considerate of others."

"Hey, I've had enough of your crap. Leave me the hell alone."

Though it hardly seems likely he would attempt to manhandle Charlotte, he does lean toward her, and the last words were spoken directly in her face.

Before either Charlotte or the worker can say or do anything else, a deep voice crashes in. "Pick up the butt, butthead!"

Charlotte looks around and sees a menacing Graziano, hands on hips, eyes leering at the man, jaw set firm, authority in his manner unmistakable.

A stolid man with wide shoulders and a square torso that causes his arms to bulge out, creating a gorilla-like, oval appearance, Graziano is at least forty pounds more massive than the offender, who, in an instant, determines it would not be in his best interest to contest the order.

He picks up the dead butt, slides it into his jeans pocket, and swaggers silently away as if, in his mind, he is the winner.

"Thank you, Mr. Graziano. I didn't see you, but I think your presence was a distinct influence on that young fellow's behavior. I told your boss, Shanna, that people do tend to break rules, especially when they think they can get away with it."

"Can't police everyone. But I hate it when a guy tries to take advantage of an older person."

"Yes. Well, I tend to confront people who flout the law. My younger brother keeps telling me it will get me in trouble."

"Didn't mean to be a bully. After all, that's not what I'm supposed to be doing with you. But—he was acting like a tough hombre, and I didn't know what he might do."

She nods and Graziano at once steps back and retreats to the far door of the ballroom, lingers for a moment, takes in the entire room, and exits without another word.

Back to the task at hand, Charlotte studies the ambiance of the large hall, a room that reminds her of a well-lit, cavernous cave, though, hopefully, no wild beasts will be using it as their lair.

Her task, as she sees it, is to insure that all the potential suspects in the two crimes are present at the show—and then agree to attend the "reception" upstairs in her suite. But how can she pull it off?

Like gears engaging, one by one, the elements of the plan begin to lock in.

Brooklyn needs to announce the gathering to her crew. Shanna needs to contact Batchelor, the two Burrus men, and even Dr. Bruce Landry. Broadway will have to see to it that China Olivier is invited. And, in the interest of thoroughness, I will tell Antoine to ask his sex mate, Toby, to attend. You never know.

Of course, the Christian Dior company putting on the show will have their large number of fashion experts and potential buyers on hand, the gathering afterward not for them.

She ponders: *I need to decide where I can sit, more easily to observe the guests. Naturally, all the models will be here—that is, if the rebel group doesn't boycott—and I'll only be able to watch them during their runway trek. Have to make sure that Brooklyn alerts the monitors to our presence, the guests we want to invite, Shanna, Broadway, and me. Mustn't hint to the Dior folks that anything is amiss. Their show must proceed without a hitch.*

Her mind leaps sideways. Since Corrine Gelly's prints were on the canister weapon, Shanna believes she must be the perp in Brooklyn's fall. But that may not, in fact, be the case. There are other possible explanations for those prints. Stout was a vicious man, and who knows how he might have manipulated the scene. Besides that, he and Batchelor could have had something going. After all, Batchelor did have something going with Charlie Burrus. Lots to uncover in the next two days.

She leaves the ballroom, catches sight of a casually meandering Graziano along a row of potted palms, heads toward the elevators, and descends to the street floor.

In the richness of the interior of the Sheraton, it is easy to forget the ragged tumult of Times Square. New York's famous, or infamous, Broadway is a jumble of attractions overwhelming the senses, some appealing, some repulsive.

A one-legged man seated on a blanket, playing a flute, catches her attention. He is bearded, gaunt, eyes a watery cesspool of anguish. Passersby tend to ignore him, his inverted fedora containing a few meager coins.

The day is clear, a sapphire blue sky, a small halo beyond the towering Manhattan skyscrapers, a cool but invigorating breeze stirring around corners, flapping the loose skirts of sidewalk kiosks.

As she briskly parades toward Fifth Avenue, thoughts tumble and toss, her typical process of unwrapping a box of conundrums. For Charlotte, to get off by herself has always been the secret to clear thinking.

The threatening phone call she got was definitely from a man, a man who likely has a partner, either male or female. Without looking about, she is comforted in knowing that Graziano is close at hand. Still, if someone is desperate enough, damage could be done before anyone could intervene. Ah, but that's it. So far, she hasn't pinned anyone down, forced any person into a corner. Corners are dangerous. Violence is a product of inescapability.

There is an enormous atrium above Fifty-Eighth Street, perhaps half a block in area, where she has sat in the past, reading or simply watching the people. Great bamboo shoots grow in one plot of earth, and in another, potted geraniums bloom red, pink, and white. The ambiance is one of outdoor freshness, though a high ceiling made of filaments of steel covers the entire expanse.

This time she orders herbal tea from an outdoor stand, sits at a spindly, wire-mesh table, produces her notepad with all the names of the players in the Brooklyn-Stout situations, and begins again to rummage through possibilities.

The Burrus father and son are—as kids say it these days— scumbags. The father is a manipulating, racist plutocrat, aligned with Aaron Batchelor, Brooklyn's once-upon-a-time mistake, who is a key figure in at least the attempt to hurt her, and maybe the murder of Stout as well. The son, Andy, is a helpless sycophant who sucks up to whoever pays the most—and, clearly, he is Kyla's shame for the bargain she struck with Stout.

Then there are the two male models: Brent is a first-class liar, though his allegiance to Brooklyn may be his one truthful element. It is still a possibility that he traded that allegiance for Stout's benediction and accompanying favors. As to Antoine Bontemps, his lifestyle marks him as a struggler, one who has questionable élan and flimsy talents. His girl-mate is a caricature and possibly a partner in whatever mischief Antoine might have done.

Corrine Gelly is a deeply frustrated, marginal model. Let go by Stout, she had plenty of reasons to resent Brooklyn, and received Batchelor's approbation to be reinstated—but for what in return?

Even Doctor Bruce Landry, if indeed he has romantic urges about Brooklyn, could have been affronted enough by what happened to her that he might have wanted to harm Stout. Not likely, but still a remote possibility.

Of course, the momma, stocky little Sarah Farivar, had

powerful motives to want to do Stout in. The question is, after a life of scrabbling to a respected summit in her field, would she resort to something so crude as murder?

Who else? The second-tier model, Phillipa, herself once victim of a fall, could have had buried reasons to attack both Brooklyn and Stout. And there are also other models—Andrea, Deanna, and Julia—who, it was common knowledge, hated Stout's style and often felt trapped in his agency web.

Yes, with Stout, it was a sticky entanglement in which several characters were suspended—and now, the web remains as a criminal labyrinth, where the task is to discard one possible suspect after another and leave only the guilty one or ones ready for Shanna's mantra about "You have the right to…"

Charlotte looks up and about. A cadre of young schoolchildren in dark blue uniforms, led by a fussing, slightly overweight teacher, is passing her table. At the rear of the troop is a harried aide, calling out to and herding stragglers like a sheepdog rounding up strays.

Charlotte smiles at one winsome little girl—reminds her of Angelica, the child in New Jersey in last year's case. This one has a long, blonde braid down her back. She returns the smile, and that inexplicable message passes between them, a message that happens all too rarely: *Though we are strangers, we have made a connection.*

As if suddenly resolved about some deep issue, Charlotte stands and says softly to herself, "Think I'll take in Broadway's rehearsal."

29

Sleepless in Seattle is a household name, the movie a mega-hit, so, if done well, this stage musical could be a blockbuster. Ian Tenant, the lead male, is a Broadway regular with his own cadre of fans, and the woman playing Annie is appealing to look at, with a Mary Martin musical-comedy kind of voice. The producer and director, at first concerned that China and Broadway would be too "beautiful" and might outshine the leads, have settled in with the comfort of knowing that they have a talented bunch, the stars sure to win the favor of audiences, and the gorgeous supporting players a five-star bonus.

The cast is all on stage, and the Director, Jamison Brown, is with them, holding court. Surprised that the front door to the theater is unlocked, with no guard anywhere around, Charlotte enters and proceeds to the auditorium. She sits in the rear, in an aisle, where it is dark enough so that the participants can't see her.

With an impressive interior, this theater, as are most in New York, is elegantly appointed, seating eight hundred, the walls, on either side, splashed with abstract designs, and a domed ceiling from which several sparkling chandeliers are suspended. The seats are a shade of deep maroon, impeccably clean, and, since no shows are currently running, the entire ambiance appears pristine.

Another surprise: in the dim light, Charlotte can make out a solitary figure seated in the opposite aisle, also near the back, and, even though she can't be positive, it looks like Kyla Pino.

"Listen up, my lovely people," Brown says, his stentorian voice again scoring his own career as a thespian. "Here we have a rare combination of a comedy that is also poignant and serious. A little boy in Seattle wants desperately for his widowed father to hook up with Annie, a New Yorker, who heard the child's tale on a radio talk show.

"What we must pull off is a sensitive production that turns the humor into joy and the pathos into pleasure. The music must be compatible with the dialogue and not seem like an add-on to the story. As you have seen—or will see—from the lyrics, the play is propelled forward at several points by the songs. Above all, we want this to be a romance of *Wuthering Heights* proportions, though without the brooding quality of a Bronte character like Heathcliff.

"In the end, when Jonah and Sam Baldwin find Annie at the Empire State Building, the audience must sigh with relief—and with a sense that true love will always find a way."

Ian Tenant says, "Amen," and stares hard at China Olivier.

The female lead, Gemma Klein, who plays Annie, adds on, "The old crooner, Bing Crosby, and Princess Grace Kelly, sang a Cole Porter song about that in the movie *High Society*. It said a guardian angel's job was to give true love to both parties."

"Don't know if we have a guardian angel," Brown says with a sardonic hint in his tone, "but hard work might be a friendly substitute. I want, personally, to have folks leave the theater saying, 'What a charming piece! It tugs at the heart. Why can't I have a love like that?' This production has to be a Cinderella story, where the prince and princess really do live happily ever after."

He stops, and, for a time, there is a protracted silence on stage. He picks up with, "So, with all that, I hope you will do some internal probing to produce the fairytale quality this creative work deserves."

Charlotte smiles. Clever director, planting seeds this way to challenge his cast to take on an enchanted attitude about their product. Make it mythic, larger than life, a modern-day fable of epic proportions.

"Hello, Charlotte."

She looks across to see Kyla sliding down the aisle toward her.

"Ah, Kyla. Nice to see you."

"I…uh, thought I'd take in Broadway's rehearsal. He doesn't know I'm here."

"Apparently no one cares if there are visitors. At least so far."

An awkward moment as Kyla sits two seats away from Charlotte and, after a pause, says, "I must seem rather childish to you."

"Oh, my dear, I don't know why you say that."

"Trailing after him like this."

She stops, and, in the dim light, Charlotte can see her shrug, then continues, "I knew all along he had feelings for me, but I compromised my life for Stout's...benediction. Tolerated that silly boy for many months, and now, well, now I think it might be too late."

"I sort of doubt that. My impression is that the object of your affection is a rather tortured soul. He doesn't know his own mind."

"But the pressure is on. This gig is a monumental step up for him, and that woman, China, look at her; she's to die for."

"Yes, and so are you, but it's not always the to-die-for women who get the prize."

A wan smile and both turn silent as the voices on stage pick up.

"But Victoria is a mean ho! She can't take Mom's place."

"Hey now, Jonah, that's no way to talk. Victoria is beautiful and, you know what? She likes you."

"But I don't like her."

"You can learn to like someone."

"Not her."

"Look, okay, so she's not your mom. But no one will take her place. If I hook up with Victoria, she'll become an adult friend, not a substitute mother."

"But, Dad, you don't love her."

There is a long silence on stage, and though the scene has not been blocked, Ian Tenant strolls about in a little circle, turns to his son, and says, "It's not always love that brings people together. Sometimes it's practicality or even necessity."

Another silence and the child says, "I'll bet you could fall in love with Annie."

"Jonah, that's a fantasy. You don't know anything about this Annie. People don't pair up with strangers."

"She's not a stranger to me."

"Enough! You're the child, and I'm the parent. Don't you have homework or something?"

"Okay," Jamison Brown says. "I like the way it's going. Let's turn to another spot with Annie and Walter. Page sixty-seven."

Broadway begins: "You're going to fly to Seattle? What the hell is in Seattle?"

A beat…then, "I'm not sure. Could be a life-changing adventure."

"You going to join a commune? Live with hippies? Seattle is where it rains. You'll get drenched."

"Walter, that's silly. It rains everywhere. I…I'm following up on something I heard about. Could be nothing. Could be a false lead."

"Should I worry about you?"

"Oh. Worry about me? You've never really worried about me before. Why would you start now?"

"What's that supposed to mean?"

"Walter, I'm your girlfriend. Your work is your mistress."

"Unfair! I go home from my work. I come home to you."

"You've got an explanation for everything. Look, our connection is pretty comfortable. We don't really fight, we like some of the same things, and we have some mutual friends. It's…it's okay."

"That's quite an endorsement."

"So, how do you see it?"

"You're a dreamer, and I'm a pragmatist. I get things done, and you float. In lots of ways that's a good combination. We cover everything."

"All right," Brown interjects. "At this point you sing the duet, our patter song, 'I Love You a Little, I Need You a Lot.' Broadway, your character is unaware of the implicit criticism in the lyrics. Annie is super-aware. The song ends with Annie facing the audience…and singing: The challenge for me is to see the choice; that he's in love—with the sound of his voice; he's not in love with me. We won't sing the song now, but keep in mind those attitudes when we do."

The actors move on to another scene, and, as if they had not been interrupted for ten minutes, Kyla says to Charlotte, "So he'll be thrown together with her for months, and I'll be on the outside, looking in."

"It's possible, however, if you pay attention to some of the lines just read, you might realize that people can be in each other's lives on a daily basis and not have true love. Broadway is a pretty discerning fellow, and I'll bet things will get clear for him."

"Sure. With or without me."

Charlotte's cellphone buzzes softly, and she reaches into her purse and silences it without looking at the correspondent's name or number.

For a few minutes, she and Kyla sit quietly, both aware of an elephant in the large hall. Charlotte allows a small smile to turn up her lips. Lovely dilemma Broadway is in, though one of his two beauties will certainly be disappointed.

On stage, Brown announces, "Half an hour break. Get something refreshing to drink. Might try a song or two when we return."

Kyla rises as if to communicate, "I need to get out of here," but Charlotte touches her arm.

"Might be a good idea for you to stay. Wouldn't hurt for Broadway to see you showing interest in him."

"More like frenzy. I'll look ridiculous."

The cast begins to stroll up the carpeted aisle toward the two women, gabbing amiably, Broadway on one side of China and Ian Tenant on the other. As they approach, Kyla steps behind Charlotte as if to hide or at least for protection. But, of course, she is seen, and Broadway says, with a welcoming tone, "Charlotte and Kyla—how neat that you're here."

Charlotte catches a frown on China's colorful face, brief and instantly gone. Broadway hugs both Charlotte and Kyla, turns, and says, "You know China, and this is Ian Tenant, our Tom Hanks character."

Tenant is astounded by Kyla, and Charlotte can see that he struggles with a Don Juan attitude toward beautiful women, pulled toward China, and now, all at once, another eye-stopping female in his sights.

"Broadway," Tenant says, "your friends are lovely, captivating women of all ages."

"Thank you," Charlotte replies. "I haven't thought of myself as captivating for some time, but it's nice to be included."

Shoring up her courage, Kyla says, "I enjoyed the dialogue. It's going to be a hit musical, I'm sure."

"Let's hope so," China responds. "Wouldn't it be fine to have a spot in a long-run Broadway show!"

Broadway adds, "For me, what a blast; Broadway on Broadway."

"Join us in the lounge," Tenant says. "There are soft drinks and snacks. Guests welcome."

Charlotte and Kyla fall in line, and Broadway says softly to

Charlotte, "Anything new on the cases?"

She whispers back, "Want to have a reception tomorrow after the fashion show. Up in my suite, room 1840. Hope to have a full complement of possible suspects for both crimes. Spread the word."

China hears the exchange and frowns.

Tenant hears part of it and looks puzzled.

Kyla's face is pale, with, indeed, a look bordering on frenzy.

Separating herself from the group, Charlotte pauses before entering the lounge room and punches in her code to retrieve her message.

It is Brooklyn's voice, with a sense of urgency, saying, "Charlotte, I think I've pacified those few models who were revolting. They aren't happy but agree not to do anything to jeopardize our show. But, on another matter, my mother seems to have taken ill. At least, she thinks she has. I didn't want to disturb Broadway during his rehearsal, but I contacted Detective Cavanaugh and she got in touch with some other policeman who is supposed to be watching out for you. I think his name is Graziano, and he passed on that you were in the theater with Broadway. He needs to call me. Thanks."

PART 3
Getting to Guilty in Gotham

30

Sarah Farivar is a classic manipulator. Her family and those who have worked with her know this very well, though, in most instances, her treatment of others ends up being benign, more like clever persuasion than exploitation. She has gone so far as to ignore the feelings of others if they met her needs. Always alert to her tactics, Brooklyn and Broadway have learned to protect themselves.

Charlotte says, "Brooklyn didn't sound panicked, but she did think you ought to know and maybe join her in some sort of response."

"Damn it. My mother would do this right before Brook's big show. I know she doesn't want her daughter to look bad, but she gets wound up in her own stuff, which no one else can explain."

"What was her mother like? I mean, was Sarah treated badly?"

"I don't think so. My mother had her kids late, and I didn't know her parents. She came to this country with only her mother, and our father died when we were pretty young, so she had to rear us by herself. Lots of expectations. Brook and I marvel at how 'normal' we are, considering the 'shoulds' and 'ought-tos' we grew up with."

"But, as far as you know, she never deliberately hurt people. Always stayed within the law."

"As far as I know."

"I heard her say how proud she was of her own achievements. Sort of contrasted that with Batchelor and probably Stout as well."

"She has a lot of disdain for silver-spoon success stories. Hers, she insists, is due to hard work and keen insights."

"Probably so. I was just wondering if she ever got, well, ruthless."

"Hid it from us if she did. She was a tough taskmaster and demanded respect for her rules from Brook and me, as well as from people who worked for her. Still does, to this day."

"Okay. I'm going to go. Have an important piece of information to track down." She takes on a wry look and, after a short pause, tacks on, "You might have to do some tiptoeing about, considering that your two young lovelies are both here."

He whispers back, "Deserting the ship."

"How about saying, 'I believe in your ability to navigate expertly, even in rough waters.'"

"Yeah, but this isn't the open sea. There's fire here and it's hot as hell."

"It's all relative. I read recently that in the center of our sun, the temperature is about twenty-eight thousand degrees Fahrenheit. Stay cool, young man."

She moves into the lobby and out into whatever slanting sunlight has made it through the towers in this late afternoon, absorbed at once by New York's incessant bustle.

Back inside, Broadway returns to the lounge area where the cast and Kyla are relaxing on soft chairs and pillowed benches, sipping sodas and munching on donuts set out on a round aluminum tray.

He catches the end of Ian Tenant's comments.

"So, you're a model. A lot like acting. Got to put on a face. Pure entertainment."

China responds, "A little different, Ian. I've done both. Models take on a mood and try to keep it constant. Actors' moods need to be transient, always adjusting."

Kyla, less assertive than China, in her contralto voice, raises the mildest of protests: "Well, we do take on different personas, depending on what apparel we're displaying."

Broadway intervenes, "Both are in the business of illusion. Creating something unique for the viewer or listener. If we're honest about it, our purpose is escape. Help the consumers get into a fashionable, magical world, totally opposite of their actual mundane ones."

"A little cynical there, young man," Ian says without reproach and with a beatific smile spreading on his Gable-like face.

"Yeah, I can get cynical. But at heart I'm pretty tolerant."

"I can vouch for that," Kyla responds, saying more than the

words mean.

The message is not lost on China, and she replies at once, "Oh, I'm sure. You two have been friends for some time."

Friends. The word skewers Kyla and she absorbs it without comment, though roiling inside. *Putting a frame around Broadway and me. Friends. Nothing else. A cage holding us in. Leaves her outside the cage, open to…whatever.*

"Old friends know a lot more about a person than new ones," Broadway says, his attempt to disarm the word.

"Well, in this business," Ian says, "we meet a hell of a lot of people, but not too many become friends."

"Amen!" Gemma says, rising from her padded bench and strolling past them to the door. "Let's go. Jamison will have a cow if we're all late getting back."

"I doubt it. We're too valuable for him to become peevish," Ian replies.

The cast spills out of the lounge, through the lobby, and down the aisle to the stage, where, indeed, Jamison Brown is waiting with an impatient scowl.

As Broadway is about to climb the few steps, Kyla says to him, "I'd better go."

He turns and looks into her hazel eyes, troubled, murky. "How about if I call you this evening? We need to talk."

Her look clouds over as if some internal fear has been confirmed.

On the stage, China turns, having heard their exchange.

—

The streets of Manhattan are seductive fingers pulling Charlotte in, and, though resistant to the label, she finds herself feeling more and more like a New Yorker. Alive with diversity: corner vendors stirring up the pungent aromas of grilling sausages, kiosks with endless framed pictures of touristy scenes, double-decker buses lined up on Broadway, waiting to be filled, Hershey's chocolate store on the edge of Times Square, authentic Jewish delis, musicians, beggars, elegant theatergoers, out-of-town gawkers—yes, alive in a way different from any other city on the planet. In her heart of hearts, she knows this is not her place, but the magnetism becomes a commanding claw, clutching at her affections.

While Broadway agrees to bring Charlotte along to confront Sarah, Brooklyn begs off, occupied with a myriad of last-minute details for her maiden fashion show, and says to her brother, "You can handle this. She's malingering, I'm sure, but I don't know why."

In Sarah's apartment, a luxurious condo on the west side, they find Sarah alone, sitting in bed, two lacy pillows behind her head. She is reading *Elle*, a fashion magazine, and as they approach, she looks up at them with heavy eyes deprived of sleep.

"It's my heart," she says at once.

"You have the heart of an elephant, Mother. Tell me what's wrong."

"I have trouble breathing, and my joints ache."

"Probably a twenty-four-hour flu, or maybe you ate something."

Charlotte's curious eye notes the pricey furniture in the room, dressers with silver handles, a wall of mirrors behind which, she is sure, are dozens if not hundreds of examples of fashionable attire, and bedposts that seem carved from mahogany. Sarah is dressed in a pink chiffon negligee that rises to her neck, its sleeves stopping at her elbows.

"All this violence has compromised my health. I never get sick, but my daughter becomes a cripple and that evil man gets killed—those things have affected my immune system."

"Terrible stuff, Mother, but life has to go on. Now tomorrow is Brook's big day, and you have to haul yourself out of bed and get over to the Sheraton."

"The police do nothing. And this Smart woman—she's trying hard, I can tell, but there is no progress. Anyway, I don't know why I have to go to the fashion show. I see them all the time."

Charlotte, who has stayed out of the family brabble, decides to offer what she hopes will be an incentive. "Sarah, I know you're impatient with the investigation, but tomorrow, after the show, everyone who might be part of these crimes is invited to my room for a post-event reception. My guess is we will learn a lot at that time and maybe even get some real answers to our search. It would be important for you to be there."

For a moment, Sarah lights up as if, indeed, there is something for her in Charlotte's plan. It is transitory, however, and she begins to wave her hand in front of her face, trying to cool down.

The consummate victim, Charlotte thinks. *This old gal plays it for all it's worth. Broadway seems pretty immune to it all, a product of years of reacting to Mama's emotional blackmail.*

"No excuses," he says. "Brook will want to see you there. And the gathering afterwards is a chance to get to the bottom of these awful events."

Like a deer, after the headlights have passed, Sarah seems to emerge from some self-induced trance, begins to nod slowly, and mutters, "It won't be easy, but I'll do my best."

"I have a question," Charlotte says, her look a steady gaze on Sarah.

"A question for me?"

"Yes. Has anyone—I mean any person affiliated with the Stout Agency or any of its models—been in contact with you recently? And if so, about what?"

"Sure," Sarah replies immediately. "That silly boy who was dating Brook's best friend. He told me his father wanted to talk to me and gave me the number. I called yesterday."

Charlotte's look does not change, but she files away the notion that Andy Burrus is not on good terms with his father, so why would he be carrying a message?

"Go on," Charlotte says evenly.

"His name is Charlie and he is a boorish fellow whose every sentence is filled with swear words."

"What did he want?"

"To make a deal. He claims he could deliver the person who hurt Brook if I would find a job for his son in my fashion business. I asked him what skills his son had, and he said none, but he could be trained. I laughed. That stupid child can't be trained. And he knows nothing about my industry. He is a prodigal son without roots. What he wants is to get close to pretty women. I told the father he should buy his son a prostitute."

"And his response?"

"He swore at me and hung up."

"Yes," Charlotte says. "Charlie's style."

Broadway looks at her curiously. "You had a notion that my mother was in touch with someone."

"I guessed. Wealth seems to think it can influence anything.

The Burrus men are having their own internal issues, and I doubt the son would work for his father. But what is interesting is that Charlie, despite disowning his son financially, keeps looking out for his welfare. A contradiction whose only explanation is that the father feels guilty."

"Guilty for?"

"Being a rotten father, trying to control the boy's romantic life, probably looking the other way about drug use. That man, Charlie Burrus, is a piece of work. He'd do anything to get what he wants."

"Even murder?" Sarah asks.

"Well, as the detectives always say, everyone is a suspect."

There is silence in the room as Charlotte's rubric settles in.

"Got to go, Mother. Get yourself some chicken soup, and we'll see you tomorrow at the Sheraton. No excuses."

Sarah grunts.

Not used to her son laying down the law, Charlotte thinks.

A light breeze stirs the leaves on a majestic mulberry tree in front of Sarah's townhouse complex as the sun plays peekaboo with patches of cumulus clouds. Broadway stands in the shade and says, "You are something else. And I'll bet you have enough of an open mind to include my mother in that notion of everyone."

"Look, young man, nothing is over until all the information is collected. I've been storing things away and making designs in my notebook. As of now, there are a dozen possible culprits, both for Brooklyn's affront and Stout's murder. What I have learned in my brief experience as an independent investigator is that the obvious is never quite obvious."

"Well put. And I don't suppose you'll give me examples?"

"I can give you a 'for example,' though it is only as an illustration. Detective Cavanaugh's team has determined that a final set of fingerprints on the heavy canister that propelled Brooklyn down those stairs belonged to Corinne Gelly. What might appear obvious is that she did the terrible deed. We must, however, not jump to that conclusion."

"Because…?"

"Because we do not have confirmation of her history with the so-called weapon."

"How…?"

"That I cannot yet say, but I think I will be able to by tomorrow."

It takes less than a minute for Broadway to flag down one of the constant flow of yellow taxis streaming down Park Avenue.

"Is there somewhere I can drop you? I have a call to make; a different topic."

"I'm sure. And my guess is it has to do with those two dazzlers interested in you."

"Good guess. I promised Kyla I'd call her this evening."

"China is worried. She's only known you a short time and would like to hold on. Kyla has known you longer and would also like to hold on. Juicy dilemma."

"There are more important things happening in the next day or so than my erratic love life. But I'd still like to have some clear direction."

"Drop me at the Sheraton. I need to meet with Shanna again before this day is over."

"Why do I get the feeling that this day is nowhere near over?"

31

They are seated in the same tavern area where Charlotte encountered Broadway and China two days before, Shanna delighted with the surroundings yet, in her modest way, feeling rather out of place with the opulence.

"Swell joint. My tastes go more to pubs than hotel lounges."

"The Farivar family gave me a wad of money, so it feels wonderfully wicked to spend it recklessly. Enjoy, and don't worry about the cost."

They sit for a moment in silence, and Charlotte says, "Last time I was here, I saw Graziano at a distance, reading a newspaper. I spoke with him, sort of embarrassed him too, since he felt ashamed that I— how do they say it?—made him."

"It's kind of remarkable that what started out as a consultation with you to uncover the idiot who hurt the girl has turned into a nasty murder investigation. I must tell you, Charlotte, I appreciate your keen insights." She pauses and adds, "We make quite a team."

"Back in Pennsylvania, Augie Hartunian once told me the same thing."

A tall, leggy cocktail waitress questions them for drinks, smiles sweetly, and, proud of her acumen, returns to the bar without writing anything down.

Wonder if she could do that if there were four or five of us at this table, Charlotte ponders. To Shanna, she says, "I've been asking around and found out that because Corrine Gelly was one of Stout's second-layer models, she was given mundane tasks around the studio. You may remember that Antoine Bontemps, also one of the less favored in the group, was made to keep the roll sheet, Stout's way of throwing these lesser talents, as he saw them, a bone or two."

"So, how does this fit in with the crimes?"

"Well, Brooklyn told me that Corrine had been appointed by the man to sign in for all mail and reordered supplies. Didn't help her become a better model, but at least in Stout's eyes, she was being useful."

"She became his gofer person."

"Yes, and, though he fired her anyway, she served a purpose while in the troupe."

The long-legged server returns, the same sweet smile fixed as if a painted mask on her pretty face, a look of pride there as well, as she delivers Charlotte's red wine and Shanna's on-duty, nonalcoholic ginger ale without error.

"Okay, so tell me the ending to this narrative. How does that help us find suspects in these felonies?"

"It is a short leap from there to presume that Corrine Gelly likely signed in for the delivery of a canister of floor wax and, as such, by either taking it into Stout's office or storing it in the closet, would have left her prints on the container. The point being that she could have been but was not necessarily the perp in Brooklyn's fall."

"Of course. And the delivery people almost always wear gloves, especially when carting around toxic materials, so they would not have left prints of their own."

"Exactly."

"That leaves us Stout as the other person with prints. But the same thing could apply to him. He might have moved the canister into the closet."

"Might have; however, the word is that he never cleaned or picked up anything around the studio. Left that work for the underlings. But, furious as he must have been when Brooklyn…dumped him, we could hypothesize that his prints were there because he used the container to attack her."

"If that is the case," Shanna says, "it's likely someone who knew what he did decided to pay him back."

"Possibly true. Now, who would have known?"

"You tell me."

"Brent White was in and out that day and might have seen what happened. And, though no one saw him, Batchelor, who was searching for Brooklyn, may have stumbled on the event and, since he still had feelings for her, could have turned on Stout. Even Corrine, once Brooklyn was no longer top model, could well have decided to do Stout in. Of course, there is still the possibility that Corrine, or even Antoine Bontemps, acted at someone else's bidding—such as Batchelor, who might have made a deal with one or the other in exchange for his recommendation.

"And we mustn't forget little Andy, who was getting funds from Batchelor and could have felt beholden to him. Finally, though a long shot, Mama Farivar was convinced that Stout had injured her precious daughter, was put off by the slowness of the investigation, and might well have hammered Stout as payback."

"Of all those, who would have access to his office and his toolbox and could sneak up behind Stout without him expecting it?"

"It didn't have to be a sneaking up. Stout and whoever was with him could have been heading toward the stairs, Stout leading. Then wham! A blow from behind. And, for me, I think it is significant that your investigating officers confiscated Stout's appointment calendar, which I want to see—because it may tell us who was scheduled to be in his office that day."

"Well, our forensics people discovered that Stout had been sexually involved not long before his death."

"Yes, and since Brooklyn was no longer his girlfriend, so far as we know, his only remaining sexual partner was a man—Brent, to be specific. Or, better to say, had been, since Brent was surely put off by Stout wanting him to harm Brooklyn."

"So, are you saying Stout might have started up with one of the other girls already?"

"Might have, however, since your people found no evidence of recent female presence in his office or on his couch, it could have been a man—maybe another man."

"Antoine?"

"No semen residue, so we probably can presume that what happened was…well, to put it into today's vernacular…oh, this is hard for me to say… A blowjob?"

Her nose scrunches up, and she says this latter phrase with delicacy as if the words are foreign, unsavory.

"It could be Antoine, then."

"Or, it could be a woman."

"Well, yes, of course."

"Keep in mind also that the note left on Stout's door suggested that a lesbian was connected to all this. If it is one of the models, she is not, as the phrase goes, out of the closet—at least not generally—though perhaps one or two others might know. Which means we might have to judiciously ask around tomorrow, either before or right after the show." She hesitates only briefly and adds, "I'm still unsure why the culprit wanted to send us notes. It certainly tipped his hand."

A designer clock high on an opposite wall reminds Charlotte of a sagging Dali painting; it sounds a single chime as its needlelike arm points down to the half hour. Four women and a man at a nearby table break into spontaneous laughter, entertained en masse by someone's anecdote. An aroma, heavy with garlic, likely hors d'oeuvres from the kitchen, curls about the lounge, stimulating the cocktail crowd to crave dinner.

"Perps have big egos, and anyway, one note was a threat to you," Shanna says, "which in my work means the guy felt threatened himself."

"Could be, yet, thanks to Graziano and you, I've felt quite safe."

"Yes, but don't get cocky. Bad guys can be very creative when it comes to dealing out hurts."

"Oh, I'm not a very cocky person. However, I am a survivor. Had to be, to live this long."

"So, you're saying we need to determine if one of the girls could be the lesbian the perp was citing."

"That would help steer our ship toward a solution. This is a tricky journey because there are so many characters with sundry needs and motives. As you surely know, we must begin to peel the onion, strip off one suspect at a time, until the remaining one or ones shine as brightly as the night lights on Times Square."

"Neat image. What I don't know is why citing a lesbian would make a difference in the note writer's mind. Why would he or she want us to know about that?"

"Maybe we'll find out tomorrow. Somebody could well be homophobic—a word I only learned about a year ago. And that person didn't try to imply that the 'dyke' was the murderer—as we discovered once we twisted the anagram around."

"No. Owned up to the murder but gave us info—for some

obscure reason."

Charlotte goes away in her thoughts for a time. In the present age of technology, she often despairs over ineffable qualities that get ignored and interactive moments that get discarded. Face-to-face confrontation is still the most revealing way of reading a person.

"Finally," she says softly, "I have a hunch that the killer was willing to admit to his deed but wanted all of us to separate that from the attack on Brooklyn. And that separation was a kind of implied admission showing his or her connection to, or even affection for, Brooklyn."

"Ah. That's it. The murderer cared about Brooklyn and most certainly was exacting some sort of punishment on Stout, the suspected attacker."

"That is the most likely scenario. Still, going into tomorrow, we need to keep an open mind."

Shanna laughs. "Pardon my French, but how in the hell did you get so smart, Ms. Smart? We cops go through all kinds of training to get us to clear away the red herrings and come up with the unvarnished truth. Here you seem to know intuitively what to look for—and, even more remarkably, what tangents not to go off on."

"I'm not all that smart. What I try to do is avoid the side roads and stay on some sort of direct path. All of this is logic, you know, and, as investigators, we need to be pristinely logical."

"You are that."

"The pundits have written that Abraham Lincoln did not have a genius IQ, more likely about a hundred twenty or so, and they try to gauge that from his vocabulary. But he did have the amazing ability to move at once to the heart of an issue, tear away the cobwebs, ignore the superfluous. I've read that people in his presence were often stunned by how acutely he saw a problem and could respond with a clean solution."

The kitchen aromas now swirling about in the air conditioning have grown in intensity, and Shanna says, "I'm getting hungry. Not that I think we ought to eat dinner here, but a hamburger would be nice."

"That's what I like about you, Shanna, a down-to-earth gal. I saw a McDonald's in the Square."

"Oh, I'm not all that down-to-earth, and you know what? I don't eat McDonald's. I like thick, juicy, gourmet burgers like they have at Hamburger Hamlet."

"Okay. Since you mentioned Hamlet, let me quote from another of Will's plays: Lead on, MacDuff!"

From a distance, this entire forty-minute scene has been monitored by Graziano, newspaper-in-front-of-face and all; monitored, yes, but perplexing as well. *Now where in the hell are they going? If boss Cavanaugh is going to hang out with the lady, why am I needed?*

Thoughts wander to his black-eyed, still raven-haired, full-bosomed woman with cherubic cheeks and welcoming arms, one Geraldine Falk. *Might as well call her. Maybe take a break for an hour and meet her for a snack of some kind, maybe a hot dog, maybe even a beer…. Or, better yet, head over to her place.*

32

Shame follows carelessness; regrets spill out in massive doses, and, from an official perspective, consequences result; disciplinary action might well stir in the precinct's pot, and Graziano will be held accountable.

Out in the chatter of Broadway's inimitable urban language, Shanna and Charlotte head for the prominent Hamburger Hamlet on the edge of Times Square.

In California, vehicles are commanded to stop when pedestrians enter a crosswalk. As well, no one is supposed to cross against a light. In New York, it is a matter of dodging taxis and other vehicles, foot traffic darting across whenever there is an opening—a risky game of Russian Roulette with automobiles.

Not being a New Yorker, Charlotte is more cautious, the experienced Shanna more bold. They have moved out into the street, standing a couple of yards from the curb. A dark sedan, possibly a Toyota or a Honda, spurts out of traffic and speeds up directly at them.

Shanna is aware at once, her training instructing her to reach for her weapon with one hand while shoving her friend toward the sidewalk with the other, all the while crouching low, knees bent, ready to leap aside.

Screams and shouts from others; pedestrians scattering like leaves in a tempest.

The driver sees that Charlotte Smart is out of range, twists the car's steering wheel instantly, and careens back toward the middle of the street.

As the vehicle zooms by, Shanna, still crouching, aims her

weapon at the receding target, thinks better of it, and stands, hoping to sight the license number.

Her concern turns toward Charlotte, and she hurries to where her friend is seated next to the curb, supported by a couple of terrified women.

"I…I'm okay," Charlotte says. "Did you get the number?"

"Blocked out. Perps do that when they know they'll be on the attack."

Shanna looks around for Graziano, her associate.

Curiously, though she can't be sure, someone resembling him appears to be in the street, almost a block away, where the fleeing vehicle had faded from sight.

Last-minute details crowd in. Brooklyn has asked the entire troupe to assemble in the early evening before the big day. The disgruntled few blend with the satisfied majority, most unaware of the friction Brooklyn had encountered. His presence constant, one might wonder if Dr. Bruce Landry has any other patients. Priority is his key word; a jewel has begun to shine in his life, invading his fixed medical routine, and his deeper layers tell him to focus in, something rare pulsing on the horizon.

On her part, Brooklyn is aware that her status as director is fragile; though appreciated by most, she knows she does not carry the weight of an older, more experienced, and certainly more authoritative Donald Stout.

Her dissidents must have believed their protests would bear fruit since change occurs through militants already on the rise and rarely from abject hopelessness.

Shanna and Charlotte agree not to burden the modeling ensemble with the attempt on their lives. Not what Brooklyn and the others need on the threshold of their grand production.

Both are surprised to see Aaron Batchelor seated on the periphery of the parquet.

The elder Burrus had mentioned Batchelor as his partner, both power-based men, each capable of manipulating others. Their alliance nags at Charlotte, especially since Batchelor seems to pop up off-and-on around Brooklyn, and Burrus was not only the broker who arranged Andy's romantic connection with Kyla Pino; he also wanted Mother Farivar to employ his son; some weird energy operating with both men.

"The Dior people will have two of their designers at the event," Brooklyn is saying, "and they will want to be in the staging area to ensure that their creations are being faithfully represented. They have consulted with me, and so far, what we have planned seems—at least in the abstract—to meet with their approval. As you all know, for the fashion world, these runway exhibits are their meal ticket to worldwide distribution. They have invited buyers from every major market imaginable. Our ability to display their work in the most magnificent light possible is what they are counting on. And, beautiful people, we will deliver!"

"How many will be in the audience?" Julia asks. Of all the models, she is the most fragile-looking, though her style on the runway is effective.

"Not sure," Brooklyn replies, "but I'll bet at least a couple of hundred."

"What time do you want us here?" Andrea asks.

"The music will start at two forty-five, mostly background instrumental pieces as people are settling in. Our cue will be a peal of bells at a minute or two before three. Often, there are trumpets, but, with this array of elegant attire, bells seem more classy."

At this, Batchelor leans forward and applauds, shrugs his shoulders in apology, and slides back into his chair.

Appreciates classy, Charlotte thinks.

Shanna's cellphone buzzes, and she rises and walks into the hall, Charlotte peering after her.

"Need to have you all here no later than one o'clock," Brooklyn continues. "The gowns and other attire will be here at noon, and Gladys, our makeup person, will be ready to go to work any time after that. Just a reminder, not a good idea to administer makeup once you don the clothing."

She looks about at the company of gorgeous people, hesitates for a moment, and adds, "Have to be prepared for last-minute changes as well. You all know the pieces you are to wear, but don't panic if the designer comes up with some alterations. We are talented professionals, and adjusting to sudden modifications will be a piece of cake."

At this moment, Dr. Bruce Landry enters, in his hand an enormous bouquet of red roses. Following the eyes of her team, Brooklyn turns her head, and as she does, Landry steps forward and presents his gift. The room erupts in applause. Brooklyn's hand is over her mouth, her cheeks turning a rosy red as if emulating the flowers.

An irritated look crosses Batchelor's face; as Charlotte watches, she sees it turn into a sneer.

Her mind embraces more than one thought, and, as if in a classroom, she tentatively raises her hand.

Brooklyn smiles at her. "Go ahead, Charlotte."

"Sorry to intrude, but I want all of you to know that, after the show, I am hosting a reception in my suite, upstairs in the Sheraton, room 1840. Everyone here is invited, and I hope you all come."

Shanna, returned from the alcove, speaks up, "And it's quite a room, at that. One of Gotham's finest."

She catches Charlotte's eye and motions with her head to accompany her into the hallway.

"What's up?" Charlotte asks.

"Big surprise. Graziano just called. He confessed that considering I was there, he was about to take a break from watching out for you. I mentioned his girlfriend to you once; well, he thought he'd meet up with her, have a drink or whatever. He felt guilty and was turning back to catch up to us, and luckily, was a block down the street when the car tried to run us over. He heard all the screams, took in the scene, and watched the car speed toward him and past him. And guess what? He caught the front license plate."

"Why, that's wonderful. How long will it take to run it through?"

"He already did. The Motor Vehicle Department told him the car is a Honda Accord and is registered to a Delbert Groode. Our people looked his name up in our archives and he is in the system; a couple of arrests for burglary. It shows his employment at Maria's Italian Kitchen in the Village; occupation: food server."

"Ah. As they say, a patsy, hired by someone else to do the dirty deed."

"Yes, but an accomplice, and we can pick him up for attempted murder."

"If you do, maybe he'll…uh, sing?"

"Good for you, Charlotte. You've got all the language down pat."

"It seems we now must figure out who wanted you and me dead—or at least out of the way—so intensely that he or she decided to employ a goon named Groode to do us in."

"Tell you what. I'll supervise his arrest. Be in touch with you later. Whatever info he spits out will help us with answers to your query."

"Okay. I'll stay with Brooklyn for now, then I'll get off by myself to do some calculating. I presume Graziano is still on my tail?"

"After almost letting us down, I don't think he'll mosey off anymore."

"Glad to hear it."

"Later."

Charlotte's thoughts wander for a moment as she reflects on how fortunate she is to have connected with another competent detective—last year, Augie Hartunian in Pennsylvania, and now Shanna Cavanaugh in New York. As an amateur, these tuned-in law people make her gifts of logic and intuition look good. Pursuing criminals is now such a technical enterprise, with electronics and DNA and fingerprint analyses so advanced that what she does from the heart combines nicely with their cognitive sciences.

When she reenters the studio, Brooklyn is closing the session. Again, as Charlotte has already realized, this young woman has both: a heart filled with love and empathy and a clever mind that seems to know instinctively what to say and do.

"Lovely friends," Brooklyn says in a voice trembling with passion, "this is a grand experiment. No Donald Stout to crack the whip, and, on the other hand, no Donald Stout to command the respect of the industry. My gratitude goes out to all of you for who you are and how we have come together to pull this event off. Goodness knows I am stunned at my good fortune; to be able to help guide you through this experience, despite my…condition." She pauses, takes a deep breath, waves both arms in the air, and shouts, "Time to shine! Let's do it!"

A few blocks away, Broadway is seated in the theater lounge across from China; both are sipping tea. Jamison Brown has decided to work with the two principals alone for an hour or two, and the supporting people are on break. The lounge is not elegant, but neither is it tawdry; the furniture is functional, snacks always in abundance, a TV monitor available for recreational viewing, and there is a CD player in the far corner, providing soft and hopefully soothing music.

China's agenda is relentless, though not resented by Brooklyn.

She is, after all, an appealing woman and, if he avoids any self-delusion, a potentially unparalleled lover. Alas, he regularly argues from conflicting perspectives: China-Kyla, Kyla-China? And he hears the lyrics to an old song: "Which one will the fountain bless?"

"Look, handsome," China says, placing her hand on his bare arm, "I know we're pretty new, and your loyalty to an old fixation isn't spent, but I'd like to put in a strong claim for your affections. Sound too formal? Okay, what I want is you—on my arm, in my bed, in my life. How's that for blunt?"

"Man, China, that tears me up. I'm more than flattered. I'm stunned. Not that I didn't catch your feelings, but it's amazing how you can know your mind so quickly while I flounder like a fish in shallow water, not able to get clear on mine."

"You're a male. Independence and freedom get in the way of connectedness and commitment. Hey, I'm no ogre. I don't believe in ball and chain. When I have a man, he's on a long leash. It's a mutual love-in, no boss, no leader, and absolutely no follower."

"I'm not worried about being controlled by a woman, I'm worried about making the right choice in a woman. Frankly, both you and Kyla are spectacular—absolutely flawless in looks, emotionally open and candid. That makes me miserable. I hate having the power to pick one and, in the process, unpick the other."

She is quiet for a moment and puts in, "Well, yes. One of us, to go directly to the point, is going to be a loser. I'm hoping it won't be me."

"Won't be you for what?" Tenant says as he strides into the lounge.

"She's hoping that, when the great spirit from Valhalla comes down to claim its next stage character for eternity, it won't be her," Broadway says with a grin.

"Bad grammar," Tenant replies. "It won't be *she*."

It is useful to know that Ian Tenant was married at twenty-four to an aspiring actress with to-die-for looks but minimal talent. They produced one child, a boy, Christopher, who, at the age of seven, was victim of a crash when his school bus skidded on ice and rolled over. Eleven children survived, but Christopher and two others were killed. Their child's death scuttled the Tenants' marriage. Ian, thirty-two at the time, went on to become a respected Broadway performer, recognized for his soaring tenor voice and what some reviewers called his appealing stage presence.

Now, at thirty-nine, he has not remarried yet and is known to have had a half dozen romances, at least three with his leading ladies. It isn't that he is shallow or frivolous about sticking with a woman; rather, he likes to explain that he has yet to find the right second chance. It was publicly broadcast that his first marriage to Wendy Trumbo was made in heaven, and only a tragedy of the magnitude they had suffered could have ended it.

Though apparent that he has a roving eye, his fellow thespians admire him, and no one knows of complaints about his treatment of the women he pursues.

China is his present female focus, and though Broadway is a nice young fellow, Ian is quite alert to competition and is wary about her attention to him.

On her part, China is drawn toward Ian, perhaps as much for his celebrity status as his male allure; at least for now, though, she is desperate to lock on to Broadway Farivar. And, of course, he knows it.

Broadway and China hug goodbye in the lobby—he begging off to help Charlotte with some details. Jamison Brown observes the scene, sees Tenant watching from the edge of the lounge, and approaches his lead thespian.

"She's a cutie. Not sure if the Broadway-China connection is solid. I've heard rumors. But you, my famous friend, need to play it cool. I don't want any complicated private pettiness interfering with our cast harmony."

Tenant laughs. "Hey, Brownie, no sweat. I only go where I'm wanted. Doesn't mean I won't follow up if the opportunity arises."

"Yes, well, make sure the 'opportunity,' as you call it, is neat and clean. Resentments ruin unity. Unity is what makes a show a mega hit."

"This show is a sure thing. No conflicts. 'Out, damned spot!' I guarantee it."

33

Each day, whether anyone sees it or not, Charlotte dutifully makes her bed. It is not so much a ritual as it is a value: things need to be in order—no loose ends, nothing put off for later. Her life has worked rather well that way, and, as an amateur sleuth, the same values apply.

Her sociogram and the many thoughts she has scribbled into her little notebook give her a focal point. It remains for her to settle in and study all her notes. Embedded somewhere in those scratches are contradictions, self-incriminating disputations that may well become indictments.

It is late in the evening and she has returned to her suite, the maid service having changed her sheets and remade her bed, which she had thought was perfectly fine. With Broadway's help, she has ordered a buffet for the next day, to be delivered and set up for when the show is over, including wine, decorations, and a special gift for Brooklyn.

All right, so maybe that Delbert fellow will reveal who hired him to try to do away with Shanna and her. But if he doesn't, who is feeling the heat, sensing that she and Shanna are closing in? There are three rich folks in this scenario, and Mother Farivar, even if she could be the one who took revenge on Stout, would hardly hire a loser to hurt the person she is paying to find justice for her wounded daughter. Charlie Burrus certainly could do it, though his motive is a bit obscure; he doesn't seem to have much invested in the Stout enterprise, and he can't seem to decide if he wants to help his itinerant son or dump him—neither option having a connection to the investigation unless the boy is truly the culprit. Batchelor. Now there is a plutocrat with a lot of issues: dropped by Brooklyn, so he might well have wanted to get even, but still seemingly drawn toward her. It's sort of a come-go situation, although, as perps are concerned, there is often an attempt to show one face while camouflaging another.

The non-wealthy actors in this drama include all the models, particularly the two males, but also Corrine Gelly, and a less-likely but still possible Phillipa, who had fallen—and, for all anyone knows, was possibly pushed—down the stairs herself a year earlier. Mustn't forget little, inept Andy, his father's bane and his own worst enemy. Aside from his nasty manner, it wouldn't be a surprise if he is also a druggie. His mantra: will do anything for money.

A sociogram sets up relationships between people, often in the form of a family genogram, with members who have died, remarried, committed suicide, been divorced, or any number of other scenarios, including exotic illnesses. Freud's genogram was bizarre. One like Elizabeth Taylor's, with all her marriages, would be mind-boggling.

Now, on the last evening before the hoped-for climax in this investigation, Charlotte sets out to draw lines between relationships, see what tangents might exist, gauge the multiple connections between many of the principals. A light will surely shine on irregularities, alibis, or motives that rise or fall and careless behavior that can lead to exposure.

An hour passes as, propped up in bed, she studies her graph and her notes, smiles inscrutably, and finally lays her head on her pillow. Something is percolating.

The morning opens up with thunder as another close-to-winter storm pushes across Manhattan. For an instant, Charlotte lies in bed, taking in the lowering clouds through her uncovered eighteenth-floor window, awed as usual by weather's indifferent abundance of energy. She thinks and almost says aloud, *Rich and poor, guilty and innocent, all get soaked by Mother Nature.*

Snuggling about in her regal bedding, she does say aloud, "Wouldn't brother Greg get a kick out of this!"

One hour later, she is leaving the Sheraton, the storm's fury dissipated, a rosy light coloring the clearing sky. After a vigorous walk through shadowy canyons, she enters Au Bon Pain and orders a croissant and green tea. With movements leisurely and deliberate, she savors her morning snack, dabs at the corners of her mouth with a soft napkin, pushes the paper plate and cup away, and lifts her cellphone from her purse.

"Good morning, Shanna. I'm curious about the Groode fellow who tried to run us down. Did he point the finger at his employer? Do we know who put him up to it?"

She waits, smiles slightly, frowns, and replies, "Of course he'd try to weasel out of any fault, but deny he was driving the car? How can he explain that?

"Loaned the car out? To whom? Do you believe that? …I agree. It's a ploy to avoid being charged. So, are you saying he hasn't coughed up any name? …He won't own up to being paid for his dirty work?

"A deal? What does that mean? …Ah, I see. You go easier on him if he delivers the true culprit. You think that will work? …Okay. Let me know. I have some ideas, but it would be wonderful to find out who put the fellow up to his nasty trick."

She signs off and, after a brief pause, like a concert pianist commencing a new movement, fingers in a series of digits, waits, listens.

"Yes, Charlotte."

"Broadway, this is the big day, and I'm wondering what you will be doing before your sister's show. Are you available to meet?"

"I'll make time, but we do have a run-through rehearsal from ten to noon. From the way things are going, I'm guessing I may need to confront one or both of my leading ladies. I doubt Kyla will show up there since she has to be at the Sheraton to prepare."

"When you say confront, are you planning to…make a choice?"

"You know, I'm not sure. You once said circumstances change and choices become clear."

"I hope they become clear for you. Go in one direction and you risk friction among your theater cast; go in another and you risk estranging your sister's best pal."

"You got it. There is still the possibility a choice will be made by one of the other people and let me off the hook—whether I like the outcome or not."

"That's it, young man. You have two remarkable women interested in you, and if you get clear, you can take your pick. If you don't, well, you live with the consequences of someone else's decision."

He is quiet, as if pondering this crafty, elderly woman's very clear pronouncement. "Uh…what do you want to see me about?"

"Questions about our pair of crimes. Like the changing weather on this beautiful fall day, we may see the stormy confusion of our investigation morph into the sunshine."

"Where shall we meet?"

"How about the Sheraton lobby-lounge at twelve-thirty?"

"How's the sun going to get into the Sheraton lobby?"

There is more than one lobby at the Sheraton, the registration floor with its casual seating, and the floor where Shanna and Charlotte had their pre-auto-assault snack, with its rather upscale café. It is understood by Charlotte and Broadway that they will meet in the latter. Charlotte—as has happened more than once—feels somewhat giddy over the opportunity to surround herself with elegance at someone else's expense.

She arrives first, waits no more than five minutes, and Broadway enters looking flushed.

"Tell me."

He scratches the back of his head with both hands, smooths down his hair with a look of agitation, shrugs his shoulders, and replies, "Damned if I know what's going on. As I expected, Kyla wasn't there, and my plan was to ask China a few key questions."

"Such as?"

"Such as why do you think you want me in your life—I mean, in a romantic way? And what do you like or love about me? But most important, since she is so beautiful and so young, are you ready to settle in with one person?"

"Ah, great questions. Do you realize that those are the same questions you need to ask yourself?"

He gives Charlotte an odd look. "Hey, you just turned that on me. No, I didn't think of it in those terms. But, yes, I do need to ask myself those questions."

"Since you seem confused, I can only presume that you didn't get to carry out your plan. So, if you do ask yourself, what are your answers?"

"That's a tough one. I think having China in my life in a romantic way would be a heady experience—erotic for sure since she has a physical presence I'd never tire of. What do I love about her? Uh…you know, I'm not sure. She's a wonderful actor and dancer, and she is almost always upbeat. I guess those things aren't really love. As to whether I'm ready to settle down with one person? I believe I am. I've had girlfriends and thought I was in love in the past. It's time for me to create a deep connection with one woman. Now there! How's that?"

"Bravo! Only one thing missing: Can you apply the answers you just laid out to Kyla? Does anything change?"

Laughter. "You nail me every time, Charlotte. Too bad my mother could never talk with me like you do. Kyla? Sure, it would change. She's a dear heart, beautiful inside and out. I've loved her for a long time. Could I see myself settled in with her? Absolutely."

"Okay. I don't make decisions for other people, but I surely hear you laying out a portrait that seems unambiguous. You only have to look at yourself with a vacuumed eye."

She stops and waits. After a moment she asks, "So tell me what you did say and how China reacted."

"We were about to do a reading when China whispered something to me. I hadn't told her anything yet, but she leaned close and said, 'Ian Tenant wants me. Not as a fellow thespian but as a companion. I want you, but I can't wait too long. He's an impatient fellow.' All I had time to say was, 'I don't own you.' At that, she moved back, tears in her eyes, and muttered, 'I love you.' We didn't get a chance to talk anymore, and when she left the theater, I saw Tenant scurry after her."

"Hmm. Well, someone in this little tableau is going to end up with a broken heart. Or at least a wounded one."

"Enough about me. What did you want to talk about? The fashion show gets started in a couple of hours."

"Yes. First, I would like to know a few things. Your mother hated Donald Stout, correct?"

"She thought he mistreated Brook."

"Okay, and she believed that he likely was the one who caused her injury?"

"She kept saying that."

"Now, I know I asked you about this already, but be candid with me. In your best judgment, do you think your mother could have either done the deed or hired someone else to kill Stout?"

He looks away, pain spreading across his handsome face. The large room, buzzing with guests, seems suddenly stifling, unwelcoming. His eyes rise from their downward focus, and he gazes at Charlotte.

"Look. I don't know what my mother is capable of. She is a fierce competitor in business and a mother bear when it comes to her two children. Would she stoop to the murder of another human being? I doubt it. But I am her son, and I don't want to believe such a thing."

"Good enough. I'm satisfied with that answer. Another question: which, of all the women models, do you think could be a closeted lesbian?"

This brings a frown as Broadway says softly, "Brook has always thought maybe Corrine Gelly might be. Other than her, I don't know. Phillipa has not been known to have any boyfriend, but that doesn't mean—"

"No, of course not. Like me, I haven't had a boyfriend in nearly forty years."

"Well, Charlotte, for all I know…"

"Tsk, tsk. So, one more important question: Corrine and Brent both seem to have had access to Stout's office, she to clean up and he to…well, whatever he and his boss did. Do you know of anyone else who could easily get in there?"

"Stout's changeable girlfriends would be there off and on. When Brook was dating him, she was welcome any time. When she kissed him off, he wasn't hooked into any female, as far as I knew, so I doubt any of the other women would enter his personal space. He was a tyrant about privacy."

"Always kept that office door locked?"

"Except when he was right outside, in the studio room."

"Very good. You've been a big help." She pauses, gets one of her faraway looks, and says, "You know, Broadway, sometimes the obvious is so hard to see, but the obscure leaps out like a specter from the shadows."

"I wouldn't be surprised at anything you come up with. Detective Cavenaugh asked me what I thought about you, and I told her you are, like, a clairvoyant when it comes to the hidden being revealed."

"I don't know about that, but it reminds me of the story of a young man who told his mother—a mother like yours, in fact—that he was going to be married, and he added that he wanted her to meet the woman, but in an unusual way. He said he was bringing three women in and he wanted Mom to guess which one was to be his bride. The three sat across from her on the couch, and after they left, the son asked, 'So which one is it?' The mother smirked and said, 'The one on the right.' 'But, how did you know?' the son asked. 'Because,' the mother replied, 'I don't like her.'"

"Yes! I can see my mother doing just that! Though, in my case, I would guess she wouldn't object to Kyla or China since both are elegant women on their way to being successful and maybe stars. My mother has stars in her eyes."

"Yes, but in either case, Mother Farivar has to give up her precious son to another woman. Okay, so let's go cheer your sister on. I'm eager to see all the folks who show up. My guess is our suspect or suspects will be among them."

In the prep room, there is the usual hum of nervous energy and also a strained hush hovering like a mantle. Certainly not the first time these beautiful people have walked this walk, yet the first time, for most, absent Donald Stout. Brooklyn, though wheelchair-bound, seems to be everywhere, suggesting, praising, offering an idea about makeup, a thought about hair style, even an appraisal of complementary jewelry.

An undercover fly on the wall might well peruse the ensemble for any sign of excessively furtive behavior, of individuals who seem either turned inward or quietly hostile. The protestors, not happy with their assignments, would be expected to show moodiness. As to the others, guilt is harder to read, and hiding such feelings is a cultivated skill.

To Phillipa, Corrine whispers, "Got to make the best of things. If that prick, Stout, was still around, I wouldn't even be here."

"That 'prick,' as you call him, seems to have had a thing about stairs. Ironic that he got his comeuppance on his own quasi-private staircase."

"Yeah. I'm sure you know about all that."

"No more than anyone else. No more than you—though I did take a tumble myself a while back."

"That's what I meant."

"I was hung over at the time, so my fall was hazy. Just like with Brooklyn, I might have been pushed."

Corrine lowers her hand, interrupting the process of applying eye shadow, stares at Phillipa, and says, "But were you one of Donald's girls? I mean, part of his parade of devotees?"

"Not in the same way. He sort of forced me a couple of times, to ensure my loyalty. He never publicly displayed me as his girlfriend."

"So, would he have a reason to want to hurt you?"

"Well, you see, I knew he was bi, and I think he got worried it would leak out. Like with Brooklyn—if he is the one—it was a matter of showing power, who's the boss, not permitting any mutiny in the ranks. He was a sadistic asshole."

"Yes, Brooklyn's case was a tragedy." She stops as though the entire subject has been exhausted.

As if mention of her name is a summons, Brooklyn wheels up.

"Hope you two are feeling prime. You both look beautiful. Anything you need?"

Corrine says, "One of the designers decided to cut off a rounded linen bouquet attached to my suit at the beltline."

"She told me. I agreed with her that the suit is designed for a businesswoman, and the fluff of an artificial posy on it seemed rather out of character. Even the greatest of designers sometimes get carried away."

"I'd like to own this piece I'm wearing. Matches my coloring. I could wear it to other people's weddings and at cocktail parties for my book club," Phillipa says.

"I didn't know you belong to a book club," Brooklyn replies with a warm smile.

"Every month. We read the *New York Times* best-sellers and critique them."

"Phillipa, that's wonderful. Maybe someday I could join up with you. I'd love to know who the new, talented novelists are. Speaking of the *Times*, they have sent their fashion editor. She's to be seated in the first row near the end of the runway. Name tag reads *Daisy Peregrin*. Give her a look. Make this whole event fun, okay? I'll be there rooting for everyone."

She wheels away as the announcing swell of carillons fill the ballroom and its wings.

34

In tallying up the scorecard, Detective Cavanaugh is acutely conscious of several pernicious happenings: her friend and co-investigator, Charlotte Smart, has been threatened by notes and phone calls and a brazen attempt on her life, in the midst of hundreds of people on the most famous street in the world. Since Graziano had aborted his furlough from shadowing Charlotte and, in fact, had been the instrument for tracking down the perp, his status at police headquarters remains solid. Now, Cavanaugh has decided that Graziano will join her at the fashion event, each on one side of the runway, four eyes alert to any mischief.

Charlotte's plan to assemble all possible suspects after the show is confirmed by the detective, and she has instructed Graziano to station himself immediately outside her room. If no negative incident occurs during the production, surely the gathering afterward will result in some kind of revelation. She, herself, will be in the room supporting Charlotte however she chooses to proceed. It is the ultimate symbol of respect when an officer of New York's finest concedes to permit an amateur to take the lead.

Attendees file into the decorated ballroom, the instrumental music Brooklyn had mentioned supplied by a string quartet made up of two violins, a viola, and a cello. At the moment, they are playing a Hayden piece, originally written to include a harpsichord. A linen-covered table in the rear of the room holds bottles of iced champagne, caviar in white china saucers, soft drinks for teetotalers, and pitchers of ice water.

Charlotte's seat, behind most of the audience, allows her to peruse almost everyone, in her lap a list, which she checks off as those she was expecting enter.

Toby, Antoine Bontemps's roommate, cruises in.

China Olivier smiles at Charlotte and takes a seat near the runway's end.

Papa Charlie Burrus enters with a slow pace, his head pivoting back and forth, taking in the scene.

Aaron Batchelor pauses at the entry, sees Burrus, and wanders over to join him.

Dr. Bruce Landry, appearing harried, scurries in and, with a nervous grin, sits beside Charlotte.

Mother Farivar and Broadway find two chairs in the front row, designated with red ribbons and printed reserved signs, complements of Brooklyn.

Andy Burrus shuffles in slowly, on his face a sneer as he sees his father, and finds a spot on the opposite side of the runway.

To Charlotte's delight, America Lobero, Brooklyn's nurse, tiptoes in, wiggles her fingers at Charlotte, and sits quietly in the rear of the crowd.

As the bells chime, the garrulous group slowly settles down, the noise level shrinking dramatically until only a few guests are left whispering to each other. Amid a healthy round of applause, Brooklyn wheels out onto the crown of the runway, its curved entry a glorious arch of colorful chrysanthemums with their double-headed blooms.

"Welcome to this splendid opportunity to see the newest fashions created by the leading designers in the world. The Donald Trout Agency is proud to feature our lovely models in what we hope and expect will show these amazing Christian Dior designs to their ultimate advantage. Please be aware that on the right side, near the back of the auditorium, there is champagne and other refreshments for your pleasure when the presentation has concluded. You haven't come to this event to hear me talk, so let the show begin."

The music Brooklyn had settled on starts to play, and the first model, Kyla Pino, stalks in, wearing a dazzling chartreuse evening piece, a cashmere pelisse lined with white silk, trimmed with embroidery. On the back of her head is a two-tone, white-green lace cap. A collective inhale fills the ballroom—not only for the uniqueness of the apparel but also for Kyla's stunning beauty.

Broadway's body grows taut—his mother at his side turns to

examine her son's sudden edginess—as he realizes, once more, how he is captivated by this young woman's easy grace. Across the way, China does not miss the slight twist of Broadway's head, the rise of one shoulder, his obvious animation.

Spontaneous applause as Kyla prances to the end of the runway, pivots dramatically, and, with hands on hips, retraces her steps back to the entry.

One by one, the young women and men promenade in front of the admiring audience, bodies and looks complementing their attire, Brooklyn's admonitions dutifully followed: sadness, affront, a look of disdain, primness, haughtiness.

Like an obedient servant, a glaring spotlight pursues every model, illuminating their handsome faces (thank you, Gladys, for the expert makeup!) and stylish fashions.

Beyond the runway area, the room is relatively dark, but Charlotte can make out the several candidates on her suspect list. What gives her pause is that Charlie Burrus and Aaron Batchelor seem uninterested in the display, their heads together as if in some grand conspiracy.

Andy Burrus—as she might expect—is absorbed with some electronic device in his lap, glancing up now and then with a salacious look.

China seems more devoted to watching Broadway than the models, her face, even in the dim light, a portrait of resignation.

To her surprise, Charlotte sees, entering the ballroom, tentative in the unfamiliar territory, peering mightily as if to pierce a hazy barrier, the classic-looking Ian Tenant. He seems to pick out his target, smiles broadly, and slides in past three folks to sit beside China.

Every few moments, Cavanaugh and Graziano, on opposite sides of the runway, whisper softly into a wrist microphone, not expecting trouble but respecting that alertness is paramount. To those who might recognize Shanna, having police in the vicinity could be seen as a comfort in case of any disruption and an alert to one or more who might be living with guilty feelings over trespasses. Not a problem either way for the detective since the primary consideration is the safety of the assembly and the assurance of peace while the exhibition proceeds.

The music is modified as the attire switches from evening to sporty to business wear, and the mood of the models adjusts correspondingly. Charlotte picks up that Mother Farivar is beaming; her little girl, after all, has engineered this magnificent fashion event, and, Charlotte presumes, as a designer herself, Sarah is surely appreciating the distinctiveness of these pieces.

Cavanaugh sidles over to where Charlotte is seated, leans down, and whispers, "Got a call from the ADA. That Groode character bought the deal: we go easy on him, he gives up his contact. Seems as if the arrangement was made with some anonymous second stringer, not any big name. My people are tracking him down and we should be able to apply pressure and find out who hired him. But what we did get was that the payoff was in cash, five grand, which means it came from a hefty money source."

"Very good, Shanna. I doubt that any of these models would have that kind of money to throw around."

"I agree." She slides away, but not before staring hard at Charlie Burrus. Different from Charlotte, Detective Cavanaugh has no hesitation in forming conclusions about criminals, her experience instructing her to grab a perp before he or she can wriggle out of a situation. Many do, she has learned, and once the opportune moment slips by, it is hard to pin a suspect down.

Doesn't clinch anything, Charlotte thinks, *though it narrows down the field, at least when it concerns the attempt to wipe Shanna and me out. I'm still pretty certain there is more than one person involved, and definitely not the same one for the two stairway episodes.*

A curious event now occurs that, at least for Charlotte, is tricky to understand. Corrine Gelly traipses down the runway in her chic, sporty outfit, moving with quick little spurts and an occasional skip— perhaps her view of what a sports-minded woman might do.

When she reaches the end of the runway, she pauses, leans over toward the row of chairs on the left side, smiles broadly, and extends her hand. Daisy Peregrin, the *Times* fashion editor, reaches up and, along with a laugh and a shrug, shakes Corrine's hand.

Titters from the crowd, as Corrine swirls about and ambles back up the runway. Broadway shakes his head as Charlotte and he catch eyes. *Ambitious gal,* Charlotte thinks, *and brassy as hell.*

Before the parade is over, some sixty designs have been displayed, and the dozen models have pranced and spun and cavorted, no glitches, no tumbles, the music a delightful companion to each outfit, the collection clearly appreciated by all.

Quite a successful marriage between designer and displayer, Charlotte ponders, *and one can only guess if it might have been the same or different if Donald Stout had been at the helm.* Perhaps a similar outcome, though, with the performers driven to aberrant emotional levels, for it is, she says to herself, *easy for tyrants to bring about results but at a certain terrible cost.*

There are also no glitches in the crowd, not a single intimation of any trouble, no looks of personal affront, remorse, guilt, or resentment. This event, as far as Charlotte and Shanna perceive it, is kept divorced from the Stout Agency crimes, though, not surprisingly, the underlying message is that the culprit or culprits are clever enough to conceal all emotion.

Kyla is the final spirited model to walk the runway, her last outfit a two-piece suit of gray tweed, with wide lapels and tapered waist, a to-die-for work ensemble that could well be the hit piece of the show. Different from Corrine, she caters to no single observer, stares, with deep-set, dark eyes, at no one and everyone, the consummate professional.

Another emotional reaction, not so curious, but nonetheless powerful, comes from Mother Farivar, as tears spill over and slide down her puffy cheeks. Charlotte understands that, despite the success of this adventure, and despite Sarah's daughter's leadership in pulling it off, it could have been Brooklyn up there commanding the attention of the principals of the fashion world, Brooklyn as the finale model wearing the favorite pieces and being adored by the multitude. That, after all, before the ugly tragedy, was Sarah's goal for her magnificent daughter: to be in the spotlight, soar with success, the ultimate star.

Charlotte sees that Broadway, finding it difficult to contain his feelings, is ready to leap up and embrace Kyla, obviously beside himself with passion. *Yes, decisions are often made for us, nothing spoken, absent any grand pronouncement, and isn't Kyla going to be absolutely delighted when today's function has concluded, triumphant as a professional and triumphant in her personal life?*

Seated beside the Broadway icon, Ian Tenant, who is looking confused and dismayed at his companion's sudden display of sadness, China cries.

More than a fashion show, Charlotte thinks. *The end of something and the beginning of something else, all accomplished without a word being said. Perhaps, with the choice being made in this way, there will be no tragedy, no outright loser, though China will certainly require some healing. Thank you, Mr. Tenant, for being on the threshold, ready to take up the slack.*

The entire show is an hour and twenty minutes long, and when Kyla retreats under the arch of chrysanthemums, Brooklyn wheels out amid a steady rise of applause. She smiles as if suddenly realizing how appreciated the entire presentation has been, also applauds, and then, to the absolute wonderment of all who know her, lifts herself out of the wheelchair and stands.

35

There are two receptions: the general refreshment spread and post-program appraisal in the grand ballroom and the more private gathering upstairs in Charlotte's room, the latter for the entire modeling cast and specifically invited guests. The first will go on for half an hour or so; the second will begin when the models can change into their own clothing, remove makeup, and gather themselves for the transition.

When Brooklyn's unconscious act of rising to her feet occurs, Dr. Bruce Landry almost leaps out of his chair. To Charlotte, he yells, "It's happening! She's doing it!"

It takes only a minute for several friends to surround her, which at first she thinks to be congratulations for a successful show. But Broadway points to her posture and whispers hoarsely, "Look at yourself. Look what you're doing."

This brings a little yelp, and, in an instant, she and her mother are hugging each other, both Farivar women letting the tears flow.

China, knowing instinctively that she is not included in the family rejoicing, pauses in the shadows, Ian Tenant at her side. As she watches, she sees Kyla join the celebration, and yes, she is welcomed in. A sad smile flits across China's colorful face, and she waves at the group, aware that no one sees her.

While the downstairs celebration is continuing, Shanna and Charlotte enter the elevator to the eighteenth floor to make final preparations for what will hopefully be a climax to the sordid crimes at Donald Stout's Modeling Agency.

"Do you believe in serendipity?" Charlotte asks.

"I might if I knew what it was."

"Let me explain it with an example. During the Croatian Wars, thousands of land mines were planted, and though many were removed at the end of the war, hundreds remained hidden underground. Because of that, people have avoided that area of the Balkans, cautious of the danger. Well, as a result, the one major lake and several streams are teeming with fish, the land's animal population flourishing. Wild groundhogs, with their excellent sense of smell, stay away from buried metal, and their numbers have soared. So, you see, because of one terrible action—the planting of land mines—and the resulting absence of humans, wildlife is thriving. That is serendipity."

"By chance, one group benefits from another group's actions."

"You got it."

"Okay, now how is that relevant?"

"We're about to find out. Because of the actions of our friend, Groode, the warning phone call I got, the scrambled notes, and even the attempt by Stout to punish Brooklyn for dumping him, we may have a pattern that will reveal what the movies refer to as the bad guys."

"All right, Charlotte! The New York City Police Department would officially like to put you on the payroll. What do you think about that?"

"Not much. I can't wait 'til this whole business is over so I can get back to my tranquil life in rural Pennsylvania."

"You'll be bored. There will be another trumpet sounding your name."

"That's what my brother in California keeps saying. I tell him to bite his tongue."

They enter room 1840, the door already open and a single server stationed near a resplendently set buffet table adorned not only with a variety of food and drink but with two elegant vases filled with long-stem yellow roses.

"Broadway knows his way around," Charlotte says.

Shanna helps herself to a turkey sandwich on a pint-sized roll, wanders about the large parlor room, and nods to Charlotte. "Easy to monitor folks in here, no visual blocks and no tricky, hidden corners."

"Say, Shanna, before we call the meeting to order, I would like to spend a few minutes with Brent White and, after him, with Corrine Gelly. There are some questions that need to be addressed. I can go into the bedroom where it's private."

"I won't even ask what the questions are. You know what you're looking for, so go for it."

"I'm not trying to keep secrets from you, but it's just that I have hunches and I don't want to mess up the facts because of them. It's a good idea for one of us to keep away from 'maybe' and 'possibly,' and hold on to what we know for sure."

"Yeah. Cops don't work that way. We go wild over the littlest clue and jump to conclusions. I'm learning a lot from watching how measured your reactions are."

"How sweet of you. I've never had a better investigative colleague—no insult meant to Augie Hartunian. Agreeable fellow, Hartunian, and a capable country cop, more cognitive than intuitive, and that, to his credit, was why he wanted me around."

Charlotte picks off three or four seedless red grapes from the smorgasbord and pops them into her mouth. "Got to have my antioxidants before facing the contamination of criminal suspects."

"For what it's worth, I do believe that Charlie Burrus has his dirty fingers in this stew. He's a wealthy and seedy crook, and I see his motive as wanting to avoid his son sullying his name. Punish the kid for being irresponsible, and, at the same time, pay people off to keep him from crashing and burning."

"Oh, I agree that Papa Burrus is an odious person. I dislike his ugly prejudices and the way he manipulates poor, clueless Andy. About his guilt in Brooklyn's fall and Stout's murder?—well, that's another story."

Through the open door, Broadway hurries in. "Did you see that? Wasn't that amazing? She didn't even realize. What a breakthrough!"

"Quite a gal," Charlotte replies.

"Wanted to get up here to be sure everything is okay."

"See for yourself. Looks wonderful."

"Feed 'em and then finger 'em," Shanna says with a little laugh.

"Pretty good day for the Farivar family. Kyla is a sweetheart."

The switch in topics catches Broadway for a moment, but he recovers quickly and says, "I love her. I've always loved her. In a different way, I've been pulled by China, but Ian Tenant savors her, so I think she'll be fine."

"Do you think China and her pal, Tenant, will join us for the party?"

"Not sure. Why? Is it important for them to be here?"

"Not as suspects, but as observers and maybe to support what we come up with. As to love, the young have resiliency," Charlotte philosophizes. "I read somewhere that many youth fall in love ten times before the age of twenty."

"Depends on your definition," Shanna puts in.

"I was in love only once before, but it didn't work out," Broadway says. "I think I've been…well, in lust with China, but really in love with Kyla."

"Guess I knew that all along."

The three in the room turn their heads to see, in the hall, a solemn China Olivier.

"China…" Broadway begins.

"No, not a problem. I told Ian to wait for me down below and came up to tell you I understand. I realize I was a late addition. You were hooked into Kyla for a long time, even when she was paired off with that boy. For a few days, I thought I had an outside chance, but…well, not going to happen."

"You're…you're spectacular," Broadway blurts out. "You know that, don't you?"

"I know I'm your second choice. In some ways, even that is flattering."

"We'll be working together for months."

"And I look forward to that." She hesitates and adds, "Ian is a good man, super talented, and fanatically adored among the groupies. I have to count myself fortunate that he wants me—though who knows how long that will last."

"Don't want to butt in," Charlotte says, "however, you, Ms. China, are positively extraordinary. Have you been listening to yourself? Do you see how open and understanding you are? This has to be a loss for you, and you're taking it with courage and a generous heart. My respect goes out to you."

These words bring tears as China strides up to Charlotte, hugs her, turns to Broadway, leans in to kiss him gently on the mouth, wheels about, and scurries out of the room.

—

The single server attending the buffet, a thin Latino man dressed in white, has been standing at attention like a palace guard, the only movement his eyes, which jiggled back and forth as each person commented. Now, as the next guest, Sarah Farivar, enters, he alters his position to behind the long table, sets a permanent smile on his face, and waits.

In a moment, the first models, Andrea and Deana, arrive, followed by Phillipa and Corrine, who, to Broadway's surprise, are holding hands.

Charlotte simply nods.

Charlie Burrus and Aaron Batchelor are next, both beaming as if the show had been their personal triumph.

Batchelor comments, "Spirited lady, our Brook. She'll be running a marathon before long."

Our Brook. Charlotte's face is inscrutable, while her thoughts consider the notion that Aaron Batchelor is some kind of narcissistic fool, spurned by Brooklyn yet insistent upon intruding into her life.

Burrus is the first to help himself to champagne, three bottles resting in buckets of ice.

The tall, fragile model Julia enters, along with Antoine Bontemps and his hippy roommate, Toby. The sight of food pulls Toby to the buffet, and she begins to adorn a plate with little tea sandwiches, strawberries, macaroons, and red grapes.

The room, now beginning to fill, attendees dividing up into various conversation groups, depending on who knows whom, Charlotte and Shanna watching carefully the way people align themselves.

"Since she's already here, think I'll invite Corrine to join me in the bedroom for a couple of minutes," Charlotte whispers. "I doubt she'll make a fuss. Hold down the fort."

"Consider it held," Shanna answers as she steps to the doorway to ensure that Graziano is in the hall.

Andy Burrus grins at her—she is, after all, an attractive woman—as he slips past her, into room 1840, sees his father, and walks to the opposite side of the smorgasbord. He is alone, and Broadway, realizing this, wonders which of the models he is likely to pick up on next.

"Hello there, Corrine. Quite an add-on to your runway work, reaching out for the *Times* critic."

"Just having a little fun." She smiles at Phillipa. "That gal doesn't know me; maybe now she will."

"I wonder if I could speak with you alone for a couple of minutes. Come join me in my bedroom."

"What about?"

"The same. Still trying to sort out those terrible events."

Her look is belligerent, yet she nods slightly and follows toward the bedroom door, which Charlotte opens to allow them both in, then closes behind them.

They are away for only eight minutes and, at one point, hear applause from the front room, Charlotte surmising that Brooklyn has rolled in.

When they return to the parlor area, all expected attendees have arrived; Shanna winks at Charlotte as a circle of people surround Brooklyn.

Broadway and Charlotte had agreed on a gift for his sister, anticipating the grand result of the show, and he now waves his hands and calls out, "Please, everyone, a moment of your attention!"

The gathering, some twenty or so, settles down, some curious, others appearing rather surprised at this call to order; a party, yes, but a formal meeting of some kind?

"Every one of you in the troupe deserves high praise for a job well done. Since you asked my sister to help guide you through this enterprise, I wish to pay special tribute to her and her efforts.

"The fact that she is healing from her injury is an unexpected bonus in today's doings. I'm sure we all are pulling for her complete recovery—and in record time.

"My friend, Charlotte Smart, and I have joined to present to Brooklyn a little gift as appreciation for her stellar work in the Stout Agency's finest achievement. Who knows where this company will go next, but for now…all of you rock!"

He produces from a corner chair a bulky, wrapped box decorated with a yellow bow on top, slides over to his sister, and with a loving grin, hands it to her.

Gratitude mixed with embarrassment light up Brooklyn's face, Charlotte aware that this lovely young woman is self-effacing and, while used to being in front of audiences, not totally comfortable being the one honored person in the room.

Carefully, she removes the bow and lifts the lid from the gift box, reaches in, and removes a statuette of a stylishly clad dancer poised on a revolving base. Broadway had wound the stem on the base and set it with a rubber band, reaches over to remove the band, and, as he does, the dancer begins to spin to music: Come on along and listen to, the lullaby of Broadway; The hip hooray and ballyhoo, the lullaby of Broadway....

Charlotte says, "An appropriate melody. You and your family of models have created a new lullaby of Broadway." She looks over at Sara Farivar, wondering if this grand recognition of her daughter's talent is enough. Sarah seems content, but with her, the outside façade often hides an inside bitterness.

"Enjoy the snacks and drinks," Broadway says. "In a few minutes, there will be another ceremony." He looks over at Charlotte and dips his head slightly.

Charlotte approaches Brent White. "Excuse me, Brent. I have a couple more questions to ask you. Would you mind joining me for a moment in the other room?"

"Why not?" Brent says as he steps away from Andrea, the tall model with almost perfect coffee-colored skin.

Again, Charlotte leads her interviewee into the bedroom, closes the door, and is gone for close to ten minutes.

Though burning with curiosity, Shanna knows that her amateur friend's business with these suspects will soon be revealed. She waits patiently for the meeting part of the gathering to begin.

Charlotte emerges from the bedroom smiling, approaches Broadway, and says to him softly, "My young friend, we are ready. Please call this little flock of beautiful people to order."

36

"Ladies and gentlemen," Broadway says in his projecting actor's voice, "alas, along with this joyous celebration, we also have to remember that there have been some terrible events shrouding our lives over the past weeks. We have with us this late afternoon a member of the New York City police"—he throws out his arm toward Shanna—"Detective Shanna Cavanaugh. She and a friend of our family, Charlotte Smart, have been investigating the two falls down the Stout Agency stairs. Since all of you here are familiar with the principals involved, as well as the locale, it seems the perfect time to pursue what these two insightful women have been researching. So. I hope you will all cooperate for a few minutes as we explore some evidence that many of you can help us with."

Shanna defers to Charlotte, who moves in front of the food table and faces the assembly. "Folks, by now, you all know that Brooklyn's fall was a deliberate act of treachery, pulled off, for some obscure reason, by a disgruntled perpetrator. That terrible act was followed by—and there is no ameliorating way to say this—the murder of Mr. Donald Stout."

"Cool," Toby says. "Sherlock Holmes tracks down the perps."

"Well, yes," Charlotte says. "In fact, you are correct. It is plural. More than one culprit is involved. In every criminal act there has to be motive. And, dear me, in these instances, there are ample motives to point the finger at numerous folks."

"Good. About time we find out who did this thing to my Brook."

"Since you spoke up, Sarah, let's focus on you for a moment. It is certain that you did not try to hurt your own daughter, but once that act occurred, you had ample motive to take vengeance on the person you kept saying did that to her: Donald Stout. Only a few of you know that Stout was killed by a blow to the back of the head with a heavy metal object, which the police forensics team concluded was a round-headed hammer. Stout kept a toolbox in his office, was the builder himself of the wooden runway in his studio, and a mock-up model of a studio he was designing—that model kept in his office as well. After his death, the police searched for the murder weapon, but there was no hammer in the toolbox. Someone had used it and either kept or disposed of it."

"So, what do I know about hammers and toolboxes?"

"Oh, no one is accusing you, Sarah. We are simply laying out the evidence surrounding both violent acts. However, it is true that when Stout's body was found, and the police and others were milling about, you appeared at the top of the back stairs and were invited to come around to the rear door of the Antwerp Building. The point being that you apparently did know your way around that edifice."

"I heard what happened, so I wandered back there to look for the scene. That's all. Nothing else."

"Yes, I imagine that is the case. And another person appeared at that scene, also an outsider and also at the back door."

She turns and fixes on Andy Burrus. "You, young Andy, showed up there as if you knew exactly where to go."

"Bullshit. Yeah, I knew there was a back entrance. Kyla told me. So what? It doesn't mean anything."

"It doesn't mean you killed Stout, is that what you're saying?"

"I hardly knew the bastard."

"True, but at first you were the beneficiary of his largess. Your generous daddy, wanting to point you away from an unacceptable woman from Washington Heights, paid Stout to favor Kyla Pino if Kyla would be your girlfriend, though, heaven knows, talented and beautiful as she is, she hardly needed any favoring. Yes, she has deep regrets over that deal; however, in the modeling business, deals are made all the time, and getting ahead is often the result.

"Your problem, dear Andy, is that when Daddy cut off the cash, you needed funds desperately to sustain your drug habit and maintain your sports car. Someone who needed a dirty task done could well have bribed you in exchange for currency. To put it frankly, since Kyla was next in line after Brooklyn, you could have had motive to hurt her and later could have had motive to polish off Stout."

"Lady, you're dreaming. I ain't no killer."

"Notice that I said 'could,' not 'did.' Sorry to be preaching, but you certainly need to get your life together. It's no wonder that Daddy Burrus is fed up with you."

"Don't speak for me, woman!" Charlie Burrus yells.

Graziano appears in the doorway to the hall, as Shanna, raising her hand to keep him away, replies, "Settle down, Mr. Burrus. Sit on your temper. This is an investigation, not a debate."

"I apologize if you think I am speaking for you, Charlie. My information about your son comes directly from you. I am only repeating what I've heard you say."

His look could terrify children, but, aware that he is in the presence of police, he does what Shanna asks—sits, though reluctantly, on his temper.

"At first," Charlotte continues, "we were investigating an ugly attempt to harm Brooklyn, but when Stout was killed, it became a double crime, and, more than likely, with two different culprits.

"You, Charlie Burrus, while on the fringe of the Stout Agency, had, and still have, mixed feelings about your wayward son, Andy. It makes sense you would want to teach him a lesson so he wouldn't sully your family's name and yet protect him from serious harm. No, you had no reason to want to injure Brooklyn, but you could (that word again) have disliked Stout for his callous manner, and you could have seen a threat to Andy after the detective and I seemed to be on his trail for Stout's murder.

"That leads me to another event, which most of you know nothing about. Out on Broadway, a short time ago, Detective Cavanaugh and I were almost hit by a car, deliberately attempting to run us down. The driver has been captured, and his disclosure will be revealed in a moment."

She pauses as the impact of her revelation stuns the group so that, if it were possible, a more intense attention is now paid to Charlotte's analysis.

Brooklyn, in a soft voice, says, "Oh, Charlotte, that is horrible. What sick people are doing these things?"

"Sorry to say it, Brook, but look around—all of you. The

culpable parties are in this room."

This cryptic truth is a massive shock to many present. Eyes dart back and forth, a few people seem to shrink away, dark-eyed Deanna eases her back against the wall, fragile Julia settles into a soft chair and makes herself small.

Sarah Farivar is the first to speak.

"So, let's hear it. Who are the rats that did all this?"

Shanna says, "Yes, Ms. Farivar, we all want justice. Charlotte is cruising now. Let her continue at her own pace."

"Thank you, Detective. Everyone has a unique pace; I'm sorry if mine is either too slow or too fast for some. But this is a tricky case, with lots of tangents and ulterior motives. It has taken a while to flesh it out, and with everybody's help, I'm expecting more of it to be revealed in the next few minutes."

"Not sure why you need me here, but, hey, this is fun," Toby blurts out.

"I'd like to turn for a moment to you, Phillipa. You were once a victim, and since the stairs seem to be the mode of attack in all these situations, it would help a bit to recount what happened to you."

"I fell, that's all."

"Ah, but that is not all. You claimed to have been either high or tipsy, so your fall was a fuzzy memory. Luckily, you were not injured as badly, but some of the pre-fall facts are eerily similar to those that occurred with Brooklyn. You had less of a connection with Stout than she, yet you were his little experiment for a time—as were several of you here. I'm not being critical when I say that; I know the pressures that build in this business and the power a man like Stout had to influence your careers."

"He was a boor and a letch," Kyla murmurs.

"And then, as with all of Stout's playmates, either he tires of them or they realize the ignominy of what they are doing. Self-respect surges up, and the young beauties—as with Brooklyn—break it off with the tyrant boss.

"Though you don't own up to it, our best guess is that you had had enough of Donald Stout and told him you were no longer interested in his office shenanigans. Of course, he could not tolerate getting dumped, so whether you were loaded or not, it is highly likely that you do recall getting a little help from 'the man' in getting down those stairs. But since your career was on the line, you shut it down.

An accident. No one's fault."

"Where are you coming up with all this?"

"You weren't as closed-mouthed as you wished to be. At least one of your friends knew the truth."

Phillipa struggles for a moment; secrets that open out to public view are surrendered with pain.

At last, she says, "Okay. So, what happened was I told Donald I would no longer be his little whore, and he blew a gasket. We were at the top of the back stairs, and sparks were flying. He insulted me so I pushed him in the chest. That pissed him off even more, and he pushed me back, only too hard, and I went down the steps. He did follow, to attend to me—he could see my arm was injured—but the first thing he said was that nobody can know about this. If I wanted to keep my job, I would have to tell people I tripped. So that's it. It wasn't like he was trying to break my neck or anything."

"Which it was with Brooklyn. A deliberate blow to the back. But, young woman, it does leave a residue of deep resentment. You had ample reason to want to hurt Donald Stout."

"So did just about everyone in this room."

"My comment was not an accusation but simply a fact. And yes, there were many who had issues with the big boss. Which leads us to another set of facts. Stout was struck from behind with a round-headed hammer. As I mentioned, in his office he kept a toolbox, and upon examination, it was found that there was no hammer in the box. The killer took Stout's own hammer, approached him from behind, delivered the fatal blow, and kept the weapon with him…or her. It must be obvious to all of you that the culprit in this terrible deed was known to Stout—not a stranger—and likely someone he had been conversing with."

37

The group is silent for a moment, the implications of Charlotte's comments slowly seeping in. Finally, Batchelor says, with a shrug, "Lots of hypotheses here, but no witnesses and no proof. What's obviously needed is to know who was in Stout's office with him before they headed out the back way."

"To be sure, Mr. Batchelor," Charlotte says at once. "And here is some information that might help with that. Forensics people have determined that Donald Stout had engaged in sexual activity a short time before his body went down the stairs. We know that he was a philanderer, and many of you also know that he had girlfriends and boyfriends. Loyalty with him amounted to nothing. However, it makes a lot of sense that, before being killed, he did not have sex with Brooklyn, who is in a wheelchair and who had kissed him off, with Phillipa, who rejected his advances many months before, or with Kyla, who was off limits to him because of a deal with Daddy Burrus."

"Peeling the onion," Detective Cavanaugh says softly.

"The examining crew also reported," Charlotte resumes, "that no residue of a recent sexual event was found in Stout's office, on his couch, or anywhere else in his room. Now, that may not be obvious to all of you, but what it tells the investigators is that Mr. Stout likely did not have penetrating sex with anyone, but rather, what has come to be known these days as, and I hope I shock no one when I say this, oral sex."

"Disgusting," Sarah Farivar mutters.

With a twist of his head, Broadway announces, "Either with a man or a woman."

"And that leads us to another important juncture," Charlotte says.

"I'm fed up with all these junctures. It's all hocus-pocus to me. What in hell are you looking for? Who needs all this crap?" Charlie Burrus rises as if readying to leave.

"Please, Mr. Burrus, stay put," Shanna says, fixing her eyes on his puffy, pink face. "We all have to see this through to the end. My guess is we will be well rewarded when Ms. Smart gets to the finale."

"Thank you, Detective. This next point has to do with who, of all in this room, had easy access to Donald Stout's office. His girlfriends, of course, until he was through with them, any boyfriends he had as well, and…a person he had assigned to be a monitor, to receive incoming mail, and be sure the studio and other areas were neat and clean. I'm speaking of…"—she turns to her right and faces Corinne—"…you, young woman."

"Hey, he fired me, remember? Yeah, I wanted back in, but he wouldn't let me."

"You wanted back in when you knew that Brooklyn was out of the modeling picture. But, before you were let go, you had ample access to all the materials in the agency and to Stout's office. Here is another maybe scenario: maybe you stashed away his hammer before Stout kicked you out or sneaked in there and lifted it when no one else was around. Maybe you planned to pay him back when the opportunity presented itself."

"Baloney! I had no options. For me, the Stout Agency was the only game in town. I'd be nuts to burn my bridges."

"You had no bridges until, thanks to Brooklyn's generosity, you were called back in, and that was after Stout's death. What we do know, and this is critical, is that you were recommended to Brooklyn by her former boyfriend, Mr. Aaron Batchelor." She gestures toward Batchelor, who opens both hands out to the side as if to say, *So what?*

"We'll get to his motives in a moment, but for now, suffice it to say that you are definitely in the mix for both Brooklyn's fall and Stout's death.

"Now, we also have a couple of little notes that the perpetrator, in his egotistic zeal, decided to post for our pleasure. One was an admission of guilt in Stout's murder, the other a threat—basically to me, or perhaps even the detective, if she got too close to fingering him. I say 'him' because the writer referred to a woman in one of his notes, a woman whom he called a dyke—and I presume you all know what that is."

"Geez, this is a complicated package," Antoine mewls.

"It gets more complicated," Charlotte answers. "For example, we know that Brooklyn was propelled down the stairs by someone from behind, striking her with a heavy object. Officers have determined that a floor wax container, kept in the closet at the head of the stairs, was the weapon. Who knew about the closet? Who might have been hiding out there? And who would know to use the canister to assault Brooklyn just as she strolled by toward the stairs?"

"Twenty questions!" Toby shouts out.

"*Dios mio*," America Lobero murmurs softly.

"The answers aren't simple, because someone on the inside could easily have told someone on the outside, so that almost anyone could have been the closeted culprit." Charlotte smiles at her own alliteration.

"But, as you might suspect, there were fingerprints on the container." She stops to let this indicting comment hang in the air.

"Fingerprints and DNA, the foolproof methods for tracking down guilty parties. What amazing developments for law enforcement! But, along with the detailed facts in every case, there are also innuendos, hunches, guesses, and, most of all, intuition. Anyone investigating a crime needs to use all approaches and also all of the senses. I, for one, have a rather keen sense of smell, which I shall address in just a moment. But first, let me turn to the male models, Brent and Antoine."

"All right!" Toby blurts out.

"What did I do?" Antoine stands suddenly, as if he has just sat on a pin.

"What you didn't do is important for this case," Charlotte replies. "Donald Stout was infuriated when Brooklyn, as they say, dumped him. And, since you, Brent, were close to Stout—more than close, actually—he tried to manipulate you into punishing your good friend. Probably not hurt her badly, but because he already knew, with poor Phillipa there, how to vault someone down stairs, teach her a lesson about who was boss. To your credit, you would not hurt Brooklyn but suggested to Antoine that you might put in a good word to Stout if Antoine, one way or another, would discipline Brooklyn. To your credit, Antoine, you also refused.

"So, neither of you was the culprit in Brooklyn's tumble. In fact, I must say that when Stout was killed, I was quite aware, Brent, that you were distraught. Well, of course. Any loss of connection, if it had intimacy at all, is tragic.

"But I also want to note that you were around on the day that Brooklyn fell, and did see her in the studio. I guessed that you might also have seen someone else hanging around that day, though you were reluctant to come forward about who."

"I didn't see who hurt Brook. For all I knew, Donald could have been the one."

"I didn't say you saw the crime, but you did see someone there that day, other than Stout and Brooklyn."

"Well…" He stops, peers about the room, and lets his gaze settle, at last, on Corrine. "Corrine had an appointment with Donald. She had told me she wanted back in, and I had said to go talk to the man. That was earlier, so I assumed she had already left."

"Assumed," Charlotte says, "but you were wrong. Corrine, who was aware of the layout of the second floor as well as anyone, knew exactly where to seclude herself when Brooklyn came by. No one really expected her to be around since Stout had let her go, but the forensics people found several sets of prints on the weapon used to hurt Brooklyn. Yes, Stout's were on it, and yes, so were Corrine's. That, in itself, might not be proof since Corrine was the monitor in charge of supplies and could have fingered the canister earlier. Ah, but I mentioned my sense of smell, and there is no way what I smelled in that little closet could have lingered for weeks. What was it? It was a gender-neutral perfume called Black Midnight, pretty strong stuff, and the same perfume I smelled when Broadway and I interviewed Corrine at her job in the museum two days ago."

"Lots of people like Black Midnight," Corrine protests.

"I don't think so. It is a perfume-slash-cologne for men or women. And you, Corrine, though reluctant to admit it, are a bisexual person and attracted to a scent that, though secretly, makes a statement about your sexual preferences."

"You're out of your mind, old lady."

"I may be a pretty old lady, but I am not out of my mind."

Shanna edges toward Corrine, not in fear that she would bolt, since Graziano is clearly visible in the doorway, but to keep her from any precipitous move against Charlotte.

"Having a propensity to love a man or a woman is no crime, and I, for one, have no issues with your love leanings. Take Phillipa, for example, who just admitted carrying on for a time with Stout and who, clearly, is enamored of you. She can love either a man or a woman. And so, Corrine, can you.

"For a time, I had a hunch that an outsider, fed information by you—or perhaps another insider—might have done the deed against Brooklyn. And it did not have to be someone who left fingerprints." She turns toward Batchelor. "You, Mr. Batchelor, like to dress fashionably, and that includes cashmere or leather gloves. Gloves do not leave prints."

Batchelor, who had been leaning against a sidewall, now takes a step forward. "This is becoming ludicrous." He turns to Detective Cavanaugh. "Why in the hell are you standing around, letting this elderly woman, who is clearly muddled, indict everyone in this room?"

"Hey, it's no fun when the toss of the dice looks as if it's going to land on your number. Best if you button up and listen," Shanna says.

"What we have here," Charlotte picks up, "is actually three crimes. One is the ugly attack on Brooklyn, the second is the murder of Donald Stout, and the third is the attempted murder of Detective Cavanaugh and me out on the street. It is now quite obvious that each of these was engineered by a different person.

"Furious as you were at Stout for letting you go, Corrine, and him not listening to your plea to be brought back in, you twisted your thinking into believing that if you could eliminate his top model, he would have to reinstate you. That day, after meeting with Stout, you concealed yourself, powerful perfume and all, in the closet at the top of the stairs, waited for Brooklyn to pass by, slipped out, and struck her from behind with the heavy canister."

A pitiful whine escapes Corrine as she places her forearm over her eyes. The entire room is stunned into breathless silence. Brooklyn's face has turned pale. Broadway's is like a thundercloud.

Sarah Farivar, her anguish over her daughter's violator now focused, says, with venom, "You vampire!"

"What must have destroyed your motive and caused much suffering was when Brooklyn, asked to coordinate the important fashion show, was compassionate and invited you to rejoin the ensemble. But we also have to remember that Mr. Batchelor here, pleaded with Brooklyn to offer you and Antoine amnesty and a chance to work with the group. Brilliant move, the inclusion of Antoine in the request! It was camouflage, though, since disgruntled about not being used enough, he was already a solid member. But it helped Batchelor to disguise the fact that he had agreed to pay Corrine back for a favor she did him.

"That favor was to give him a complete picture of the second floor of the Antwerp Building, the intrigues that were going on, Stout's latest conquests and losses, how to access the back and front stairs, the exits, and the ingress into Stout's private area."

Batchelor's voice is hoarse and noxious. "There a vendetta against any who oppose the Farivars? Who's paying her, after all? They are. She's gloriously earning her salary."

"For your information, Batchelor," Broadway growls, "Ms. Smart is receiving zilch for her help with these awful crimes."

"You see," Charlotte continues, "Mr. Batchelor here, informed by Corrine that Brooklyn had dumped Stout, simply assumed that it was Stout who had assaulted her on the front stairs. We now know that he was wrong. Corrine, in her distorted attempt to win Stout's favor, had done that. But Batchelor, egotist that he is, and with the disdain he has for women in general—and lesbian women in particular—decided to avenge Brooklyn's fall.

"The disdain part is that the very person he used for information, Corrine, filled him with revulsion. The egotistic part is that he was compelled to brag about what he did, with a posted note written as an anagram and another trying to intimidate me, along with a threatening phone call.

"Okay, so we can give him one plus, and that is that he carried a wounded heart around for the past year over Brooklyn telling him that they were incompatible. Of course, she is a magnificent woman, so who wouldn't want to hold on to her? When she was hurt, he showed up with flowers and a check, offering to pay her medical expenses.

"Poor, gullible Corrine provided him entry into Stout's office, where, when no one was around, he may have either pilfered Stout's own hammer or had it presented to him by Corrine. The timing here is everything because Corrine, still intent upon getting back in, made an appointment with Stout—yes, Corrine, he jotted it down on his calendar—to plead her case. How did she plead it? By servicing him! Alas, not a pleasant thing to discuss.

"He, of course, still rejected her and, as she told me herself, laughed with disdain.

"Also on Stout's calendar was a penciled-in note that an Aaron Batchelor wanted to take him to dinner to discuss financial support for the Stout enterprise. On that pretext, Batchelor entered his office only half an hour after the frustrated Corrine was gone, and yes, Mr. Batchelor, clever as you are with finances, you are an amateur when it comes to crime.

"You failed to consider that, when you asked to meet with Stout, like any dutiful entrepreneur, he jotted down the appointment on his calendar pad. Also, America Lobero, Brooklyn's nurse, at my request, saved a drinking glass with your prints on it, and the police were able to match it to prints found in Stout's office, on the edge of his desk. You and he were about to leave through the back stairs when you viciously struck Stout on the head. Payback, you thought, for hurting the love of your life, Brooklyn Farivar!"

"You have nothing! No weapon, no proof. So what if I was interested in supporting Stout's agency? It would help Brooklyn."

"Yes, you might argue that; however, for one thing, you are the last person to be in Stout's presence, the last appointment on his calendar pad, and, for another, Brooklyn once mentioned that you are a pack rat, never discarding anything, and that your home, as well as your office, are like jam-packed storage spaces. Given your involvement in this business, Detective Cavanaugh was able to secure a search warrant, and as we speak, officers are poring through your private areas. Already, they have reported that they are prying open a locked cabinet in your office, and I will lay odds that you have stashed your nasty murder weapon in there."

"You can't do that! Police can't invade someone's privacy. There are laws. It won't fly in any court."

"That remains to be seen. But sir, it is contemptible to use your hands in a close encounter to destroy the life of another human being, and sad that you must live with that image for the rest of your life. I dare say it will haunt your dreams and infiltrate your thoughts. Because of a spurned romance and an ugly vindictive bent, a man of your status will spend twenty years in a prison cell. A killer has no peace."

As happens so often, when faced with truth, a perpetrator

discomposes and blurts out what amounts to a confession.

"He was scum. He had it coming!"

Shanna answers him: "Even scum are protected by law."

Broadway is smiling. He was right in calling Charlotte in. This perspicacious woman is pulling the whole thing together the way Agatha Christie might have written it. The crowd is subdued, and, surprisingly, one might expect the accused to be more frantic, go crazy with protest. Could be another twist or two since Charlotte is full of surprises.

As if reading his thoughts, Charlotte turns to the elder Burrus and says, "You, Mr. Burrus, have obviously not been pleased with little Andy, your wayward son, getting financial aid from your business associate, especially since you desperately want him to learn self-reliance. Aaron Batchelor buying information from him, or, for that matter, from Corrine or even Antoine, goes against your tough-love doctrine. But, no mistake about it, tough or not, you are intent on protecting your indolent son from crashing and burning."

"Lady, you're speaking for me again."

"Not really. I'm speaking about you. Your actions speak for you. Since Detective Cavanaugh and I implied that Andy could be a suspect in one of these two terrible acts, you have chafed with concern that he would be arrested and the Burrus name would be dragged into the gutter.

"Alas, the detective and I got a little too close, and, in your exaggerated sense of power—both you and Batchelor believing money can solve every problem—you decided to buy a way to eliminate the threat. You, Charlie Burrus, are the culprit behind the attempt to have a hired hand run Detective Cavanaugh and me down."

Burrus waves his hand in disgust. "I agree with Aaron. A meddling old fool. You don't know what the hell you're talking about."

"Oh, it's not what I'm talking about. Your once-removed attempted-assassin did what the police have a name for. He sang. And the payoff contact he named works for you. The indictment is clear, and instead of Andy sullying the Burrus family name, you did it all by yourself."

"Hah!" Andy blurts out.

"Three crooks," Sarah mutters.

"Two attempted murders and one murder," Shanna Cavanaugh says. "And, with the car event out on Broadway, if attempted murder won't stick, the D.A. can file for conspiracy."

For Brooklyn, this entire climactic scene is bewildering. Corrine was never an enemy. Why had she taken out her frustration that way? Ambition trashes decency, corrupts any sense of humane behavior. And Aaron—a frustrated womanizer, wealthy to a fault, a vengeful misanthrope—distorted their relationship and confused Donald's anger with Corrine's desperation. And Charlie Burrus? She didn't know him enough to comprehend his ugly act. Sad family, and good that Kyla is free of them.

Kyla is the next to speak. "Get yourself a job, Andy. Sell that overpriced sports buggy and, with the forty grand you get, try to begin a new, decent life."

All at once, Corrine begins to sob. "Brook, I…I'm not a bad person. You've been good to me. I wish I could take back what I did and make you whole again. Donald's shadow hangs over all of us."

To the amazement of everyone in the room, Brooklyn pushes herself up, out of her chair, and as she does, Broadway takes a step toward her, but Charlotte reaches out and restrains him. Dr. Bruce Landry, on the other side, has one hand on the wheelchair and the other extended, as if ready to catch Brooklyn if she falls.

For a moment, she stands still, a single finger lightly touching the chair's arm, then, without a word, she moves her left leg forward several inches, following with the right. She repeats this five times until she is facing Corrine, who has dissolved in anguish, a hand over her face.

Brooklyn opens her arms, and Corrine leans in.

"It's okay, Corrine. I forgive you."

38

On the television show *Law and Order*, as soon as the detectives weave through the evidence and nail the bad guys, the uniforms appear, as if by magic, to haul them away. In this instance, Shanna had alerted her precinct people to send three officers to Charlotte's room, wait in the hall with Graziano, and march in at a signal from her.

As the police enter and cuff the three exposed culprits, Brooklyn, back in her chair, wheels up to Detective Cavanaugh.

"Look, Detective, I don't want to press charges against Corrine Gelly. She's as much a victim here as anyone."

"Oh," Shanna replies, "well, that's fine, but the district attorney will have to sort all that out. She did commit a crime, and whether she's held accountable or not, she has to be booked—at least for now."

Charlotte, listening to this exchange, touches Brooklyn on the shoulder. "Sweetheart, you are something else. I'm no expert on precious gems, but I'd call you the rarest of diamonds."

"You want to let that rotten girl go?" Mother Sarah asks rhetorically, her disapproval of the matter unmistakable.

When no one chooses to answer, Broadway faces his mother, his posture combative.

"Mother, it's about time you hear this. You are a punitive person. You criticize and control. Whether you realize it or not, Brook and I are not like you. I'm not saying you're hopeless or anything, but you need to soften your manner and throw away the whip. Compassion is a virtue. Forgiveness builds character. I love you, and I know Brook does too, but we also want to like you better. Can't you see that Brook's gesture toward a person who hurt her is an act of supreme generosity, a towering display of grace? I hope you are as proud of your daughter as I am of my sister."

For the briefest of moments, as she processes her son's critique, Sarah's face clouds over. Criticize and control. Punitive. But also, love you, and want to like you better. These polar messages dance about like cartoon characters on a screen. With her lower lip trembling, she mumbles, "I'm not a bad mother."

"You aren't," Brooklyn says, "but Broadway is only trying to tell you to mellow out."

Not wishing to intrude, Charlotte hesitates but decides to add one comment. "I'm around your age, Sarah, and the most important thing I've learned is that life is like this smorgasbord, filled with goodies, which, at every stage of life, from one to a hundred-and-one, offers something slightly different. We take from the buffet what is appropriate to our stage, what fills us with nutrition and joy."

"Well said, Charlotte!" Broadway nearly shouts.

The assembled models and guests begin to file out, and when only a handful are left in the room, Brent White seems to dawdle, finally saying in a modulated tone, "You know, Donald wasn't all that bad. I knew him better than most, and I doubt that anybody was aware of his childhood. Beaten by his father and pushed away by a mother who was trying to hold on to her marriage, he built up a defensive shell. Never wanted to be vulnerable. Had to be the one who gives the orders and distorted the sense that those in charge can't get hurt. He got hurt plenty. Made him even more of a bully."

"Oh my," Charlotte says. "Armor allows for no intimacy. I can imagine how alone the man must have felt."

Brent simply nods.

"You know, Kyla, you've never been in my apartment before," Broadway says.

"You never invited me."

"Would you have come if I had?"

Kyla shrugs, wanders about, and examines the books and CDs stacked on almost an entire wall of shelves.

"*Les Mis,*" she says, "the novel by Hugo."

"One time, I thought I'd like to be in the musical, so I read the original story. Beautifully written."

"My favorite is *Pride and Prejudice.* I've read it three times, and

Mr. Darcy never changes."

"He turns out to be a good guy in the end."

"It's neat," Kyla says, as she settles into a two-seater couch with a back row of soft pillows, "how the old stories wrap up so well. Don't necessarily turn out happy, but they do get resolved."

"Life isn't always so copasetic," Broadway says, as he joins her on the couch. "In my experience, there is always unfinished business."

"Speaking of unfinished business, I want you to know that my adventure with that little creep, Andy Burrus, was not anything like love. It was sort of a business deal, and since I wasn't involved with anyone at the time, I went along with it. It's definitely at an end, and there is nothing unfinished about it. I hope the guy straightens out, but, as far as I'm concerned, it's a sad part of my history."

Kyla has removed her shoes and pulled her legs up so that her feet touch Broadway's thigh.

He, too, discards his shoes, turns to face Kyla, and, with socks still on, begins to massage her toes with his. She copies him, and both begin to giggle.

"Even when you were out of reach, with help from Brook, I did my homework on you. I know your favorite color is jade green; favorite food baked salmon with dill; best classical composer, Serge Rachmaninoff; number one song, "American Pie; and top three movies, *Serendipity*, *When Harry Met Sally*, and ironically, *Sleepless in Seattle*."

The giggles build, then fade away as they bend toward each other, slowly, slowly, until their lips touch.

Kyla throws her arms around him, and a little cry escapes. This time, he copies her.

The police found no hammer in Aaron Batchelor's locked cabinet. His angst over them going into his private area was, however, justified because the officers did find a small diary of sorts, in which Batchelor had written: *That Stout prick destroyed Brook's career. He has to pay. The fag model that Stout fired will help me.* In a later entry, he wrote: *Got the asshole's own hammer from the lesbo. Payback time.*

"Crazy and ugly, that's what it is." They are in Brooklyn's apartment, seated on the edge of her bed, the wheelchair set off to the side several feet, like an automobile that has run out of gas and been abandoned.

"Hopefully, the whole disgusting affair is over. That Charlotte woman your brother invited in is amazing," Landry says. "But, as your doctor, let me caution you to proceed slowly with your walking. The exercise is needed for muscle tone, yet too much could irritate the surrounding nerves."

"Bruce, do you feel sorry for me?"

"Why would I feel sorry? You're the most remarkable woman I've ever known."

Tears form, making little mirrors of Brooklyn's eyes. "How could I have been so stupid to take up with Donald Stout?"

"Seems as if several of the models did the same thing. He had control."

"Yes, and all of us were vulnerable, fooling ourselves that our careers depended on his approval."

A long pause and Landry says, "With me, no trade-offs, no favors for favors. If you let me, I want to love you, plain and simple."

"Oh, Bruce, I want you to…"

She interrupts herself and twists toward him, lips slightly parted.

The cacophony of Times Square surrounds Charlotte and Shanna: hawking vendors, street musicians, gawking tourists, honking taxis, flashing neon, sputtering corner grills.

Charlotte's thoughts wander. Her brother, Greg, in California, needs to be told about this latest caper unwinding. Otherwise, he'll worry. Perhaps, at sixty-nine, it's time to say no to any new solicitation. After all, crime is everywhere, and one cannot be expected to step in on all of them. This one was unusual. Being housed at the Sheraton was a treat. Detective Cavanaugh has been a supportive co-investigator.

Now it is resolved, and, yes, there is an empty feeling, as there is after a war is won, after a race is over, when a compelling piece of theater ends. Challenge gone. Something larger than yourself had a life of its own and now has died. Uncovering material and the intricate details of the conundrum are no longer required. Thank goodness for being an optimist, for viewing endings as opportunities. As they say, a door closes and a window opens.

Shanna says, "So now what, Charlotte? Back to Pennsylvania, to the peace and quiet of retirement living?"

A taxi's warning horn postpones an immediate answer, but, in the after-silence, Charlotte says, "For the most part, it is rather tranquil.

However, for the last year or two, I have been asked to step in on these mysteries. I'm wondering if I've had enough."

Shanna laughs. "You're too good at it to quit."

"You know, Camille Saint-Saens was distressed that his musical creation, *Carnival of the Animals*, pitched as it was for children, was too amateurish to be considered a serious composition. He fretted that it would diminish his stature as a serious composer. ...Although, it is true that it remains one of his most treasured works."

"The point being?"

"That I'm an amateur. My contributions so far have been to track down amateurs. I also fret that, if thrust into a crime situation with hardened criminals, I'd be in over my head. In other words, my successes so far would mean nothing."

"Yes, but keep in mind that this Camille composer fellow was proven wrong. His more basic creation is apparently as valued as any of his other compositions. The main thing about hardened criminals is that they are more dangerous, and we investigators have to keep our guards up. The methodical pursuit of evidence is still the same."

"Thank you, Shanna. You know the right things to say."

Both are silent as the Broadway bustle, teeming with energy, assaults their senses.

"Anyway," Charlotte says, "before I go home, I intend to spend time at the United Nations. Never been there and want to see where the countries of the world try to settle their conflicts."

"Well, if they're smart, they'll hire you to do the job. No conflict too big for Charlotte Smart."

They are quiet again, and Shanna offers, "I'll drive you over to the East River. Beats taking a wild ride in a cab."

As they settle into her unmarked auto, Shanna says, "I'll miss you."

"You know what? I'll be back in New York in about a month, when Broadway's musical has its premiere. He's promised to get me an opening-night seat."

"People suddenly breaking into song isn't my thing, but I'm willing to make an exception in this case."

"Then we'll ask Broadway for two tickets."

Shanna's phone buzzes. "Cavanaugh. ...Amy? ...To New York? ...Well, that's wonderful. You and the little one. ...I know, she's not that little anymore. ...Okay. See you day after tomorrow. I'll show you the sights…And Jessica too."

She signs off, grinning as if she has just won the lottery.

"I can't believe this. My sister and her daughter are coming!" she says with a squeal.

"I'm delighted, Shanna. How nicely things are wrapping up."

In the late morning sunlight, removed from the deep canyons of Broadway, buffeted by a crisp wind flying in off the East River, visitors are delighted to see, silhouetted on the expansive approach to the United Nations building, two women, one gray-haired, the other black-haired, standing face to face, wrapped in a deep embrace.

STAN CHARNOFSKY is a retired professor of psychology atCalifornia State University, Northridge (CSUN), where he taught for more than fifty years. But that's just the tip of the iceberg. In addition to his work at CSUN, Stan also writes books, and it could be said that his life reads like one.

Before teaching, in the 1950s Stan signed with the New York Yankees where he played in their farm system for six years. He later managed teams in Edmonton and St. Petersburg. Later still, Stan worked as the assistant coach at USC under the famous Rod Dedeaux, who was voted College Baseball Coach of the Century. Stan also served as head coach at CSUN from 1962-1966, with one champion-ship team.

He was the founding director of the Educational Opportunities Program at CSUN (then known as Valley State College). Stan was inducted into the CSUN Athletic Hall of Fame in 2016. This was followed, in 2018, by his induction into the USC Baseball Alumni Hall of Fame. Stan is the former President (and a current board member) of the National Association for Humanistic Psychology. In 2016, Stan received the Distinguished Teaching Award at CSUN.

And of course Stan writes books. His numerous publications include *When Women Leave Men: How Men Feel, How Men Heal* (New World Library) *The Deceived Society* (Trafford), and the Charlotte Smart Mystery Series. Stan resides in Northridge, California.